KADE

Also by Cheyenne McCray

KADE

Armed and Dangerous

Cheyenne McCray

 ST. MARTIN'S GRIFFIN
NEW YORK

This is a work of fiction. All of the characters, organizations, and events portrayed in this novel are either products of the author's imagination or are used fictitiously.

KADE: ARMED AND DANGEROUS. Copyright © 2010 by Cheyenne McCray. All rights reserved. Printed in the United States of America. For information, address St. Martin's Press, 175 Fifth Avenue, New York, N.Y. 10010.

www.stmartins.com

ISBN 978-0-312-38668-9

First Edition: November 2010

10 9 8 7 6 5 4 3 2 1

To Mom and Dad and the HJL Ranch

Acknowledgments

Thank you to all of the Border Patrol agents, ranchers, and residents of southeastern Arizona who aided me in my research. And to my editor, agent, and crit partners—couldn't do it without you.

To My Readers

Kade: Armed and Dangerous is a novel I wrote several years ago and published with a small e-publisher.

This novel holds a special place in my heart as it was my first romance. The characters are special to me, as is the location in south-eastern Arizona, where I was raised. Even the ranch where a good portion of the novel takes place mirrors the ranch I grew up on.

Kade was formerly titled *Wild Borders*. It is my hope that you enjoy reading this book as much as I enjoyed writing it.

Author's Note

When I began research for this novel I was given the utmost courtesy by members of the U.S. Border Patrol. The agency has since been reorganized under the umbrella of Customs and Border Protection within Homeland Security. I enjoyed going on a ride-along as well as interviewing Border Patrol agents.

Many ranchers and residents of Cochise County in southeastern Arizona were especially accommodating, giving me their views and opinions on the climate of living in a border community and how the situation affected them.

Many changes have taken place in the world since I originally researched and wrote this novel. Although I have attempted to accommodate as many of these changes as I could, some things have not been addressed.

I have taken liberties with buildings and locations throughout the towns of Douglas and Bisbee. However, the histories of both Bisbee and Tombstone are well-known and what I included in this book should be fairly accurate.

In this same corner of Arizona, I grew up on a ranch much like the JL Star. I hope you enjoy your visit to this little part of the world that I'm originally from, a place that I still love to visit from time to time.

KADE

Chapter 1

Kade Owen dragged his hand over his stubbled face as he settled into the plastic airport seat while waiting to board the plane he'd be taking to Tucson. He was ready to get out of dreary San Francisco, back to Arizona, and home to his son.

And then catch those damn *coyotes,* the people-smugglers who'd managed to elude him for far too long. Especially the bastard known as El Torero.

It was dark outside, a slow drizzle rolling down the large panes of glass, and he was looking forward to Arizona sunshine. He pulled his black Stetson low so that he could observe people around him without being obvious. In his line of work as an Intelligence Agent with the U.S. Border Patrol, people-watching was a necessary skill. But now he was doing it to pass time before his plane was scheduled to depart.

Hair at Kade's nape prickled—he had the distinct feeling *he* was being watched. He looked casually to his left to see a young woman staring at the screen of a small laptop computer. Something in his gut told him she'd been studying *him* a fraction of a second earlier.

Kade pushed up the brim of his Stetson and raked his gaze over the woman. She sure was pretty, her shoulder-length hair the golden color of an Arizona sunrise. She had the type of shapely figure he preferred, nicely rounded and sexy as hell.

From a gap in her pink silk blouse he could see a bit of lace covering her generous breasts, beneath the soft material. His gaze traveled down to those long legs beneath the skirt that hit a couple of inches above her knees. Yeah, she sure had terrific legs, and he'd bet she had a great ass—

He broke off his appraisal as the woman glanced up and her gaze met his. She had gorgeous eyes, warm and deep brown. The connection between Kade and the woman, for that fraction of time, was tangible. Like she'd lassoed him with that one look. She immediately blushed a pretty shade of pink and looked back at her computer.

Kade couldn't help but grin. Damn, she was cute. She might be worth getting to know.

Well, hell. Wasn't it just last night he'd told his sister, Dara, that he didn't want a relationship? In the five years since Lorraine's death, he hadn't met a single woman he was interested in pursuing. Not one. He'd gone on dates, but few and far between. Yet there he was, fascinated with a stranger in an airport a thousand miles from home.

"Flight twelve-sixteen with nonstop service to Tucson is now boarding everyone with an A card," announced a voice over the intercom. This particular airline had "cattle call" boarding with no assigned seats.

Kade stood, and he noticed the woman had slipped her laptop into a bag and was already walking toward the gate, giving him a nice view.

Yeah, she definitely had sexy legs, and she had a great ass.

Several passengers crowded in front of Kade, so he had to wait awhile longer for his turn to board. When he finally made it onto the plane, he worked his way back. He noticed the pretty blond in a window seat, staring outside, and no one was sitting in the middle seat next to her.

He took off his Stetson and set it in the overhead compartment. With his big frame, he usually disliked sitting in the middle, but this time it would be just fine. Careful not to bump the woman, he eased into the seat next to her, extended the seat belt, and buckled it.

A flight attendant helped an elderly lady put her bag into the overhead compartment and then the lady sat next to Kade. He nodded to her and said, "Ma'am."

The woman's pale blue eyes held a hint of amusement. "You're too polite to be a Californian."

"Just spent a week in Frisco with my sister and her twins." He smiled, wishing he'd been able to spend more time with his niece and nephew. If he hadn't had to go to that briefing in San Diego beforehand, he could've taken his son, Trent, to Dara's with him. He sure missed the kid and looked forward to getting home.

"I'm visiting my grandchildren in Tucson." The lady shook her head and sighed. "Hellions, all. Love them, but a weekend is about as much as I can handle. Now *those* kids could use some lessons in manners."

She punctuated her statement with a jab of her fist in the air, then began digging through an enormous purse. "In here somewhere, I have pictures their father sent. . . ."

Kade held back a grin and glanced at the woman in pink on his other side. Her forehead was pressed to the pane, and she was apparently lost in her thoughts. She sure smelled good. Real good. Like honeysuckle and soap, clean and fresh.

* * *

The windowpane felt cool against Kelsey's forehead as she stared into the darkness. She sighed and turned her thoughts back to that gorgeous hunk of man in boots she'd seen in the airport.

She'd been so embarrassed to find him studying her from beneath his black cowboy hat. What incredible blue eyes he had—and that sexy grin could melt a woman's soul. Thank goodness he hadn't noticed her watching him a minute before. As a journalist she'd become a people-watcher, and lord, was that man something to watch.

Kelsey groaned. What was wrong with her? She had no interest in men after being married to the biggest creep of the century. Thanks to what her father had put her mother through when she was growing up, Kelsey should have known better. She should never have let Davis Johansen's lies make her believe in happily-ever-afters.

But as far as that cowboy in the airport, what harm was there in looking? Kind of like window-shopping with no intention of sampling or buying the merchandise.

She was finally free, finally divorced from Davis.

"Good riddance, creep," she grumbled, her breath fogging the pane.

"Beg pardon?"

Kelsey jumped at the sound of the husky voice, so close that a shiver sprinted down her spine. As she whirled in the cramped seat, her elbow rammed hard flesh. Heat crept up her neck when she saw the cowboy's blue eyes wince.

"I'm so sorry." Her gaze swept over the tanned face, strong chin, and the chestnut hair that had been hidden under the cowboy hat earlier. "Did I hurt you?"

The man grabbed his side and grimaced as if in mortal pain. "I'm not sure I'll live."

He winked.

That familiar flush spread throughout Kelsey, the telltale blush that would redden her face from the roots of her hair to the tips of her toes. She offered a half-smile and turned back to the window.

Lights flashed on the wing and reflected on the wet asphalt, a steady rhythm in time with her throbbing pulse. She watched as a man on the tarmac guided the plane onto the runway. Her heart rate rocketed, her palms slick with sweat. The scar on her upper thigh ached and she rubbed it through her skirt.

"I'm sorry if I embarrassed you," the man beside her said, his voice low and disturbingly close.

A thrill rippled in her belly as she forced herself to face the man. "Not at all."

"Kade Owen." White teeth flashed against tan skin as he smiled and offered his hand.

Kelsey caught his earthy scent of sun-warmed flesh and apples, and she fought the desire to dry her moist palm on her skirt before his callused hand engulfed hers. His grasp sent tingles throughout her and she quickly pulled away.

"What's your name, ma'am?" he said in that slow and sexy voice that sent a shiver straight through her.

"Oh." She swallowed, feeling flustered and on edge. "I'm Kelsey. Kelsey Nichols."

"Kelsey," Kade drawled, a slight, almost imperceptible country edge to his voice, and she shivered. "A pretty name for a pretty lady."

Just the way he was looking at her, the way he said her name, made her want to squirm in her seat. Good lord. If just talking to this man was making her feel like this, what would it feel like to really be with him?

Nope. Not going there. She'd had it with men, and that was that.

The plane started to taxi down the runway, throwing Kelsey into her worst fear. All she could do was close her eyes tight, pray, and try to shove the heart-wrenching memories from her mind. Every muscle in her body tensed, and she gripped the armrests as if the mere act would guide the plane into the air and keep it there.

At least until it was time to land.

"You all right?"

Kelsey heard his voice but refused to open her eyes. Not until they were safely at cruising altitude.

Kade Owen's hand closed around hers, and he gave her fingers a comforting squeeze. The stranger's touch startled her, but not enough to make her look at him or speak a word. It surprised her how his warm grasp calmed her nerves, if only for a few minutes.

As the craft lifted, her chest tightened, and her breath rasped out in shallow huffs. The rumble of the plane, the roar of the engines, the smell of burning fuel, the pause in the air-conditioning, the way pressure clamped down on her head . . . she hated it all.

Ten morbid thoughts later, she felt the plane level out, and in a rush, she released the breath she'd been holding. "I knew I should have driven," she muttered.

The man gave a low laugh. "All the way to Tucson from San Francisco?"

Kelsey opened one eye and peeked at him. "Yes."

"Don't you know flying is safer than driving?" He smiled, and she opened her other eye.

She sighed and allowed her muscles to relax. "Yeah. Right."

"If it makes you feel better, I'm a pilot."

"It doesn't." Sensation was coming back into Kelsey's limbs, and she brushed a wisp of hair behind her ear. "You can let go of my hand now."

"Sure." A spark of mischief lit his blue eyes. But he didn't move.

"What'll you two have to drink?" the flight attendant asked before Kelsey had a chance to tell Kade exactly what she would do if he didn't release her.

"I'll have orange juice," he said, and turned to Kelsey. "What'll you have, darlin'?"

She'd darlin' him in a minute.

Kelsey asked the attendant for a diet soda. After the woman had taken their drink orders and moved to the next row, Kade said, "That stuff'll kill you."

"When I get my drink, it's going in your lap if you don't release my hand, cowboy." She gave him a dangerous smile. One that could leave no doubt she intended to follow through with her threat.

"I give up." He raised his hands in mock self-defense, coming within a breath of hitting the woman on the other side of him. He was truly too big for the seat, his broad shoulders and chest spanning the width.

"Excuse me," he said to the elderly woman, who patted his knee and then returned to showing a stack of photographs to the man across the aisle.

Kelsey reached up to open the air vent, then punched the button for the reading light. Yes, the cowboy was definitely too handsome for his own good.

While she dug in her laptop bag, she felt the intensity of Kade's presence but avoided looking at him. Where was it? Ah, there. She withdrew the slim laptop computer and slipped on her gold-rimmed reading glasses.

Theresa had loved the idea of the immigration feature. It would be the most comprehensive feature Kelsey had written, and she intended to make it the best series of articles any reporter had done on the subject of illegal immigration along the Mexican border.

Kelsey was looking forward to the experience with desperate enthusiasm. What better way to distance herself from Davis and all the bad memories?

"What're you working on?" Kade asked as she began jotting down questions for her feature. "If you don't mind me asking."

"I'm a journalist." She shifted her attention from her notepad to the cowboy. "I'm making a few notes for an article I'm writing."

"For a newspaper?" He looked genuinely interested, and Kelsey found herself warming to his friendliness.

"I write for *City by the Bay.*" She rustled in her bag, pulled out a copy, and handed it to him. "It's a San Francisco–based magazine that primarily carries local-interest stories, but occasionally runs features on national topics."

Kade's fingers brushed hers as he took the magazine. Kelsey caught her breath at the tingle that skittered within her at the contact. Her eyes cut to his, to see if he'd noticed, but he seemed intent on flipping through the magazine.

"That's the current issue." She pulled off her glasses and slid them back into their case. "I wrote a feature on single parenting. My pseudonym is Kale C. Nichols."

He cocked an eyebrow and his gaze met hers. "You're a single parent?"

"My editor assigned the story." Her smile faltered. "I don't have any children. But I wish I did."

Before Kade could ask her anything more personal, she said, "So, what do you do?"

"Law enforcement," he replied with a shrug.

Surprised, Kelsey blinked. "And here I thought you were a cowboy."

He smiled. "Grew up on a ranch, but following in my folks' footsteps never appealed to me. As a kid I always wanted to be the good guy tracking down the bad guys."

"I'll just bet." Her mouth quirked as she imagined him on a white horse, tracking down desperados.

Lightning flashed outside the plane and her heart dropped. She turned away from Kade to glance out the window. Another flash illuminated the swirling mass of a thunderstorm.

The plane bucked and dropped, then leveled out, shooting her stomach straight to her toes. She gasped and clutched the armrests, her heart pounding so fast she thought it would jump out of her chest and the cowboy next to her could lasso it.

When Kelsey had looked to the window, Kade took the opportunity to study her. What was it about the woman that interested him, more than anyone else he'd met?

Was it her velvety brown eyes? The way she blushed? When he'd embarrassed her, every bit of bare skin that he could see had gone pink, from the V of her blouse to the tips of her ears. He wondered if the rest of her turned that attractive color.

What would it be like to kiss those full lips?

As skittish as she seemed, he'd probably have better luck kissing the old lady on his other side. Kade grimaced at the thought.

Lightning lit the sky outside and Kelsey gasped as the plane dropped and shuddered. She turned from the window to face forward, her eyes scrunched tight, her face as pale as his mom's lace tablecloth.

Over the intercom a man's voice drawled, "This is your captain.

Y'all sit tight with your seat belts fastened until we ride out this storm."

Poor kid, Kade thought as he studied Kelsey.

He couldn't stop himself. He eased an arm around her and pulled her head to his chest. She remained rigid, trembling. In a few moments, he felt her relax. A bit.

"Everything'll be fine," he whispered into her hair, and squeezed her cold fingers within his warm grasp.

His gut tightened at the smell of her and the feel of her soft body in his arms. Somehow he felt like he knew her. That he'd always known her.

The plane bounced and rattled amid the turbulence, and she pressed her face closer. Tears soaked his shirt, and he fought the urge to slip his fingers into her hair.

Why was she so terrified?

He moved his thumb over the back of her hand and noticed a band of pale flesh against her skin, where she must've worn a wedding ring. A broken engagement? A divorce?

The rest of the flight to Tucson was one of the roughest he'd taken. The thunderstorm raged and turbulence tossed the plane like a toy caught in a dust devil. But Kade found himself glad for the storm, glad for the excuse to hold the woman that he barely even knew.

Kelsey woke to a whisper in her ear. "We're here, Kelsey. We made it."

Disoriented, she blinked, then heat burned through her when she realized she had her head against the cowboy's chest. When she pulled away from Kade, she couldn't think of a thing to say.

How could she have let a stranger hold her to begin with? But it had helped calm the terror that churned inside her like an earthquake in the heart of San Francisco.

Davis had never held her. *You're being stupid,* he would say. *Get over it.*

Not this man. Kade didn't even know her, and yet he held her as though he truly cared.

"Such a sweet couple," the wispy lady croaked from the other side of him. She reached across with her frail hand and patted his, still covering Kelsey's. "You two remind me of my Wilbur and me. Sixty years of marriage and still dancing." She gave a watery smile and eased herself up to enter the aisle.

Kade grinned and Kelsey wanted to drop through the floor of the plane.

She ducked and reached under the seat in front of her to grab the laptop bag. When she looked back, her eyes kept going up, traveling those long legs in snug Wranglers and, good lord, that very nice package. . . . Her cheeks burned again at the turn of her thoughts.

He put on his cowboy hat and allowed her to go in front of him in the aisle. What did he think of her after that terrifying plane ride? Did he think she was some weepy woman who couldn't take care of herself? Why did she care what he thought?

While she exited the plane onto the ramp, Kade strode at her side. "How long'll you be here, Kelsey?"

The way he said her name sent shivers throughout her. A gentle drawl, a husky tone.

"Three weeks." She chanced a look at him and saw his smile, a smile that caused something within her to burn. An ache, a wanting.

She didn't tell him that she was considering moving to Tucson. Too many memories shrouded her in the Bay Area.

While they walked toward baggage claim she was surprised at the comfortable silence between her and the stranger. He had such an easy, relaxed presence that she found herself drawn to him even more, despite the pinging in her belly.

As he stood next to her at baggage claim, Kelsey tried not to think about the effect he was having on her. She was afraid he'd felt it, too, and that was dangerous territory she had no intention of exploring.

With relief, she saw her bright pink bags tumble down the slide to the conveyor. She snatched them one at a time and set them on the floor beside her. She turned to face Kade and saw him grabbing his own suitcase.

She took a deep breath and met his intense blue gaze. "It was nice of you to—to—well, help me make it through that flight."

"Anytime." In one swift movement, he gathered her two hefty suitcases along with his own and made it look like he was carrying a couple of hatboxes.

"What are you doing?" she demanded, hands on her hips.

"Helping you to your ride." He managed a small bow and sounded quite gallant.

"I can carry my own bags," she insisted to his retreating back.

"Is someone picking you up?" he asked as she trailed after him.

"I'm catching a cab." The clean smell of rain hit her and thunder rumbled in the distance as they exited the terminal. An odd thrill tingled within her at the tension in the air. She loved thunderstorms—as long as she was safely on the ground.

Kade didn't stop until he reached the short line of cabs and handed the driver her belongings while she stood under the awning. Rain rolled off his cowboy hat onto his shirt as he held the cab door open for her. "Where're you headed?"

"Tucson Larson Hotel," she replied as she dodged into the pounding rain and pushed her laptop case and purse into the cab's backseat.

Wrinkling her nose at the smell of stale cigar smoke, she scooted over the cracked vinyl seat, to the far side that had fewer tears in it. She wiped raindrops from her face and pushed her damp hair behind her ears.

Kade leaned in the cab door. "I'm staying the night at the Larson, too. Mind if I get out of the rain and share your cab?"

He was already soaked from the storm and she hated to see him get any wetter. In fact, the thought gave her a little thrill. She nodded, then worried her lower lip with her teeth as he disappeared again and she felt the trunk of the cab being slammed shut.

As the cabdriver hopped into the front seat, Kade climbed in the backseat next to Kelsey. Her pulse picked up. Spending any time with a man who made her feel like taking a chance on romance was definitely not a good idea.

Chapter 2

The cabbie pulled into traffic as Kade set his Stetson on his knee and studied the woman next to him. "I'm having breakfast at the Larson in the morning," he said, trying to set her at ease. "Otherwise I'd head home tonight."

Kelsey jumped as lightning split the sky, the crack of thunder not far behind.

"Scared of thunderstorms also?" Kade asked, hoping she'd need a shoulder to lean on.

"No." She shook her head. "I'm just not used to them."

He smiled. "If you're frightened, you could hold my hand again."

She pursed her lips, and he felt desire burn in him. So soft, so inviting, those lips.

"Listen, Kade." She hesitated. "You were kind to me on the plane. More than kind. But I don't let strange men hold me." She turned to the window, where he could see streetlights blurring in the rain.

"Kelsey," he said. She turned back with obvious reluctance. "I have no doubt that you would've made it through that flight without me lending a shoulder. There's nothing wrong with being in-secure sometimes. We all are."

Sighing, she stared at her lap, reaching for her ring finger as if to twist a band no longer there. She thrust her hands to her sides and looked at him. "Someone always told me how weak I was for my fear of flying. He even knew what happened."

The cab lurched to a stop in front of the Larson, and before he had a chance to respond, to ask what kind of jackass would say something like that to her, she flung open her door and darted out to the curb and into the rain. He followed, banging his forehead on the door frame and uttering a curse that was sure to turn Kelsey's pretty ears blue.

By the time he managed to get his bulk out of the cab, she'd stuffed bills in the cabbie's hand and was hauling her suitcases through the impressive doors of the Tucson Larson. Kade shoved his fare at the driver, grabbed his own bag, and followed. He couldn't help admire Kelsey's curves and the toss of her head. In a matter of a few strides, he'd caught up to her at the registration desk.

She tapped her nails on the marble countertop in a nervous rhythm that reminded him of rain falling on the cab's roof.

The clerk typed in a command and studied his computer. "Ah, yes." He handed Kelsey a key card. "Room eleven-ten."

Kade moved beside her. "Wait for me and I'll help with your bags, darlin'." He told the clerk, "Owen."

Kelsey frowned. "I'm not your darlin', cowboy. I can handle my own bags." She walked toward the elevators, across the acres of in-dustrial carpet. But he had no doubt his ruse would get the results he wanted—at least with the clerk.

"Wedding jitters," Kade said to the young man, who gave a know-ing grin.

"Hmm, let me see here, Mr. Owen. Good. The room next to your fiancée is available. Room eleven-oh-eight."

"Come on, come on," Kelsey muttered, tapping her foot, anxious for the elevator to arrive before Kade caught up. Something about him was starting to wear down her defenses and she couldn't afford to let that happen with any man. No matter how kind and attentive he might be.

No such luck. The doors opened, and Kade darted in before they had a chance to close. It was a slow elevator, taking its sweet time to head up the eleven floors.

"Have dinner with me tonight." He smiled and she noticed a dimple in one cheek.

Kelsey's body heated. *Why not? Why not spend one evening in the company of an attractive man?*

She gritted her teeth in an effort to fight off her attraction to the cowboy. *I'm not ready. I need more time.*

"It's just dinner between two new friends," Kade said, as if reading her mind.

The elevator groaned to a stop and the doors opened. *It's only dinner,* her thoughts echoed. What could happen?

Definitely not a good idea. There was no room for someone as handsome and charming as Kade Owen in her life.

"Thanks, but no." She gathered her bags and stepped into the hall that had the same peculiar odor that all older hotels did. Like ancient carpet, mothballs, and freshly laundered linens. It didn't surprise her that he followed. He was as tenacious as San Francisco fog.

"How about I make you a wager." He hooked his thumb in his belt loop. "I'll guess something personal about you, and if I'm right, you have dinner with me. If not, then I'll eat by my lonesome."

She sighed and stared up at the outdated popcorn ceiling, then shook her head and looked at Kade. "Okay."

"If I'm right, you're having dinner with me."

Kelsey smiled despite herself. "Yeah, yeah."

He took her hand, and that strange energy jolted her at his touch, sending vibrations straight to her toes. His hand was much larger than hers, his callused palm rough against her soft skin. She shivered at his mere touch.

"You're afraid to have dinner with me," he began, " 'cause you just went through a rough time. I'd say you're divorced and your ex-husband was a real jackass. You deserve better, Kelsey."

A chill pebbled her skin and she snatched her hand away. "How did you know?"

With one finger he pushed up the brim of his Stetson, and grinned. "I won the bet."

Anger burned away the frost of her surprise. "How did you find that out?"

Kade gave a gentle smile that had the odd effect of relaxing her. "I noticed that you still have a line from where you wore a wedding ring, so it couldn't have been too long ago. You talked about a real idiot who treated you poorly, and you shy away from me like a horse spooked by a rattlesnake."

She took a deep breath and gripped her laptop bag tighter. "You figured it out just from that?"

"Like I told you, I'm in law enforcement. Figuring out clues is part of what I do." Kade's expression took on a more serious look. "I'll behave. Promise."

"I must be out of my mind." She shook her head and sighed. "All right. But it's not a date."

Kade strode to the start of the hallway, then stopped before the first door. "I'll meet you in fifteen minutes. I'm starving. Those dang airplane peanuts just don't tide me over." He stuck a key card into room 1108 and was through the door before she had a chance to reply.

Slick. He even managed to get a room next to hers. She stood before her own door and groaned. Should she take her bags downstairs and demand another room?

Instinct told her that he wasn't the type of man who would hurt or take advantage of her. With the exception of the mistake she'd made with the man she'd married, her instincts were usually right on. She could always change her mind and ask for a different room if she felt it necessary.

And since Kade was in law enforcement, he spent his time protecting people.

Maybe she should ask to see his badge.

Despite her many misgivings, fifteen minutes later Kelsey was ready. She'd managed to blow-dry the rain from her hair, curl a few wisps with the curling iron, and touch up her makeup. She'd changed out of her wrinkled blouse and skirt into a pink sundress and sandals.

When she was dressed, she dabbed honeysuckle perfume at her wrists and throat. Like the color pink, the scent made her feel feminine. Davis had hated her perfume and hated her in pink.

She wore pink and the honeysuckle perfume as often as possible.

A knock at the door interrupted her thoughts. Before she opened it, she took a deep breath and checked the peephole. It was Kade, and if that skewed image of him held true, he definitely looked too handsome for his own good.

When she swung open the door, she saw that he looked incredible in his black cowboy hat, his white teeth flashing against his deep tan, his navy shirt enhancing the disturbing blue of his eyes.

"Beautiful." Kade's gaze ran the length of her, and she blushed. "Do you like Mexican food? They serve the best enchiladas north of the border in one of the restaurants downstairs."

She smiled despite the melting sensation in her bones. "Love it."

As he escorted her to the restaurant, she was intensely aware of him. What was it about him that sent jolts of hunger through her every time they touched?

When the hostess showed them to a corner table, Kelsey was surprised Kade pulled out her chair and helped her seat herself at the table before taking his own seat. Davis had never done those small gentlemanly things. She'd never considered it necessary, but she found the gesture touching coming from Kade. He then took off his hat and set it on the chair beside him.

Her stomach twisted. She hadn't been on a date since college.

No. This wasn't a date. Just dinner with a man she'd never see again.

When Kelsey finished studying the menu, she saw Kade watching her. He gave her a slow, sexy smile that made her heart stop, and she almost forgot to breathe. To her relief, the waiter arrived to take their order.

"You ought to try one of their margaritas," Kade said. "They're wicked."

She nodded. "Frozen with salt on the rim."

"Gracias." The waiter hurried away with their orders.

The restaurant had the perfect atmosphere for a casual evening out. Mexican hats, serapes, and decorated gourds plastered the walls, the floor a dark Saltillo tile. Mariachi music played in the background, and Kelsey found herself tapping her toe to the beat.

"You live in San Francisco?" Kade asked, drawing her attention back to him.

Kelsey tucked a strand of hair behind her ear. "All my life. What about you?"

"I'm an Arizona native." He shrugged. "A rare breed. Most folks you meet around these parts are from anywhere but here."

The waiter returned, placing a basket of chips, pots of salsa, and large margaritas in front of each of them.

"Goodness. It's enormous." She sipped her drink and smiled. "Delicious."

He took a swallow of his. "One of these things equals two and a half regular ones. It'll knock you on your a— butt if you're not careful."

Kelsey grinned, partly at his avoidance of the word "ass," obviously to be polite to a female. She dipped a corn chip in salsa. "Were you on a business trip?"

Kade nodded before he put a handful of chips on his plate. "And visiting my sister and her kids. I don't get to see them much, so I try to get out there at least once a year."

As soon as she bit into the corn chip, she knew it was a mistake. Her mouth flamed and her eyes watered. She grabbed her margarita and drank it, trying to cool the burning sensation.

"Careful," he said. "You'll be dancing on the tabletops if you drink that too fast."

Kelsey set down the drink and tried ice water instead, but her mouth still felt like it was on fire.

"Should've warned you about that salsa. Chips with salt might help."

She fanned her warm face as she ate a plain chip with no salsa. "I've had hot sauce before, but nothing like that."

It wasn't long before the waiter arrived with their combo plates of enchiladas, tacos, refried beans, and Spanish rice. Everything tasted fabulous, but there was so much food that Kelsey was able to eat only half of what was on her plate.

While they ate, she was surprised at how much she wanted to know about him. She purposely steered clear of personal topics, and was glad he didn't press her. He answered questions about Tucson, the best tourist attractions, and those frequented by the locals. She didn't bother to tell him she would be leaving Tucson in the morning.

In turn, he asked her about living in San Francisco. They talked about the areas he'd visited around the city, and she shared her favorite places.

Kelsey enjoyed how Kade focused on her when they spoke, like he was intent on hearing every word. The way his eyes lit up when he laughed. The infectious grin that held a bit of the devil himself in it. She enjoyed being around him too much and had to remind herself that there was no room for a distraction or complication in her life like Kade Owen.

"I'd better get to bed." She drained the enormous margarita and wondered at her reluctance to part with him. "I have an early appointment."

He agreed and called for the check. When it was paid, she stood and realized that he'd been right—drinking the entire margarita had been a mistake. Her head spun, and when Kade laced his fingers with hers, she didn't object—she was afraid she might fall. The feel of his hand sent tremors throughout her body, enhanced by the mellow, tipsy feeling the drink had given her.

On the elevator ride up to their floor, Kelsey's legs wobbled and she found herself leaning too close to Kade. She knew she needed to put distance between them, but when they reached her room, he took the key card from her hand and opened the door.

"Can I come in?" he murmured. "Two minutes."

"Okay." Where did that come from? Her heart pounded out a staccato that she could almost bet he was able to hear.

"I want to see you again." Kade flicked on a light as he drew Kelsey through the door, and it slammed shut behind her.

Her throat tightened and went as dry as the Arizona desert. "I—I . . ."

But her words vanished, her mind blank, as Kade took her face in his palms and captured her gaze with his.

"Kade, I—" But she no longer knew the meaning of up or down, and she melted against him, wanting him. His earthy scent intoxicated her, filling her senses, confusing her beyond the effects of the alcohol.

"Darlin', what you do to me," Kade said against her lips. "Let me taste you."

"Yes," she whispered.

He brushed his lips over hers. Just a whisper kiss. The light touch of his lips and the feel of his fingers on her skin made her nipples ache. A wave of longing crested, then crashed within her soul.

She pressed herself closer to him and heard a soft moan.

Coming from her.

The tip of his tongue outlined her bottom lip, a feather caress that sent desire spiraling within. She parted her lips and his tongue met hers, a velvet softness that she savored like golden honey. "You taste so good," he murmured.

Citrus from the margarita was still sweet on his tongue and she wrapped her arms around his neck as their kiss deepened. She smelled the light apple fragrance of his hair and slid her fingers into the soft strands, knocking his cowboy hat off.

With a jolt, Kelsey became aware of Kade's erection against her belly. A voice inside her shouted, telling her she couldn't go any further. Not with someone she barely knew. But her mind and body refused to listen.

As if he heard her thoughts, he let out a ragged breath and stepped back, leaving her feeling almost empty. Alone.

Kade traced one finger along her cheekbone and she shuddered with longing. "Say you'll see me again."

He looked so handsome, his chestnut hair in disarray, passion in his eyes.

"I—I don't know if that's a good idea." It took all her willpower not to throw her arms around him and tell him to spend the night. She had never been with a man other than Davis in a sexual way, and it frightened her how much she wanted Kade.

Right here. Right now.

Kade caught both her hands in his. "Have breakfast with me."

She shook her head. "I have a meeting, and then I'm going out of town."

He brought her hands to his mouth and trailed his lips over her knuckles, sending shivers throughout her, those intense blue eyes never leaving hers. "How do I reach you?"

Trying to regain even a modicum of self-control, Kelsey freed her hands and absently rubbed the scar on her upper thigh through the material of her dress. "I'll sleep on it. If I see you before I leave, I'll let you know."

"All right." He kissed her again, a soft, lingering kiss. He smiled and caressed her cheek, then turned and slipped out the door.

And she was really alone then.

Dazed, Kelsey moved toward the bed and almost tripped over Kade's cowboy hat. She picked it up, wondering if she should take it to him.

No. Tomorrow morning would be soon enough.

Kelsey ran a shaking hand through her hair. What had she just done? She'd experienced the most incredible kiss of her life—from a virtual stranger.

She sat on the edge of the bed, then flopped onto her back, Kade's hat still cradled to her chest. She inhaled deeply, drinking in the intoxicating smell of him that clung to the felt Stetson. That masculine scent that made her ache for him.

What would it have been like to make love to Kade? The thought caused a thrill to skip around in her belly.

Kelsey closed her eyes, still holding Kade's hat close to her chest. She imagined actually letting herself go and being with that tall, dark, sexy cowboy who managed to break through the ice of resistance coating her heart and soul since her divorce. She couldn't let him all the way in, but it wouldn't hurt to fantasize about him, right?

Heat filled her body and her cheeks flushed. No, that was ridiculous.

Still clutching Kade's Stetson, she slipped into a restless sleep and dreamed of cowboys, mustangs, and the Arizona desert.

Chapter 3

The next morning Kade woke early, ready to find Kelsey before she fled.

What had come over him? The confirmed-bachelor father. Hell, even if Kelsey did agree to see him again, what would she think of him having a son? He and Trent were a package deal. Usually Kade talked about his son all the time, but for some reason he'd stayed away from personal subjects, much the same as Kelsey had.

At seven he knocked on her door, hoping she'd still be there. The door opened, rewarding him with the sight of Kelsey clad in a pink T-shirt and shorts, and a glimpse of her shapely legs.

"What are you doing here so early, Kade?" She ran a hand through her tousled hair.

He leaned against the door frame. "You all right?"

"I'm fine." She gave a cute little yawn. "What time is it?"

"Seven."

"Seven?" She turned away, clearly distracted, and he caught the door with his boot. "Darn hotel drapes," she muttered. "Always make it too dark."

Kade followed her into the room, the door slamming behind him as she pulled open the drapes and flooded the room with sunshine. "Kelsey, we've got to talk."

She spun around, almost colliding with Kade, those dark eyes looking up at him. "About what?"

"Us."

"There's no us." She raised her hands as if in amazement and sounded agitated. "You were nice to me on the airplane and we had dinner. That's it."

He reached one hand up and smoothed hair from her eyes. "What about the kiss we shared? You have to admit, it was more than a little peck."

For a moment, he saw yearning in her eyes, mirroring every desire in his soul. But she pulled free and pushed him away.

"No." She pointed to the door. "And you need to go."

Was she upset with him? Or did it have something to do with her ex?

"What happened?" he said softly.

She shook her head. "Nothing. I need to get ready for my appointment."

"Kelsey—"

"Please leave." Her expression looked both sad and distant. "I've really got to get ready for this get-together and I just don't have it in me for any kind of complications right now."

Kade stood there for a second, his thumb hooked in his belt loop. "Can I at least give you my card? I'll leave it up to you to get ahold of me. If you want to."

Kelsey sighed and nodded. "All right."

He dug out his wallet and pulled out one of his cards from the agency and handed it to Kelsey. She took it without looking at it and slipped it into a pocket of her backpack.

Well, at least she hadn't tossed it into the garbage.

Just as he was about to tell her good-bye, she said, "Hold on."

He paused, wondering if she'd had a change of heart.

She leaned over and picked up his Stetson from a chair beside the bed. "You forgot this last night," she said as she handed him his hat.

He put it on and tipped the brim at her. "I hope you'll call," he said, and then turned and headed to the door.

Kelsey followed him and he stood and looked at her as she held the door open a moment.

Her eyes softened. "Thank you for letting me join you for dinner. I had a nice time." And then she let the door close quietly behind her.

Well, hell.

Maybe she'd call him after all.

Kade rubbed his clean-shaven jaw. What he needed was to get his mind back on his job and start thinking about what he had to do to track down those damn *coyotes*. He was getting closer to catching the bastards. He could feel it. Almost taste it.

He headed down to the hotel's restaurant and waited for Chuck to arrive. Sun shone brilliant through the beveled glass of the Larson Hotel and spilled onto the carpeted floor. Groundskeepers worked at cleaning torn palm fronds and other debris left from the previous night's storm, and housekeepers polished rain splatters from the windows and vacuumed dirt from carpets.

After he made his way into the restaurant, Kade was escorted to a table and let the hostess know he was waiting for another person to join him. He took a seat and tried to get his head back on the intelligence work waiting for him when he returned, but his thoughts kept turning to Kelsey.

"Howdy, son." Chuck's voice brought Kade out of his thoughts about a certain blond who'd given him the brush-off.

Kade smiled at his stepfather. "Mornin', old man."

"Old man, my ass." Chuck removed his gray Stetson, plunked it on top of Kade's, and took the seat across the table. After swiping his head with a meaty hand, Chuck eyed him with his penetrating stare, the same one that always could tell when Kade was up to no good as a kid. "You haven't been sleeping."

Kade leaned back and folded his arms. "Dad, I'm fine. Just had a restless night."

Chuck tugged at his turquoise bolo tie. "How're your sister and my grandkids?"

"Dara's doing great and the twins are ornery as all get-out." Kade laughed and shook his head at the thought of his niece and nephew. "Stevie takes more and more after his grandpa every day. The spittin' image of you and a little devil."

"Humph." Chuck pulled his pocket watch out of his jeans. "Reporter should be here by now."

Raising an eyebrow, Kade asked, "What's this about?"

"Supposedly one of those in-depth feature type reports." Chuck took a drink of his ice water and settled back. "Didn't your mother tell you? This reporter fella will be staying with us awhile, talking with ranchers, showing our side of the story and not just those damn militants that make us all look like a bunch of uneducated redneck yeehaws. He'll probably want to interview you and others from the department. He's supposed to be one of the best."

Kade's attention wandered from his stepdad as Kelsey entered the room, brushing her hair behind her ear as she spoke with the hostess.

Fire burned in his gut as he thought of last night. Those lips. The taste of her.

Bright as a summer day, her honey-blond hair tumbled loose to her shoulders, the soft pink blouse and faded jeans hugging her body, showing off her curves. He could almost smell her honeysuckle scent.

"What's the matter with you, boy?" Chuck turned and followed Kade's gaze. "Ah. A looker, that one."

The hostess grabbed a menu and led Kelsey straight to Kade's table. Her jaw dropped as she reached him, and her eyes locked with his.

"These handsome gentlemen are your party, Ms. Nichols." The hostess winked at Chuck. She set the menu in front of the empty chair between the men and left.

Chuck stood and took Kelsey's hand. "I'm Chuck Turner. You're the reporter, Kale Nichols?"

She moved her gaze from Kade to Chuck, and gave him a polite smile. "Please call me Kelsey."

What's Kade doing here? Kelsey's body tingled as if his hands were on her now. She did her best not to look at him but at the man she was scheduled to meet instead.

"Nice to meet you, honey." Chuck Turner's hand swamped hers, and with his good ol' boy personality, she almost expected him to slap her on the back and offer her a chaw of tobacco.

He released her and gestured to Kade. "This is my son. Kade, this is our reporter, who'll be staying with us at the JL Star. It'll be nice having a pretty lady as our guest."

"Your son?" That horrible flush rushed over Kelsey.

Kade's answering grin and the sweep of his eyes told her that he'd noticed. He stood and took her hand, and she felt that dangerous tingle skitter along her entire body.

Why did he affect her every time they touched?

She found her voice, and tried to sound like the professional reporter she was. "I thought your last name was Owen, not Turner."

Kade gave a slow nod and smiled. "It is. Chuck's my stepdad."

Chuck lifted his bushy brows and looked from Kelsey to Kade. "You two know each other?"

With only a little difficulty, Kelsey extracted her hand from Kade's. "We, ah, met yesterday on the plane."

"And had dinner last night," Kade added with a spark in his blue eyes.

Chuck's eyebrows shot up farther. "Well then. Let's have us some breakfast."

After Chuck pushed Kelsey's chair in, they ordered from the waitress. Kelsey chose the fruit plate, not sure the butterflies inhabiting her stomach could handle anything stronger with Kade so close, pressing his leg against hers. When she tried moving the other way, she managed to ram into Chuck's knee. She flushed with heat as she mumbled an apology.

When the waitress took their menus and left, Kelsey picked up her water glass and cut Kade a look that told him exactly what she intended to do with it. He grinned and moved his knee. The remainder of the meal he only *accidentally* brushed up against her thigh on occasion.

During the little knee waltz, Chuck explained how large the ranch was, and sure enough, Kade lived at the ranch, in the same house.

Wonderful.

Providence?

Get real.

Kelsey groaned inwardly, wondering if she should say that she had changed her mind, then flee back to San Francisco.

But to what? The jerk? Her little apartment above the Italian bakery?

No. Not going to happen. She could keep Kade in his place, finish the feature, conquer the Wild West, and be on her way.

As the waitress served their breakfast, Chuck launched into his concerns on the illegal immigrant situation and with his permission, Kelsey adjusted her cell phone's recording feature and put the phone on the table.

Chuck speared a sausage and gestured with it. "The problems have been there for years. They've got to get a handle on it, before more of those poor immigrant souls lose their lives, dying of thirst in the desert."

"Can Border Patrol increase its efforts?" Kelsey said.

"Ask Kade." Chuck waved his sausage at Kade. "He's with the agency."

She raised her eyebrows. "You're a CPB agent?"

Kade gave her that easy smile. "I told you I'm in law enforcement."

Kelsey tilted her head to the side. "You didn't mention which branch."

He shrugged. "You didn't ask."

Chuck's chair scraped against the tile floor as he stood and drew a cell phone from the pocket of his western shirt. "Need a moment to call your mother and let her know we'll be on our way in a few."

When Kelsey was alone with Kade, she wiped her mouth with a

napkin. "If I thought it remotely possible, I would bet you planned this."

"Who says I didn't?" He smiled. "You missed a spot."

As she speared a strawberry, she gave him a puzzled look. "What?"

He reached up and rubbed her chin with his thumb. "There, all gone." But he didn't stop, he continued on, trailing his thumb over her lips in a slow, sensual movement.

She froze, trapped by the brilliant azure of his eyes.

No. No way could she allow herself to become vulnerable to any man again.

Kelsey pulled away. "Kade . . . that kiss last night was a mistake. I'm going to do this feature, and then I'm going to leave. There is no room for any kind of relationship with you in this equation."

"All right." His lips quirked. "If you say so."

Chapter 4

Kade practiced keeping his hands off Kelsey as his stepfather maneuvered her into the front passenger seat of the SUV. Before she had a chance to argue, Chuck took the backseat. While Kade drove the hundred miles to the ranch, Kelsey turned and spoke with the rancher most of the way.

How the hell was he supposed to keep his hands off her when she'd be sleeping down the hall every night?

Every night.

That thought certainly held promise.

Although being around her seemed to be short-circuiting his brain. He managed to keep forgetting the reasons he was still single. And his intent to stay that way.

Maybe he'd just been waiting for the right woman . . . and his gut told him Kelsey might be that woman.

The interstate cut through rolling hills dotted with prickly pear and cholla cactus, paloverde trees, and mesquite bushes. Kade had traveled the route so often he usually took it for granted, but Kelsey's fascination with the desert made the drive far more interesting. He enjoyed the way her eyes lit up, the way she absorbed everything Chuck told her.

An hour and a half later they reached the CPB checkpoint just north of Tombstone. Kade rolled down the window to say hello to a couple of agents he'd known for years.

Kade gave a short nod. " 'Mornin', Sal. Don."

Don Mitchell raised his hand in a gesture of acknowledgment but stayed at his post to speak to the next vehicle coming up from Tombstone way.

"What the hell you been up to, Kade?" Sal sauntered over and clapped a hand on his shoulder. " 'Bout time you get your lazy ass back to work." His gaze flicked to Kelsey. His black brows rose and his mustache twitched. "Excuse me, ma'am. Didn't see you."

"Sal, this is Kelsey Nichols, a reporter from San Francisco." Kade gave Kelsey a smile when he looked at her. "Kelsey, this is Sal Valenzuela, one of the biggest pain-in-the-ass agents there are."

"Nice to meet you, Sal." She reached across Kade to shake Sal's hand. Kade's gut tightened as she leaned close, the soft curve of her breast brushing his shoulder.

As Sal shook Kelsey's hand, Kade scowled. He didn't particularly like the way Sal's dark eyes roamed over Kelsey.

After Sal and Chuck exchanged greetings, Kade nodded toward the checkpoint. "What're you and Don doing at this CP today? Get transferred while I was gone?"

Sal shook his head. "No. Short staffed. Talk about one hell of a mind-numbing day."

When he thought about the man responsible for smuggling illegal immigrants and drugs across the border, Kade narrowed his eyes. "Any new leads on El Torero while I've been gone?"

"The man's a ghost." Sal shrugged. "I'm beginning to think he doesn't exist."

Kade checked the side-view mirror. "Car coming. We'd better head on out."

"Get your ass on out of here." Sal smiled in Kelsey's direction, tipped his hat, and headed back to the checkpoint.

"Do they use that huge trailer to detain illegal immigrants?" Kelsey asked, finally addressing a question to Kade.

"No." Kade fixed his gaze on Kelsey's beautiful brown eyes. "The UDAs sit on the ground until we can ship them back to the border to process."

In the most adorable way that made Kade's heart rate pick up, Kelsey twisted her lips into a questioning expression. "What does UDA mean?"

"Our politically correct term for undocumented aliens," he said, "sometimes referred to as illegal aliens, or just illegals."

Kelsey's expression went scholarly, as if she were making notes in her head. The shift was almost imperceptible, from wide-eyed girl in a new place to sharp-as-nails reporter. She'd probably be a bear in an interview, if she had a mind to eat her subject instead of stroke his ego.

Tombstone eased into view, rising off the desert floor like a mirage. Kelsey smiled and looked out the window, still giving off that combination business-pleasure attitude. "How did Tombstone get its name?"

"There's an interesting story," Chuck piped up as they drove through the town. "A prospector named Ed Schieffelin discovered rich silver veins in the Goose Flats area in 1877."

As Chuck continued, Kade held back a grin. Chuck loved a

good story. "That old boy named his first mining claim 'The Tombstone,' after soldiers told him the only thing he'd find in those hills was Apache Indians and his own tombstone.

"On our left," Chuck went on, "is the Boothill Graveyard. So many of the folks buried there died suddenly or were killed with their boots still on, so it became known as Boothill."

Chuck launched into a story about the town's first mayor and the gunfight at the O.K. Corral.

"Fascinating," Kelsey murmured, then looked back out the window. "Is that all there is to it? I think I missed the rest of the town."

Kade grinned and said, "If you blink you miss it. From the highway there's not a whole lot to see of 'The Town Too Tough to Die.'"

Kelsey smiled and Kade pointed to the gentle swells of land. "When I was a boy and Mom and Dad would drive through here, I used to imagine a dusty road replacing the highway, and wagons instead of cars. I'd picture gunslingers on horseback, plodding along the gritty trails, and prospectors mining for silver."

"It's so . . . empty . . . so open and free." Her gaze traveled over the desert valley where it was easy to see as far away as fifty miles or more.

Kade glanced at her as she stared out the window, drinking in the landscape. "I can almost picture what you just said, Kade. Take down those telephone poles, get rid of the asphalt, replace the soil that was blasted out to make room for the highway, and nix the occasional passing car. . . . I bet it would look much like it did over a hundred years ago."

He smiled. So, she could see it. She did get a sense of how it was out here, half-old, half-new—just from this little car ride. Ms. Kelsey Nichols wasn't just a big-city girl after all.

And he still couldn't believe his luck, getting to bring her home with him.

Images whirled through Kelsey's mind as she pictured what Kade had shared. She tried to imagine him as that little boy who made up stories about cowboys, outlaws, and prospectors whenever he was in this part of the country.

"What do you think of the Wild West?" Kade asked as they headed deeper into rural country.

"It's beautiful." Southeastern Arizona had a rugged magnificence she'd never imagined that captivated her completely. No wonder settlers came out west to start a new life in places like this. The land had a way of calling to a person's soul and claiming it.

Clouds had built up around the mountains, but the sky in between was an endless cerulean blue. The final road they took was paved, too, but they had to cross several washes, some full of mud from flash floods.

Kelsey still couldn't believe that she was in a vehicle with Kade, and that it was his house where she would be staying. Her attraction to him was staggering, but she kept reminding herself that men were men, and the memory of Davis was still way too fresh.

No more mistakes. And no mixing business with personal, either.

Her heart rate increased when they finally drove up a dirt road to a sprawling ranch home. It was an absolute oasis in the desert surrounded by enormous weeping willows, cottonwoods, and junipers. Nothing but ground-hugging mesquite bushes and tumbleweeds survived for miles outside the fenced-off yard, but inside the yard everything grew lush and green from the expansive front lawn to the extensive flower and vegetable gardens.

As they reached the ranch house, a black rottweiler bounded toward the vehicle, followed by a grubby little boy. Kelsey studied him with a reporter's eye, sizing him up at around eight or nine. Kade parked the SUV, and as soon as he opened the door, the boy launched himself at the man.

"Dad! I missed you."

Dad? Kelsey's jaw dropped. Kade was a father? He had a son?

There was no doubt that boy was Kade's, from the vibrant blue eyes to the chestnut hair, to the dimple in one cheek.

Damn it, Kelsey. Don't go wide-eyed over a cute kid and a dog. And a cowboy hunk. You're a reporter. A professional. You can do this.

She grabbed her purse and laptop bag, and followed the others out of the SUV.

As she stood beside the vehicle, the rottweiler sniffed at her jeans and slobbered on her shoes.

Even the friggin' dog is cute. And I thought rottweilers aren't supposed to be cute.

"Trent." Kade gave the boy a fierce hug and set him back down on the ground. "I missed you, too, kiddo. Did you behave?"

"Yup." The child nodded so hard his hair flopped into his eyes. "I did all my chores and helped Grandma in the garden, fed the pigs, and found a rattlesnake, but I didn't get close to it, I ran and told Grandma and—"

"Slow down." Chuck crouched down, eye level with Trent. "What's this about a rattler?"

The boy squirmed. "I found it this morning and told Grandma and she chopped its head off with a shovel and she gave me the rattles. They're really long and so cool, you wanna see?" He grabbed his dad's hand and tried to pull him toward the house.

"Hold on." Kade looked like he was holding back laughter at his son's constant verbal stream. "Trent, this is Kelsey. She's the reporter who'll be staying with us."

The adorable little dynamo actually paused for a second and looked at her. "Whoa, you're a girl. We thought you were a boy. Isn't Kale a boy's name?"

Kelsey grinned and extended her hand. "It's nice to meet you, Trent. My real name is Kelsey but I go by Kale C. for my work."

He gave her a gap-toothed smile and shook her hand, and she noticed he smelled of bubblegum and dog. He would easily be as handsome as his dad when he grew up. "You wanna see my snake rattle?"

Chuck patted Trent on his shoulder. "Take Kelsey to the guest room, and then you can show her the rattle."

"Okay." The boy grabbed her hand and started for the house, hauling her along like he'd probably hauled his dog when the big brute had been a puppy. "How old are you? I'm nine. Well, almost nine. My birthday is in four days on the Fourth of July. It's summer, so we don't have school now. Grandma says there's six more weeks until school starts and she can't wait, 'cause then she'll get some peace and quiet. She calls me Taz. She thinks I'm like the Tasmanian Devil. Ever heard of him? He's on *Bugs Bunny*. I watch it all the time on Cartoon Network."

Kelsey laughed. "I'm twenty-five and I think Taz is a good nickname for you."

"My dad's old 'cause he's thirty-four now. But Grandma and Grandpa are lots older."

"What's this about your grandma being old?" came a voice from the porch before a mature yet youthful woman stepped through the screened door. She had the same blue eyes as Trent and Kade although her brown hair was streaked with gray.

Kelsey had a feeling she'd have a hard time holding back a smile around this kid whenever he was on a roll. "Grandma, this lady is

Kelsey, the reporter who's staying with us. She's not a man, though, and she's twenty-five. I'm going to show her my snake rattle after I take her to the guest room so she knows where it is."

The woman clasped Kelsey's hand in a firm grip. "I'm Sadie Turner. I see you've met the welcoming committee."

Kelsey returned the woman's warm smile and thanked her for her hospitality. "You look too young to be Kade's mother," she added, "and certainly not a grandmother."

Sadie laughed, a genuine sound that made Kelsey feel comfortable at once. "I'm plenty old enough, and have the battle scars to prove it."

Trent nodded solemnly. "Grandma's real old, 'cause she's over fifty and Grandpa's really, really old 'cause he's older than that."

"Off with you, and show Kelsey her room." Sadie gave Trent a playful swat on his behind. "And wash up. You're filthy."

"Okay." He pulled Kelsey through the screened-in porch, then the glass-and-oak double doors of the house, jabbering all the way. Kelsey could tell he was the kind of kid who could wear a person out with his enthusiasm and chatter, but he'd already won a place in her heart.

The house was spacious, with exposed beam ceilings and acres of unglazed Saltillo tile. The furnishings were Southwestern and casual, the type of home where a person would immediately feel comfortable. Country music played in the background on a stereo in the family room. They passed a wood-burning stove that Kelsey assumed would work in the winter since the stovepipe climbed into the ceiling and the stove looked well-used.

Trent pulled her through a spotless kitchen that smelled of fresh-baked cinnamon rolls. They headed around a corner, then down a long hall, and he stopped at the first room.

"This is the guest room. Dad's is that one right next to yours, and the one at the end of the hall is mine. Grandma and Grandpa's room is way over on the other side of the house. Do you wanna see mine now?"

"Sure." Kelsey tried to calm the nervous flutter stirring in her belly at Trent's words.

Kade's room, right here?

"I think he'll be a good chaperone, don't you?"

Kade's voice startled Kelsey, so close his breath tickled the back of her neck, and she caught his earthy scent. She whirled, sending her elbow into his hard stomach. "Oh. I'm sorry. No—no, I take it back. You deserved that."

He rubbed his side. "It's dangerous startling you, darlin'."

"Next time you might not be so lucky, cowboy." She couldn't help be mesmerized by those blue, blue eyes. She wanted to kiss him again, to taste him.

She shook her head, shaking the thoughts from her mind and turned away. "Hold on, Trent, I'll take a look at your room once I put my bag and purse in here."

Antique furniture of a deep mahogany filled the guest room. Cream brocade with a rose design covered the bed, matching drapes hung at the windows, and a beautiful Victorian lamp perched on the nightstand. It looked like a picture-perfect room at a bed-and-breakfast. A four-poster bed occupied the far side of the room, and she plopped her belongings beside it.

Kade followed, setting her two suitcases on the rose-colored throw rug as Kelsey turned to face him. For a moment neither of them moved.

The tension in the room tripled.

Emotions warred within her and she didn't know whether to kiss him or kick him in the shin and make a run for it.

He winked, then headed out the door. "Let's see that snake rattle, Trent."

Kelsey didn't have any problem showing interest in the rattle as Trent presented it to her. Although the thought of the rattle-snake that had once owned that rattle made her a little squeamish.

After they checked out the rattle, Trent grabbed Kelsey's hand and took her on a tour outside the house.

Warmth stirred in Kade's gut as he observed Kelsey with his son. She listened to Trent's nonstop jabbering and looked suitably impressed at everything he presented to her, including Roxie the rottweiler, a dead june bug, and Rock, his pet turtle.

When Trent dashed off to search for one of the barn cats, Kelsey grinned at Kade. "You have a wonderful son. So much energy and utterly honest."

"To a fault." Kade returned Kelsey's smile. "The kid doesn't know how to lie. I wonder how charming you'll find him once you've been around his endless talking for a while."

"He might wear me out, but I can tell he's one great kid. I've always wanted to have at least a couple." Her voice went soft and her thoughts seemed far away. "But my ex-husband insisted we weren't ready and he worried that I would get fatter." She bit her lip and blushed, obviously embarrassed from letting something slip he was sure she hadn't intended to.

"Your ex sounds like a stupid ass." He thought about punching the shit out of a man he didn't even know. "You're perfect." He put his hand on her upper arm and looked into her sensual brown eyes. "Personally, I wouldn't want you any other way."

"Thanks." She shrugged away from his touch. "I'm not sure any man could truly love a woman as she is. I heard more than enough lies from Davis to convince me of that." Her expression darkened. "Not to mention all the lies my father told my mother."

Kade caught her hand, bringing her eyes back to him. "I'm not lying, and I'm not your ex or your father." He squeezed her fingers. "They both sound like bastards."

Kelsey looked startled, then laughed. "That's them, all right."

He dropped her hand before she could pull away, and they walked through Sadie's apple and peach orchard toward the barn. The air was completely still, a prelude to a monsoon storm. Thunderheads had built up all around the valley and it smelled of rain.

Her gaze drifted around the orchard, barn, and cattle pens. "How long have you lived here?"

"I grew up in this house." He sidestepped a watering hose and sprinkler head hidden in the grass and made sure Kelsey didn't stumble over them.

"When I graduated high school," he continued, "I moved to Tucson to attend the University of Arizona for four years, then went into FLETC, the Federal Law Enforcement Training Center, in Artesia, New Mexico. Once I was officially an agent, I was stationed along the Texas border."

Kelsey ducked under the branch of an apple tree. "How did you end up back on the ranch?"

"When Trent's mother died five years ago, I felt he needed his grandparents," he said. "So I managed to get a transfer here and we moved in with Mom and Chuck for what I thought would be temporary."

She glanced up at him and he met her gaze. "I'd have already built my own house on a stretch of property I own if Trent hadn't needed his grandparents so much. I just couldn't separate them with him being so young."

"I didn't mean to pry." Pink flushed her cheeks. "About your wife and—"

He squeezed her shoulder. "You didn't."

"Dad Dad Dad Dad." Trent charged toward them. "Come see. Come on, come on." He grabbed Kade's hand.

Trent led the way, pulling his dad toward the barn. "Wait till you see." When they entered the dusty barn, Kelsey sneezed and Trent said, "Bless you. Come on now and see."

He pulled Kade around the saddles and tack to a cardboard box in one corner as he continued his endless but endearing chatter. "Look, Barny had kittens. Lots of kittens. It took me a long time to find her, but I did, and I counted five kittens, and one is orange like her and two are black and I think one is calico, and the other is white."

"Adorable babies." Kelsey crouched next to the box, then sneezed. "The mama cat is beautiful." Her eyes watered and she sneezed again.

"Cute kittens." Kade stroked one of the ratlike things as the mama cat kept her narrowed gold-green eyes on him. "I think Kelsey is allergic to cats or the barn, so maybe we'd better scram."

"I'm—" She sneezed. "Fine. Really—" Sneeze. "I am." Sneeze.

With a laugh, Kade grabbed her hand and pulled her up. "Come on, Sneezy."

Trent looked at his dad. "Kelsey's like Aunt Dara. She always sneezes when she comes out to the barn, too. Come on. I wanna tell Grandma and Grandpa about the kittens." The boy charged out the door and headed back to the house.

"I don't think I've"—Kelsey sneezed—"ever sneezed so many times in my life." Sneeze.

"Let's get you some allergy meds." Kade nodded toward the

house. "And I think I smell Mom's tacos. They're the best in the West. Hell, the best anywhere."

They headed back to the house and sure enough, tacos it was for dinner. It amazed Kade how comfortable Kelsey was with his family. After dinner, she insisted on helping clean up, and he joined her in washing and drying the dishes.

"I'm going to sleep like a baby." She put her hand over her mouth and stifled a deep yawn. Trent was tucked in bed, and Sadie and Chuck had retired for the night. "Those allergy tablets made me a little drowsy."

"I'll call it a night, too." Kade kicked off his boots at the front door, next to Trent's. "Back to work tomorrow."

Kade checked her out as she walked ahead of him. *Definitely one sexy ass.*

She stopped before the door of the guest room, looking at him with those sensual brown eyes that made him burn. "There is a lock on this door, isn't there?"

He slid his hands into his front pockets and studied her face, remembering how soft she'd felt in his arms the night before. How delicious her lips had tasted. His voice was husky as he replied, "You'll be glad to know that I have the only key."

"Kade." She narrowed her gaze and gave him a mock frown.

He moved closer to her. "The door locks from the inside." A strand of her honeyed hair fell forward, and he brushed it behind her ear. Just the slightest touch of his fingers against her skin made him want her even more. "You have one hell of an effect on my self-control," he whispered, his lips nearing hers.

"Dad." Trent's voice shattered the quiet, and Kelsey jumped. The boy peeked around the corner of his room. "I can't sleep. Will you read me a story?"

Kade stepped back and nodded to his son. "Sure, kiddo."

"Good night, Trent." Kelsey smiled at Trent. She turned to Kade and blushed.

He made his words low enough that he was sure only Kelsey could hear. "Sweet dreams, darlin'."

"Ah, right." She backed up and closed the door in his face. He heard the lock click and he grinned.

Chapter 5

Emotions raged within Kelsey, holding her on the edge of sleep. She couldn't stop thinking of last night when Kade had kissed her. His earthy, enticing smell. Her fingers against his muscled chest, and his lips burning hers . . . so sensual. Everything about him was sensual.

Kelsey's eyelids fluttered.

Kade's arms, holding her to him . . . the hammer of his heartbeat against her chest . . . wanting him, so much. Such warmth. Fire, burning her skin wherever his lips trailed. Her breasts aching beneath his slow and deliberate touch. Kade's mouth on her nipples, his tongue swirling across one and then the other. His naked body pressed against hers, his arousal melting her resolve.

She surrendered, losing herself—

Kelsey woke with a start, her heart pounding an uneven rhythm. She took a deep breath and blinked away the sensual dream and stared up at the ceiling. Moonlight and shadows flickered and danced across the white textured surface.

Lose myself. That was exactly what would happen if she surrendered to any man, and exactly why she couldn't allow it to happen with Kade.

And yet, she wanted more of him.

Damn. Even her dreams betrayed her.

Kade's words whispered through her mind. *I'm not lying, and I'm not your ex or your father.*

"I can't believe I slept so late," Kelsey told Sadie as she sat at the breakfast table in the copper and verdigris-green kitchen. The aroma of baked bread and cinnamon met her nose, and her stomach growled. "It must have been those allergy pills."

"You probably needed the sleep." Sadie handed Kelsey a glass of orange juice. "Nothing like country air to give you a good night's rest."

"Thanks." Kelsey took a long drink, then set the glass on the table. "Must be true. I don't think I've ever felt so relaxed. Where are Kade and Trent?"

"Kade left early for work." Sadie grabbed a set of oven mitts, opened the oven door, then pulled a shallow pan out of the oven.

A strange wave of disappointment flowed through Kelsey. Why should she care that Kade left before she could see him? She didn't need an adolescent obsession and she refused to think about him another second. Not one.

"Trent's feeding the pigs." Sadie set a pan on the stove and nodded toward the window. Kelsey looked out to see the sunshine warming a rose bed and willow branches dancing in a breeze.

Sadie blew a strand of chestnut hair out of her face as she wrapped up a square of cooled coffee cake and added it to a growing stack. "Would you like some Polish coffee cake?"

"I've never heard of Polish coffee cake, but it looks wonderful."

Kelsey's mouth watered as she breathed in the aroma. "It smells heavenly."

Sadie handed her a plate with a thick slice. As soon as Kelsey tasted it, she realized it was more than heavenly. Thin yeast bread with anise seeds baked in, then a cinnamon, sugar, and butter topping crumbled on top, and another topping drizzled over that.

"It's to die for." Kelsey sighed around a mouthful of the treat. "I'm going to gain ten pounds just from the smell of your cooking."

Laughing, Sadie whisked off her apron. "I wouldn't worry about pounds around here. Lots of walking. Good for the body—and the mind and soul. What're your plans for today?"

Kelsey swallowed a delicious bite before answering. "I'd like to start with interviewing you."

The woman plopped a wide-brimmed hat on her dark curls. "Let me know when you're ready. I'll be in the garden." She grabbed a metal bucket from the counter. "I'm dumping these scraps in the compost heap. Nothing goes to waste here, so don't throw away any leftovers."

"No danger of a crumb of this going to the compost." Kelsey smiled and rubbed her stomach. "Only problem is, it'll be going to my waist."

"You'll see how much exercise you get, just hanging around this place." Sadie laughed and headed out the back door with the scrap bucket.

Kelsey couldn't help like Sadie, not to mention Chuck and Trent. What a wonderful family Kade had.

Her heart gave a twinge. A family . . . she'd had a family, too, before her parents and sister were taken away. And if Davis loved anyone besides himself she could have had her own family. If he'd been the person she'd thought he was.

A son like Trent, energetic and bright. They might have built a tree house, played soccer, and every Christmas made construction-paper rings for the trees. He would have hugged her each night, after a bedtime story. *Mommy, I love you. . . .*

Enough. It was better that they hadn't had children. The divorce would have been an even greater nightmare, and no son of Davis's could have grown up healthy.

Kelsey decided to start with a shower and in the bathroom she discovered Kade's apple-scented shampoo. She smiled. No wonder he smelled of apples.

While she washed her body her mind went places she hadn't intended, imagining what it would be like to have Kade soaping her, touching her.

With a groan, Kelsey sagged against the wet tile behind her while warm water sprayed on her chest. Fantasizing about Kade was the wrong direction to take. If she let herself go, how would she manage to keep her hands off him during her stay at the ranch?

After showering, then dressing in jeans and a blouse, Kelsey headed to the den. The country air certainly did relax her, as if there was no hurry in the world to get to work. That's probably what Theresa had in mind when she'd agreed to giving Kelsey the assignment.

Kelsey sank into a swivel chair in front of a rolltop desk. She slid on her glasses and skimmed the latest news headlines on the Internet. The only sound in the room was the ticking of the wagon wheel–shaped clock, and the click-clack of her laptop keys.

Outside, chickens clucked and Rain Bird sprinklers went *ch-ch-ch-ch.* A wave of memories washed over Kelsey. The lazy sound of the sprinklers took her back to her childhood, when she and her sister, Naya, would run, in their panties, through the water sprays from sprinklers in their backyard. Kelsey could smell fresh-cut grass and feel water splashing her legs.

She rubbed the scar on her thigh as she stared out the window. How she missed Naya, and her mother. If only . . .

Kelsey jerked her attention away from things that couldn't be changed and downloaded her e-mail. She wanted to turn off the computer as soon as she saw the hundred-plus e-mails that had accumulated in the two days since she'd last checked.

Several were responses to her recent feature on the former California governor, a couple were from friends, three from her editor, and the rest were spam. She deleted all the unsolicited mail and responded to the others.

After she finished her replies, Kelsey leaned back in the swivel chair and closed her eyes. Her thoughts turned to Kade. His was a powerful presence, yet he was so gentle with her. Definitely a man she could lose her heart to, and it would make it all the harder when it was time for her to head home.

"They're not suffering, Kade," Don Mitchell said. "Just a bit of dehydration, and we've been making sure they're getting plenty of water."

Kade nodded and wiped sweat from his forehead with the back of his hand. The merciless sun cooked the desert as agents rounded up a group of thirty-three undocumented aliens at the Ford Ranch, at the foot of the Mule Mountains. Men, women, and children made up the miserable group, but they were too beaten by the heat to do more than crouch in the dust and wait to be processed.

Ford had reported the group when they stopped at his ranch for water. The rancher was a good man, and had allowed the UDAs to drink from his irrigation hose.

The stench of sweat and body odor was almost unbearable, and the heat only intensified the smell. It was obvious they'd been on a long and difficult journey, not uncommon for illegals trying to cross the U.S. border. Kade was not usually called in on a routine process, but one of the UDAs had claimed to have information on a key smuggler Kade was after.

In Spanish, Kade questioned Juan Dominguez, who'd insisted he knew the smuggler.

"Gordo," Juan said. He continued rattling in Spanglish, the border version of Spanish and English. The *coyotes* had left the UDAs to die, and Juan was angry. Gordo was the name the *coyotes* had called the smuggler. Juan gave Kade a description that matched what Kade knew of the man.

"Gordo," Kade muttered as he pushed his Stetson back and scratched his head. The name kept coming up, and in his gut he knew he was closer to tracking the bastard down.

Sal Valenzuela strode toward Don, looking like he was sweltering in his rough-duty uniform. "The kid on the end says an old guy couldn't keep up and they had to leave him behind. I'll call it in."

Don Mitchell radioed for a transport van after he and Sal determined that all the members of the group were indeed UDAs. They advised the men and women of their administrative rights and took down their personal information.

While they processed the UDAs a helicopter was utilized to help search for the missing man. Agents located him where he'd crossed Sweetwater, the ranch of the former county sheriff John "Bull" Stevens. The UDA was to be evacuated to Douglas Hospital, but he died from dehydration before the copter took to the air.

Kade tossed his hat into his truck as they got ready to leave the ranch. "Damn *polleros*."

"To hell and back." Don scowled. "Those *coyotes* deserve to die in the desert, instead of the people they leave stranded."

Sal gave a short nod as he looked over his shoulder at the UDAs.

Kade rubbed his hands over his face, trying to wipe away some of the exhaustion and frustration. "Only getting worse."

With a shrug, Don walked back toward the group of UDAs. "The *coyotes* run people and drugs. Both are profitable enough to be worth the risk."

"Need any help here before I take off?" Kade asked.

Sal shook his head. "We've got it handled."

"Then I've got to head on home." Kade climbed into his truck, lowered the window, and slammed the door.

"How long is that pretty reporter staying with you?" Sal's dark eyes gleamed.

The possessive feeling that grabbed Kade surprised him. "Not long enough." He buzzed up the window, his friend's low whistle fading as the glass rose.

Kelsey settled with her laptop computer at the dining room table for her interview with Kade's mother.

Sadie stretched a block of fabric across a hoop. "I hope you don't mind if I quilt while we talk."

"Not at all." Kelsey pulled her cell phone out of her bag and set it on the table after she'd prepared it to record.

She admired the furnishings, including an oak china cabinet filled with crystal glasses, goblets, and decanters. It surprised her to see crystal on a ranch, one of her many preconceived notions of life in the country to be shattered since meeting Kade's family.

Margarita glasses caught her attention. Heat rushed through her at the memory of what her last margarita had led to. Kelsey shoved thoughts of Kade from her mind, praying his mother wouldn't notice the flush in her cheeks. She ran her hand over a quilt block, admiring Sadie's work.

"Incredible." Kelsey traced one of the circles designed with small blocks of cloth. "I love the materials you've chosen and the way the rings loop together."

"You're sweet." Sadie slipped on a pair of half-glasses, adjusted the hoop, slid a thimble on one finger, and started stitching. "It's a wedding ring quilt, and the materials are hand-dyed."

Kelsey picked up a corner. "The circles do look like wedding rings intertwined."

"I've been working on it for years, off and on. I keep hoping Kade will find a young lady he wants to settle down with, so that I can give the quilt to him and his bride as a wedding gift." She glanced up and smiled. "There's been no shortage of women who've been interested in Kade. He's just never fallen in love with anyone."

Kelsey snatched her hand away as if it had been scalded. An image of Kade's kiss came to mind and a furious blush engulfed her to the soles of her feet.

"Can you tell me about your ranch?" She tried to keep her voice steady as she steered the conversation to safer ground.

Sadie quilted with deft strokes as she spoke. "Since Kade had no interest in going into the ranching business, a couple of years ago when we retired, Chuck sold off all the commercial cattle. We keep enough livestock for personal use, and raise most of our own vegetables and fruit."

Kelsey shifted her computer as she jotted down notes. "Do immigrants travel through your land?"

"We're fortunate that illegals don't cross our property as often as they cross the Carters', or the Grands'." Sadie adjusted her glasses and continued stitching. "Then there's the Mitchells' ranch—why, Don estimates five hundred or more go through their back pasture every night. Like a highway. Kitty put bars on her back window 'cause she's worried for her granddaughter."

She sighed and shook her head. "That's why Kev Grand bought himself a shotgun. Shoots up in the air—away from them, of course—just to scare them. I don't agree with his tactics."

"By Carter are you referring to Trace Carter's family?" Kelsey asked.

Sadie nodded. "One and the same gal who arranged for you to stay here."

Kelsey smiled. "Trace is a terrific friend. I'm going to miss seeing her while I'm here."

"Trace took off for Texas with her husband, Jess," Sadie said.

"Yeah, that's what she told me in her last e-mail." Kelsey tapped her fingertips on her laptop. "She won't be coming back until Christmas."

Sadie clipped a loose thread and started to rethread her needle. "Do you have any more questions about illegal immigration?"

"A few." Kelsey glanced at her notes again. "Do you come in contact with these people—the UDAs—often?"

"The illegals we get, most of them just want water," Sadie said. "Not too long ago, we discovered a hole cut into our fence beside a water trough. Rather than reaching over the fence to get water, they cut right through the wire."

Kelsey tapped her stylus. "I wonder why they do that."

Sadie twisted her lips in obvious disapproval of the practice, but for the woman it was still a mild expression that fit her personality.

"Sweetwater Ranch has sustained the most damage that I know of." She adjusted the quilting hoop in her lap. "Bull—that's John Stevens, who owns Sweetwater—lost thousands of dollars in cattle when *coyotes* tore down his fence to run illegals through."

Kelsey frowned and stopped taking notes. *"Coyotes?"*

"The smugglers," Sadie said. "Also called *los polleros,* who are paid to sneak illegal immigrants into the U.S."

Kelsey's thoughts whirled. "What do you do when illegals stop by?"

Sadie glanced over the rims of her glasses. "Usually my husband gives the immigrants water while I call the authorities."

Kelsey looked at the dog at her feet and smiled at the large sad-eyed rottweiler. "I'm sure Roxie is a good watchdog."

"Nothing like a rottweiler to keep people at a distance." Sadie smiled. " 'Course she'd as likely slobber all over your shoes than bite you, but we'll keep that to ourselves."

Kelsey and Sadie talked for about an hour longer. Sadie explained how deep passions ran among people when it came to the subject of illegal immigrants, no matter which side of the issue the person might be on.

"When does Kade get home?" Kelsey asked when they finished the interview. He'd been gone since at least six A.M. It was closing in on a full twelve hours from the time he'd left the house until this moment.

"Anytime now." Sadie glanced out the front window. "Looks like he's here."

A low thrill invaded Kelsey's belly, and when Kade walked through the door her senses ran sky-high. His presence filled the room and the tired smile he gave her made her knees quiver.

"Mom. Kelsey." Kade hung his Stetson on the hat rack, then

kicked off his boots and left them beside the front door. He wore a faded blue shirt over a black T-shirt and snug jeans.

"Shower?" Sadie asked as he strode by.

"Uh-huh." Kade walked past, straight for the laundry room.

"He usually won't say two words after work until he's had his shower." Sadie began folding her quilt and packing it away. "At least on days when he's detained illegals."

"Why is that?" Kelsey asked.

Kade stepped out of the laundry room, his shirt off, and he was removing a black vest. A tickling sensation rolled over her skin as she realized it was a bulletproof vest. It had never occurred to her that Kade would ever be in that kind of danger.

"I come in contact with hundreds of people from all over the Third World." He walked to an oak cabinet and opened one of the doors with a key. "Due to the conditions of their trip, who knows what viruses or diseases they could be carrying. I've seen HIV, hepatitis, plagues, malaria, typhoid, cholera, TB . . . you name it."

Kelsey checked to make sure her phone was still recording, forcing herself to take her eyes off Kade's muscular chest.

"Diseases and sickness are things that never occurred to me," she said, her eyes drawn back to him.

He withdrew his handgun from a holster at his side and placed the weapon in the cabinet, followed by a second handgun he had secured at the back of his jeans. "In Douglas, a few agents a year contract TB at work and someone always ends up sick. The last thing I want to do is bring anything home to my family."

"I see." Kelsey chanced a glance at his face. "Why aren't you wearing the green uniform that CPB agents usually wear?"

He gripped the back of a chair and eyed her with that intense blue stare of his. "I work intelligence, so I wear civilian clothing.

It's easier to obtain information when I don't look like law enforce-ment."

"Ah." She struggled to think of something to say, her brain seeming to have gone on vacation with him standing so close. Half-naked at that. "I—uh, I'll have to pin you down for an interview."

He winked. "Darlin', you can pin me down anytime."

A hot flush seared Kelsey. With Kade's mother sitting next to her, she couldn't think of a suitable reply.

"Time to finish dinner." Sadie slid her glasses into a case as she stood. She settled her quilting materials into a corner and headed into the kitchen.

Kelsey pushed back her chair. "I'll help."

As he returned to the laundry room, Kelsey's gaze followed Kade while she noticed the powerful lines of his naked back. With a mental shake, she trailed after Sadie into the kitchen, trying not to think about how good Kade looked without his shirt on. Trying not to imagine what it would feel like to run her palms over his chest and down, down the flatness of his hard stomach, down—

Kelsey. She clenched her hands and took a deep breath. *Enough of that.*

"What can I do to help you?" she asked Sadie.

"Why don't you peel the potatoes?" Sadie gestured toward several brown-skinned potatoes on the countertop, and then reached up into a cabinet filled with jars of spices. "Now where is the oregano . . ."

The washing machine hummed as it started, and Kelsey grabbed the potato peeler off the counter. She almost dropped it when Kade walked through the kitchen clad only in black boxers. He winked at her but didn't pause and went straight to the bathroom.

He had one of the most gorgeous male bodies she'd ever seen.

Hard, muscular thighs and calves. Powerful arms, and definitely a nice backside.

Kelsey blushed, realizing that Kade's mom was right behind her. If Sadie hadn't been there, she probably would have stood with her mouth hanging open.

Awhile longer.

Chapter 6

During dinner Kade sat beside Kelsey. The family chattered and laughed, but Kelsey could scarcely think with the hair on Kade's forearm tickling her arm every time he moved. He pressed his leg to hers beneath the table, and even when she shifted in her seat he still managed to brush up against her. It was almost a relief when dinner was over and she could escape his constant presence.

After they all helped Sadie clean off the table and straighten the kitchen, Trent grabbed Kade's hand and tugged him toward the back door. "Come on, Dad. Let's show Kelsey my hideout."

"You game?" Kade asked, looking at Kelsey in a way that made her heart skip a beat.

She smiled. "Sure. I'd love to see your hideout, Trent."

"All right." The boy snatched her hand, too, and pulled her and Kade out the door.

She laughed and looked over Trent's head at Kade. "You have quite the dynamo here."

"You have no idea." Kade's dimple appeared when he smiled, and her stomach flip-flopped.

The boy's hand felt small and warm in Kelsey's as he dragged them through Sadie's orchard and into the windbreak. The late-afternoon sun hung just above the mountains and the air smelled of cut grass and marigolds. A breeze cooled her cheeks and twigs snapped underfoot as they walked through cottonwood, eucalyptus, and juniper trees.

When they reached a grassy area, Trent pointed to a muddy pool of water. "That's Grandma's duck pond." It smelled of moss and algae, and the sounds of quacking filled the clearing. "Don't they sound like they're telling secrets? That's what Grandma always says. And look, there's Momma duck and her babies."

Kelsey smiled. "I bet Momma duck is chatting about how adorable her babies are."

They halted as the duck family waddled in front of them, about a dozen fuzzy ducklings trailing the mother.

"Come on." Trent pulled Kelsey's hand and led her farther into the windbreak. "Here it is," he announced when they came upon a playhouse painted in cheerful primary colors. "My dad made it for me when I was five and he painted it in my favorite colors. It's on the ground 'cause the trees around here aren't big enough to build it up high, so it's not a tree house, it's a ground house, but I call it my hideout."

The yellow house stood about five feet tall, had a green chimney, scarlet door, and bright blue trim around the windows and eaves. It was perfect for a kid to have loads of adventures in.

"The craftsmanship is beautiful." Kelsey glanced at Kade. "Your father must be talented with his hands."

The second she said it, a hot flush swept over her, and it was all she could do not to clap her hand over her mouth. Instead she studied the playhouse, trying to regain her composure.

Kade's laugh was soft, sensual as he leaned close. "Thank you, darlin'."

"Come inside." Trent dodged through the door. "I want to show you all my stuff."

Kelsey followed, doing her best to ignore Kade. No easy feat considering the effect his presence had on her erratic pulse.

The playhouse was snug, but the three of them managed to squeeze inside and sit on the green floor. She scooted beside the child-sized table and chairs, and she was sure Kade made a point to press as close to her as possible.

The warmth of his skin seared her as his arm rubbed against hers, and his jeans were rough against her bare thigh. His masculine scent surrounded her. She considered telling him to move away, but she was afraid her voice would betray the desire he stirred inside her.

"This is a great place to hide, so that's why I call it my hideout." Trent pushed open blue shutters and pointed out the window. "You can see the driveway from here and the front door, but no one can see us. So if I want to be a spy, I can check out things from here."

He dug in a toy chest under the window, tossing out toys left and right. An orange ball bounced across the room and action figures clattered to the floor. "I have these old binoc—binoco— How do you say it, Dad?"

"Binoculars."

"Oh, yeah, binoc-ulars." Trent didn't miss a beat resuming his chatter. "Anyway, I can see really far with these. Grandpa gave them to me. I've got all kinds of spy stuff. Dad said that if something ever happens and I need to find a hiding place, I should come here and he'll know where I am."

Kelsey captured the orange ball with one hand as it rolled across the floor. "Do you play out here a lot?"

Trent nodded, his brown hair flopping into his eyes. He swiped the hair away with his grubby hand. "Mostly when Grandma says her ears need a break."

Kelsey giggled and Kade grinned. He said, "Why don't we show Kelsey around the ranch?"

"Sure." Trent started to head out the door.

"Hold on," Kade said. "Forgetting something, Trent?"

Trent turned back. "What?"

"Your toys."

The boy scrunched up his face, wrinkling his nose. "Do I have tooooo?"

"Yes." Kade gave Trent a look that said, *right now.*

Trent scooped up all his toys and tossed them into the box, the crash loud enough to bring down the roof. After they were all picked up, he whirled and scampered out the door and vanished into the windbreak.

Kelsey pitched the orange ball into the toy box, wondering where Trent had disappeared to.

As she went through the little doorway on her hands and knees, she felt Kade's gaze on her backside. She didn't know what got into her, but she paused for a moment. She imagined Kade's palm on her bottom, a slow rub that made Kelsey want to moan. Heat burned her and she scrambled out into the trees.

After Kade crawled out, he shut the door and stretched his limbs. His muscles rippled beneath his snug T-shirt, and she couldn't help remember how good he had looked earlier, clad only in boxers.

Trent came crashing through the windbreak and grabbed Kelsey's hand, bringing her attention back to the boy. "Dad, let's show her the plane."

Kelsey's voice pitched a little higher as she glanced at Kade. "Plane?"

He shrugged. "I told you, I'm a pilot. I have a twin-engine Cessna."

"And it's really, really cool." Trent pulled her hand.

Goose bumps broke out up and down her arms as she forced herself to go with him through the trees until she saw the small craft sitting on the dirt landing strip.

Kelsey stopped abruptly and Trent almost fell backward. "It's, uh, nice." As she grabbed the boy's shoulders and steadied him, her heart pounded and she felt blood drain from her face. She swallowed, trying to force the lump out of her throat. "Ah . . . anything else you want to show me? Your grandma's garden?"

Trent pulled her hand. "I'll show you the inside of the plane."

Panic gripped her and she couldn't get out a word.

"Trent!" Sadie's cry came from the house. The woman had a mild easygoing manner about her, but could she ever yell.

Kade watched Kelsey with a thoughtful expression as he patted his son's shoulder. "Better see what Grandma wants."

Trent frowned and put his hands on his hips. "But, Dad, I wanna show Kelsey the plane."

"Go." Kade's stern tone obviously meant he didn't expect any further argument. "You know your grandma doesn't like it when you don't answer right away."

"Trent!" Sadie called again.

"But, Daaaaad."

"Now."

"All right," the boy grumbled, and took off for the house, disappearing through the trees.

Kade studied Kelsey for a moment before he said, "You like small planes less than commercial airlines."

"Far less." She smoothed a strand of hair behind her ear and tried to stop her hands from trembling. She turned her back to the plane and gestured toward the house. "Why don't you show me something else?"

"Want to talk about it?" His voice was calm. Grounding.

She almost wished she could tell him, but the pain was too great for her to get the words out.

She shook her head and started walking through the windbreak. "No."

When she glanced at him, his eyes were dark, concerned. "All right."

Gradually, her tense muscles relaxed as he took her on a tour of the ranch. The farther she got from the plane, the better she felt. He showed her Sadie's greenhouse and garden, then the henhouse and corrals. Kelsey laughed when she saw Trent's family of potbellied pigs, and at the antics of Sadie's baby Alpine goats.

When it was dusk, they strolled back toward the house. Kade came up short and studied her. "Enjoying your stay?"

"Very much." She smiled and nodded. "It's wonderful here."

"Have dinner with me one night." His voice was low and husky, sending shivers down her spine. "We'll head into town to a nice little restaurant I know. Just you and me."

A fluttering sensation gathered in her belly and she struggled to calm it. She took a deep breath of clean evening air and said, "I—I don't know."

They stood in front of the house, just outside the porch. Light poured through the windows and teased the gold in Kade's chestnut hair. An overwhelming urge came over her to run her fingers within that thick hair, to press close against his hard body and kiss him like the world was on fire. Like there was no tomorrow, only today. Only the two of them.

Kade trailed his finger down her arm and she gasped at the sensual contact. "It's just dinner, Kelsey."

She stepped back, away from his disturbing touch. "I'll think about it." She forced herself to turn from him, and hurried into the house.

Even as she left him outside, she wondered why she couldn't just let go and spend some time with this man.

What's wrong with me?

Why don't I just go for it?

And the answer came to her as clear as day.

She didn't want to lose her heart, and with Kade, that was something that would be only too easy to do.

Kelsey tucked her glasses into their case, then rubbed the bridge of her nose. Her temples throbbed from spending the afternoon transcribing notes from her interview with Chuck. Since her deadline was a couple of weeks off, she had time yet to start writing the feature.

She closed her eyes and relaxed in the study's leather chair. Against her will, her thoughts wandered to yesterday evening, when Kade had suggested they go to dinner. Alone.

No matter how much she tried to tell herself it would be a mistake, she couldn't help wonder what it would be like to be with him. That one kiss she'd shared with Kade had unraveled her more than any amount of intimacy she'd ever shared with Davis.

With Davis it hadn't been making love, it had just been sex, and she'd never enjoyed it. He'd called her a cold fish. Told her she was terrible in bed. She'd never known what to do, and with him it was over before it started. No foreplay. No cuddling. Just Davis relieving his needs.

She'd thought that was all there was to sex until Theresa and her friend Calinda had started in on the topic one day at lunch. Kelsey started wondering if she'd been missing something. Perhaps Davis had been not only a sorry excuse for a husband, but a poor sexual partner as well.

Why did she believe it would be any different with Kade?

Well, let's see. The way he'd kissed her, as though he wanted to taste her everywhere. The way he touched her, and how careful and protective he was with her. The way that he looked at her, like she was the only woman on earth. The way he made her feel, like a fire burned deep within her soul—an ache, a need that only he could fill . . .

And she could imagine him filling her in every possible way.

With a shiver and a sigh, Kelsey opened her eyes and looked out the window. It was a beautiful day, and she was tired of being cooped up. She stood and stretched her stiff limbs, then wandered out of the study and into the kitchen. Delicious smells came from a pan of ground beef simmering on the stovetop, next to a pot of bubbling red sauce.

"Need help?" Kelsey asked when she saw Kade's mom at the counter shredding a head of lettuce.

"You can grate the cheese." Sadie pointed to a block of cheese on the counter as she scooped lettuce into a colander. "I'm making a batch of enchiladas for the Frontier Homemakers' dance and pot-luck tonight."

After Kelsey washed and dried her hands, she started grating cheese onto the plate Sadie provided. "Sounds like fun."

Sadie took a bunch of green onions and chopped them into small pieces on a wooden cutting board. "I was hoping you might like to join us."

Kelsey glanced up from the growing mound of cheese. "I don't know how to dance to country-western."

"Nothing to it." Sadie shrugged and scraped onions into a small bowl. "If Kade's not too tired after work, I'm sure he wouldn't mind showing you how to two-step."

Heat warmed Kelsey's face at the thought of dancing with Kade. "I wouldn't want to impose." She finished her task and set down the grater. "What else can I do to help?"

"Would you mind chopping these?" Sadie handed Kelsey two plump tomatoes. "And nonsense about imposing. I'm sure Kade would enjoy it. He's quite good."

"I'm sure he is," Kelsey murmured as she took the knife and cutting board Sadie handed her.

Sadie scooted an enormous baking dish onto the counter. "Besides, you'll have a chance to meet some folks you'll be interviewing."

"True." Kelsey nodded as she sliced one of the tomatoes. Who knew, she might enjoy herself. An image of Kade holding her close flashed in her mind, and her hands trembled. The knife slipped and she barely avoided cutting her thumb.

She needed to get her mind off Kade or she'd end up slicing off a finger.

Before she could think better of it, Kelsey asked, "Does Kade usually go?"

"When I can convince him." Sadie began filling and rolling tortillas and placing them into the pan. "He tends to shy away from these things."

Kelsey gave an inward sigh, mentally shaking herself. She couldn't allow herself to trust so easily and to want so much so soon. Especially a man who continually invaded her thoughts and made her feel as if she were melting inside every time he looked at her. She was only there for three weeks and then she would be gone.

Kade would be out of her life forever.

Why did that thought make her feel so hollow?

Chapter 7

After debating whether to wear a skirt or slacks, Kelsey opted for a new pair of jeans and a silky blouse in shell pink.

Her stomach clenched at the thought of Kade asking her to dance with him—if he went. She could almost feel the warmth of his body close to hers, his arms wrapped around her, his lips brushing her ear. . . .

Kelsey rolled her eyes. "Get a grip, Kelsey."

She was acting like she was in high school again, getting ready to attend one of the functions where boys lined one wall and girls grouped together against the other.

Memories of her younger sister's first school dance abruptly came to Kelsey. She closed her eyes, remembering how pretty Naya had looked in her indigo dress. How her brown eyes had sparkled and how nervous she'd been the first time a boy asked her to dance.

Kelsey had been fiercely protective of her younger sister and had refused to let Naya out of her sight that night. But in the end, just a couple of years later, Kelsey hadn't been able to protect her. She hadn't been able to do anything to prevent her sister from dying.

As she wiped away a tear, Kelsey forced the thoughts from her mind. It didn't do any good to dwell on the past. No good at all.

While she jerked a brush through her hair, she studied her reflection in the mirror. She couldn't help see herself as Davis did, remembering all the times he told her how fat she was.

Stop it. She took a deep breath and tried to relax. Funny that he used to tell her she was beautiful before they were married. But how quickly things had changed, and how controlling he'd become. She'd been stupid. Naïve.

She slammed the brush down on the bureau and clenched her fists. She'd finally come to her senses and ditched the jerk. Taking several deep breaths, she cleared her mind of all unwanted memories.

The only problem was that the image that filled her mind next was of Kade walking through the house in his boxers yesterday. He was so good to look at. Not to mention good to taste.

With a groan, she touched up her makeup, going to a little extra effort on her appearance. At the last minute, she decided to paint her toenails bright pink with quick-drying enamel polish. When she finished, she tucked her blouse into her jeans, slid on a pair of sandals, and headed to the kitchen.

"Now don't you look nice," Chuck said when she entered the room.

Kelsey smiled, enjoying his country charm. "You're quite the dashing gentleman."

"Hey, Kelsey." Trent whirled into the room. His hair was combed and parted on the side, and he wore jeans and a western shirt. "Are you going with us?"

"Yes, sir." She put her hand on his shoulder and smiled. "You're so handsome. Will you save a dance for me?"

"Okay." Trent bounced on his toes and turned to his grandma.

"Is it time to leave? Jamie Perez is coming and I wanna show him my snake rattle. I've got it in my pocket."

"We're ready." Sadie picked up the foil-covered pan of enchiladas. "Chuck, will you take this out to the car?"

"Sure thing, sweetheart." He kissed Sadie and took the pan.

Sadie grabbed a pen and notepad off the counter and scrawled a quick note, then laid it on the table. "I'm letting Kade know where we'll be. Who knows if he'll remember about the dance tonight. Since he's late, it's possible he'll be too tired."

Kelsey nodded, pushing away a wave of disappointment that she didn't want to feel.

After they drove the two miles to the clubhouse, they all piled out of Sadie's SUV. It was early evening and lights were blazing through the windows, the dirt and gravel parking lot crammed with vehicles. The clubhouse wasn't much to look at from outside—a long, narrow building that must have been at least fifty years old and had the scars to prove it. Scraggly trees grew behind the clubhouse, and if Kelsey wasn't mistaken, there were "hers" and "his" outhouses in the back.

She hid a smile as she followed the Turners up the concrete steps to the clubhouse. Country-western music blared into the night, along with laughter and conversation. As they walked into the building, everyone they passed greeted Sadie and Chuck, and Kelsey's head spun with the names of all the people she was introduced to. The clubhouse smelled of fried chicken, sawdust, and sweat. Couples danced on the sawdust-covered hardwood floor, people were laughing, talking, and eating, and children dodged underfoot. In the corner a band was set up with a couple of bales of hay around them. For atmosphere, she supposed.

"This is Sal, a Border Patrol agent and friend of Kade's." Sadie gestured as the familiar dark-haired man walked up to them. "Sal, this is Kelsey, the reporter who's staying with us."

"Hello, Sal." Kelsey had to raise her voice to be heard over the toe-tapping song the band was playing.

"Buenas noches." His mustache curved upward as he squeezed her hand. "It's nice to see you again."

Kelsey turned to Sadie and explained how she and Sal had met at the CPB checkpoint outside of Tombstone. The song ended, and the band started another tune. "How about a dance?" Sal asked Kelsey.

Her cheeks grew hot—she hadn't danced with anyone since high school. "Ah—"

"Get out there." Sadie ushered them toward the dance floor. "I'm going to make sure Chuck set the enchiladas on the buffet table. I wouldn't be surprised if he decided to keep the whole pan for himself."

Kelsey's gaze darted from Sal to the dance floor and back. "I, ah, don't know how. . . ."

"It's easy enough." Fine lines at the corners of Sal's eyes crinkled and his mustache twitched as he guided her onto the floor.

Sal turned out to be an excellent teacher, and he didn't seem to mind Kelsey stepping on his boots at least half a dozen times. Soon she was getting the hang of it and actually enjoying herself. Every now and then, though, she couldn't help glance at the door, wondering if Kade would show.

When they stopped to drink a cup of punch, Kelsey was asked to dance by a man who was chewing on a toothpick. Before she knew what was happening, she was swept onto the dance floor again.

John Stevens introduced himself as they danced around the

room. A pleasant-looking man, he was built like a bulldozer, had hazel eyes, a slightly receding hairline, and long sideburns.

He leaned close and said over the music, "I hear you're staying with the Turners."

Kelsey tilted her head while at the same time trying to avoid getting jabbed by the toothpick. "Sadie mentioned you. Don't you own a ranch by the name of Sweet—"

"Sweetwater." He drew her out of the way of a couple twirling into their path.

Her interest perked up. "I'm interviewing ranchers about the illegal immigrant situation. Would you be free to chat with me?"

A flicker of something passed across his features, but it was too brief for Kelsey to get a feel for what it might be. He shrugged and said, "You're welcome to come on out to Sweetwater anytime. Just give me a heads-up."

By the time she finally made her escape to grab something cold to drink again, Kelsey had danced with a few men and once with Trent. Droplets of sweat trickled between her breasts, the heat of exertion warmed her face, and the backs of her heels surely had blisters.

Sal eased up to her as she ladled punch into her cup. "All danced out?"

Kelsey laughed and sipped her punch. "I haven't had this much fun in ages."

She agreed to one more dance with Sal, but when he led her to the floor, she realized the band was playing a slow tune. A twinge of nervousness gripped her stomach. It had been fine dancing to fast numbers, but being too close to any man made her uncomfortable.

Any man but Kade. The moment she amended the thought, she immediately chastised herself. She just couldn't get that man out of her head.

Fortunately, Sal held her at a respectable distance, one hand on her shoulder and one at her waist, with plenty of room between them. "I'm surprised Kade isn't here," Sal said as they moved across the floor.

Kelsey shrugged, pretending it didn't matter. "Apparently he had to work late. He's probably too tired, anyway."

Sal winked. "I'd bet next month's paycheck that nothing will stop him from coming, just knowing you're here."

Face heating even more, she shook her head.

Tingles erupted at the base of Kelsey's neck. She cut her gaze to the doorway and caught her breath. Kade had his shoulder against the door frame, his arms folded across his chest. His blue eyes were focused on her, his expression unreadable. He looked so good, dressed in a dark blue western shirt, faded jeans, a black cowboy hat, and worn brown boots.

Good enough to eat. *Whole.*

Sal leaned close, and she forced herself to turn away from the sight of Kade to hear what Sal had said. When she glanced back to the doorway, Kade was gone.

Fire simmered in Kade's gut. He clenched his jaw as he watched Kelsey dancing with Sal, her face flushed and her eyes bright. She smiled and blushed at something Sal said. She was obviously enjoying being with him. She'd barely been giving Kade the time of day, yet there she was, dancing too damn close to his friend.

He'd studied Kelsey awhile before she noticed him, and then their eyes locked. Until Sal drew her attention back to him.

Even though Kade knew he wasn't thinking clearly, at that moment he would've liked nothing better than to smash his fist into Sal's jaw. He tossed his Stetson onto a hat rack, then moved through the dancers until he was behind Sal. Kelsey was looking to the doorway, where he'd been standing.

He touched Sal's shoulder, trying not to look like he was ready to kill him. His friend glanced up and with a nod, let Kade cut in. Kelsey turned her gaze back from the door just as he replaced Sal, and her jaw dropped.

"Kade," she said, her eyes wide.

"You don't mind me cutting in, do you?" He studied her incredible brown eyes. "Or would you prefer Sal's company?"

"No. I mean yes." Kelsey shook her head and turned a pretty shade of pink. "Yes, I would like to dance with you, and no, I don't prefer Sal's company."

"Good." He smiled and eased his hands around her waist. "I'd hate to be out here all alone."

The song ended, but they remained at the center of the floor as a mellow tune began. Kade drew Kelsey to him, her head under his chin, her body close to his.

She pulled away enough that she could look up at him. "I don't know if this is a good idea." Her voice was low.

"Trust me." Kade leaned close to whisper in her ear. "It's a great idea."

She remained stiff in his embrace as they moved in time with the music, but gradually she relaxed, her head against his chest, his arms secure around her. He drank in the scent of her, reveled in the feel of her soft body against his. The swell of her breasts against his chest, the curve of her waist beneath his hands. Her hips and thighs were so close to his he was all but making love to her on the dance floor.

Well, hell. Damned if he wasn't getting rock-hard just dancing with her. He muttered another curse under his breath and eased away from her as the song ended and the band stopped to take a break.

"Did you say something?" she asked as they parted.

He took a deep breath and willed his body to behave. "Would you like a cold one?"

She nodded, her honey-blond hair brushing her shoulders.

Kade put his hand to her elbow and guided her to the buffet tables. "Looks like the folks are getting ready to leave with Trent." He inclined his head toward where his parents stood talking to Stan and Marnie Perez, and their son, Jamie. Sadie held her empty enchilada tray and Trent was showing Jamie his snake rattle.

"Would you like to stay?" Kade asked, hoping she'd say yes. "I'll drive you home."

Kelsey glanced at him for a second before looking away. Was that fear mingled with desire in her eyes? "I should be getting back with everyone else."

"Why?" Kade tilted his head and gave Kelsey that sexy smile that made her toes curl and her insides melt into pools of liquid silver. "Afraid of being alone with me?" His tone was low and husky.

Kelsey sighed. "Yes. I am."

"Don't be." He took her hand, his incredible blue eyes looking at her as if they were the only people who existed. "I'll be the perfect gentleman."

"I know. But . . ." Her heart pounded as she glanced toward his parents. "It's late."

He squeezed her hand, sending shivers throughout her body. "The dance won't last much longer. I promise to take you right home."

"Are you two staying?" Sadie asked as she came up behind them.

Kelsey jumped and snatched her hand away from Kade. She was

sure she managed to turn ten shades of red for the umpteenth time.

"I was just convincing Kelsey to stay," Kade said, never taking his eyes from her.

"Maybe a little longer." Kelsey glanced from Sadie to Kade. "But not too long. I'm worn out from all of this dancing."

Sadie smiled. "We'll leave the light on."

"Thanks," Kelsey murmured as Kade laced his fingers with hers and led her to the buffet.

He released her to ladle punch into a plastic cup and then handed it to her. She accepted it and swallowed the drink that tasted of pineapple and sherbet. When she finished, he tossed their cups into the garbage, then led her onto the dance floor.

A song with a fast beat was playing, and she said, "I just learned to dance to country-western tonight, so I'll probably stomp on your toes a few times."

He smiled and slid his arm around her waist. "You can step on my toes all you want."

"Stomp." Kelsey gave a mischievous grin as they started to two-step. "I figure I owe you."

Kade smiled. "Thanks for the warning."

By the time they'd danced to a couple of songs, she was relaxed and enjoying herself. Kade was an excellent dancer and teacher, even better than Sal, and she managed to stomp on his boots only two or three times.

At the end of one particularly fast number that she'd had a hard time learning, Kelsey was laughing so hard she stepped on Kade's foot and she almost fell. He caught her and slid his arms around her waist. Her laughter died in her throat as the lights dimmed and a slow tune started—and she saw the look in Kade's eyes. So intense. Burning with desire. For her.

She tried to back away, but he held her tight. "I'm all sweaty, Kade."

"So am I." He moved his lips to her ear. "Just relax and enjoy the dance."

Kelsey nodded, the top of her head brushing his chin. She allowed him to hold her snugly to him and rested her head against his chest. Kade felt solid and warm, his masculine scent so earthy, so potent to her senses.

His breath feathered her hair as her body merged with his and the heat of his muscled form burned through her blouse. Judging by his erection against her hip he was most definitely attracted to her. Heat rose in her cheeks and she was glad he couldn't see her face. Despite his obvious desire, she didn't feel threatened. Deep within she knew he wouldn't push her. He could have the one time they'd kissed—but he'd been the one to back away.

When the song ended, Kade lifted his head and lightly caressed her shoulders. "Ready to head on home?"

"Yes." Kelsey let him take her hand and he linked his fingers with hers.

He plucked his cowboy hat off the hat rack as they left. A single light illuminated the small parking lot as he led her to his truck. Gravel crunched underfoot and music from the clubhouse pounded out into the night. He opened the passenger door of the big black Ford truck and helped Kelsey up and in, then closed the door behind her before climbing in on his side and starting the vehicle.

Kelsey studied Kade in the amber glow of the dashboard lights as they headed back to the ranch. She was fascinated by the strength of his arms as he drove, the dark hair curling from his wrist along his forearm. His masculine profile, his strong jaw.

Yearning curled in Kelsey's belly. It was more than lust. It was the desire to be wanted, needed, and loved.

Warmth crept over her when he caught her watching him. "I had a great time," she said, her voice slightly husky.

He reached across the seat to squeeze her hand, his touch electrifying her.

Releasing Kelsey's hand to take the wheel, he brought his attention back to the road and the short drive to the JL Star. When they drove up to the house, Roxie bounded out to the driveway. Kade parked the truck and Kelsey climbed out, only to be waylaid by the rottweiler snuffling her greeting over the seat of her pants.

"Gee, thanks." Kelsey couldn't help a grin. "Just what these jeans needed. Dog slobbers."

With a soft laugh, Kade came up beside her and leaned down to scratch the dog behind her ears. "Roxie's a regular slobber monster."

Kade took Kelsey's hand and he felt an electrical spark build between them. She looked up at him with her lips parted, her expression telling him she felt the same sensation he did as they walked to the house. He stopped beside the screen door, leaned against a pillar, and brought her into his embrace. "You drive me crazy, woman."

She relaxed for a moment and then looked up at him. "I'm only going to be here a few weeks."

He didn't bother to answer. Instead he lowered his face, slow enough that she could turn away if she didn't want what he was offering.

"Kade," she whispered before he kissed the corner of her mouth and she sighed. He lightly nipped at her lower lip and she gave a little moan. She smelled of honeysuckle and her own unique woman's scent and he wanted her bad.

He slipped his tongue into her mouth and she allowed him inside. It was almost intoxicating. Her sweet taste mixed with the pineapple flavor of the sherbet punch she'd had before they left the dance. She leaned into him, her arms gripping his biceps hard enough he could feel her nails pressing through his shirtsleeves.

Damn but he wanted Kelsey. It felt almost impossible to keep his hands off her, as badly as he wanted to touch her in every way possible.

Kelsey pulled away, her lips parted and moist from his kiss, her eyes glittering in the dim light. "I can't do this, Kade." She released him and backed away.

He hooked his thumbs in the belt loops of his Wrangler jeans. "Do what, Kelsey? Kiss?"

Kade imagined a flush staining her cheeks in the darkness. "A casual relationship." She cleared her throat. "I'm just not a casual kind of woman."

"And I'm not a casual kinda man." Kade tried to step toward Kelsey, but she moved back again. "All right, darlin'. First things first. Let's get to be friends and see if it takes us anywhere. Is that fair?"

"Friends." Kelsey raked her hair away from her face. "Okay."

Kade held the screen door open. "Have you thought about dinner with me?"

"No." Avoiding his eyes, she ducked past him and entered the house.

He shut the door slowly, keeping it from slamming and making any noise. "Why not?"

Kelsey's heart pounded as she watched Kade kick off his boots and toss his hat onto the rack. "It's not a good idea. I don't want to go there." *Now that is a bald-faced lie,* she told herself, trying not to show it in her expression.

"You keep saying that." He caught her hand and pulled her to him. "But I haven't heard a single good reason. We can go as friends."

Kelsey studied her pink-painted toenails, struggling to calm her raging desires. She had to remember why she couldn't develop a relationship with him.

He lifted her chin with his finger, forcing her to look into his azure eyes. "What does it take to cross your border, Kelsey?"

With a slight shiver, she stepped back and pulled her hand away from him. "This border is closed. Indefinitely."

Kade smiled and gazed at her with a look that turned her heart inside out. "I can wait."

Chapter 8

Douglas had seen its better days at least three decades ago. Memories from Kade's childhood flickered through his mind like a series of postcards as he sauntered toward the place that had once been the town's only drugstore.

The building had changed. Hell, the whole town had changed since those times he'd perched next to his father at the drugstore counter, drinking a malted milkshake. Every Saturday when he was a kid it'd been their routine, when the man who fathered him was still around.

Smoke and sour beer filled his nostrils as he stepped into the dim recesses of Mario's Cantina, the drugstore-turned-bar. He waited for his eyes to adjust and forced himself to focus on the upcoming meeting with Jorge Juarez, a flighty contact he'd been developing.

The seedy tavern/discothèque bore no resemblance to that sunny milkshake bar of Kade's childhood. Bright-red-and-chrome chairs had been replaced by black vinyl bar stools, cracked with neglect and pitted by cigarette burns. It was midafternoon, and the only occupants were a couple of habitual barflies he recognized from previous visits. The men were hunched over as they sat on stools and nursed beers.

Kade slid into a corner booth where he could keep an eye on the front door yet remain close enough to the bar's back room, so that he could slip out the rear door if necessary. He'd already scoped it out and the alleyway was clear. He laid one hand on the scarred table-top, the waxy buildup under his palm a good indication the sur-face hadn't received a decent scrubbing in a long time.

The waitress was new, younger than the woman who usually worked the day shift. With a practiced eye for detail, he sized her up in one glance—young and accustomed to using her body to get what she wanted.

Not much over five feet, she wore a tight blouse, unbuttoned just far enough to expose the tops of her full breasts. Her skirt stopped at her upper thighs and hugged her hips so high that she'd be giving peep shows if she didn't pull the material down. Black hair flowed to the middle of her back, and she'd applied her makeup with a heavy hand.

If Kade hadn't noticed the fine lines at the corners of her eyes and mouth, the years of experience in her eyes, he would've wondered if the woman was old enough to be employed in the bar.

She tossed her hair back and stood with one hand on her hip and her breasts pushed forward. "A drink, señor?"

He nodded. "Michelob on tap."

Within a couple of minutes, the waitress returned with a hefty mug and slid it in front of him, her rows of gold bracelets clatter-ing as she moved. She stood so close he could smell the cheap per-fume she wore. "You are alone, señor?"

"Yeah." With his drink in his left hand, Kade leaned back in the seat and felt his gun dig into his lower back. Out of habit, he kept his right hand close to his side, within reach of the closer weapon concealed beneath the unbuttoned blue shirt that he wore over his T-shirt.

"Mari," a man shouted from the back room.

The woman called Mari scowled but managed to brush one hip against Kade as she turned away. Amusement flickered within him at the not-so-subtle message.

His thoughts turned to Kelsey and he smiled. Damn but she'd felt good in his arms when they'd danced. Too bad he'd had to work so late last night before dropping by the clubhouse. He would've liked nothing better than to have been with her the whole evening. She was fighting it, but he knew she was attracted to him. He could see it in her eyes, and the way she watched him when she didn't think he was looking.

He glanced at his watch, and just as he wondered if his contact would show, Juarez slunk in through the open door.

With a nervous glance around the bar, the slight man hurried to Kade's booth.

"Juarez." Kade took a sip of his beer.

The man answered in Spanish, his black gaze darting around the room. "This is too dangerous. I could be killed."

"Tell me what you know," Kade replied in the same language, keeping his voice level and never taking his eyes off his informant. The man owed him too much to back out now.

Juarez shifted in his seat. "The smuggler is someone who has long been known in this town. I do not yet know his name, but I am afraid. I've heard too many stories of how he deals with those who cross him."

"What do you know?" Kade repeated as he saw Sal Valenzuela and Don Mitchell walk into the cantina. Neither man glanced in Kade's direction before taking seats at a table in the far corner of the bar. Both knew better than to acknowledge Kade and take the chance of disrupting his work.

Juarez licked his lips. "This man. He owns a business and has many friends. Few enemies because no one knows what he truly is." He clenched his fist, and his dark features contorted, but he kept his voice low. "A monster who cares little if the people he smuggles die. Like they are nothing more than animal skins to lie upon the floor and trample."

Kade gripped the handle of his still-full beer mug. "I can't bring back Maria, but I can bring this scum to justice. What else have you got?"

"One of the *coyotes* called him El Torero," Jorge whispered. "The matador, a killer. I am very afraid, amigo."

"What else?"

"Nada."

The tap of heels on the scored linoleum alerted Kade to Mari's return. Before Kade could thank him, Juarez slipped out the front door to vanish into the hot summer afternoon.

Mari stopped at Kade's booth and pressed her pelvis to the edge of the table. "Do you need anything else?" The lustful glint in her eyes told him exactly what she meant.

He stood, towering over the petite woman. "No thanks." He dropped a ten on the table and headed out the door.

Later that evening, when Kade arrived home, he was disappointed to find Kelsey wasn't back from her interview. He hadn't realized how much he'd been looking forward to seeing her.

When he climbed into the shower, he ran it as hot as possible, cleaning the day's grime from his body. All he could think of was Kelsey. That kiss the night they met and then the one after the dance. The flames that raged beneath her skin and set him on fire.

He had to switch the water from hot to cold. That or take care of business in the shower.

After he'd gotten it about as cold as he could take, he finished up, then toweled off. His thoughts never strayed from Kelsey, and his erection throbbed as he squared off in front of the mirror to comb his hair. He was buck naked when the door opened and Kelsey walked into the bathroom.

She froze, her gaze riveted below his waist and the erection he still had from thinking about her. Her eyes shot up to his face and she turned a deep shade of crimson.

Kade raised an eyebrow and tried to hide a grin.

"Oh, my God," Kelsey said with a horrified expression. "I—I'm so sorry." She backed out the door and shut it behind her, and then he heard her own door close across the hall.

Kade dressed in clean jeans and a T-shirt, and felt a whole lot better—not to mention a whole lot more turned on after Kelsey had walked in on him. He was still smiling when he wandered into the kitchen and saw her at the table. She had on her gold-rimmed glasses that managed to make her look even sexier.

He hitched one shoulder up against the door frame and just watched her as she scribbled notes into a notebook. A strand of golden hair fell across her forehead and her lips were pursed as she concentrated. Her nipples were hard beneath her pink blouse and he wondered if she was thinking about seeing him naked.

"Kade." She glanced up from her notebook and turned red

again. "I'm sorry. I didn't hear the shower and I expected it to be locked if someone was in there."

He gave her a lazy smile, taking in her curves and sensual lips. "No problem."

"Another tough day?" She seemed desperate to change the subject.

"Yeah, but it's been getting better by the minute." He winked.

She bit her lower lip before she grabbed her things from the table and pushed back her chair to stand. "Do you have time for our interview?"

"I always have time for you, darlin'." Kade moved away from the wall and stepped so close to Kelsey that she had to look up to see his face.

She placed her hands on her hips and narrowed her velvety brown eyes as if she were angry. "Listen, cowboy. You'd better behave." But he saw the warmth and humor that warred with her desire to keep him at a distance.

"Come on outside, and I'll show you Mom's goldfish pond." He jerked his head toward the front door. "We can sit in the swing, and you can ask whatever you'd like."

She hesitated, then nodded. In comfortable silence, they walked through the house and out the front doors, and then the short distance to the pond.

The sky was overcast and the air was muggy and warm, the sun just settling above the Mule Mountains. Cattails and flowers sprouted from Sadie's pond, and lily pads floated on the surface. Kade and Kelsey stopped before the small waterfall that tumbled into the pond, and water splashed over their shoes.

Kelsey knelt beside the pond. "I didn't know goldfish grew to be that large."

Kade squatted next to her and pointed to an almost translucent fish speckled with bluish black. "That one and the black ones with gold stripes are Japanese koi."

"This is all gorgeous." She took a deep breath and sighed. "I love it here on the ranch. So relaxing and peaceful. What a difference from living in the city."

With his head cocked to one side, Kade studied her. All he could think of was how much he'd wanted her from the time he caught her watching him in the airport. This wasn't a woman to simply enjoy sex with. This was a woman to spend a lifetime with.

"Think a city girl like you could get used to living in the country?" he asked.

"Who knows." Kelsey seemed oblivious to the desire that burned beneath his words, beneath his skin. She shrugged and stood. "I've only been here a few days, but I think I could easily fall in love with this part of the world. Although I'd probably miss shopping in the Embarcadero and going to my favorite little place near the wharf for clam chowder and sourdough bread." She ran her tongue along her lower lip, and he had to restrain himself to keep from leaning over and kissing her.

Kade more than liked the thought of Kelsey staying in Arizona. "Thinking about moving away from Frisco?"

Kelsey didn't answer for a moment, as if deciding how much she should say. "Before I left, I considered moving to Tucson, but I wasn't sure if I would like Arizona. Now that I'm here, I know I would, and I'm ready for a change. When I finish this feature, I plan to interview with *Tucson Today* magazine."

With a sigh, she turned to Kade. "Now about my questions for you . . ."

"Why don't we sit in the swing and you can fire away?" He

hooked his thumbs in his belt loops, which helped him keep his hands off Kelsey. He'd probably only scare her off, and that was the last thing he wanted.

She glanced to the swing and back to Kade.

He smiled. "I promise I don't bite."

Chapter 9

"I know for a fact you do bite," Kelsey said, then heat crept up her face as she remembered his kisses and how he'd nipped at her lower lip.

"Got me there." Kade eased his big frame into the swing that was wide enough for three grown adults. "How about I promise I won't bite . . . for now?"

She tried to glare at him, but the mischievous glint in his eyes made it hard to be irritated or even mad at him.

His face grew serious as she settled into the cushioned swing. "I can tell you about the Border Patrol, and some of what we do, but due to the nature of my job you can't use my name."

Kelsey tipped her head to the side. "Do you mind if I ask why?"

"I work intelligence." He watched the intent expression on her face as he spoke. "A lot of what I do is classified."

She nodded. "I understand."

Kade stretched out his long legs. "I can put you in touch with Miguel Martinez, Special Operations Supervisor. You can talk to him on the record."

"Thanks." Kelsey turned her cell to record mode. "What's a day like for a Border Patrol agent?"

"Among other things, tracking and cutting sign," Kade said.

Kelsey adjusted her glasses as she glanced at him. "Can you explain?"

"A trail begins when we locate sign of people crossing the desert." Kade leaned back and relaxed against the swing's cushions. "We usually start our search along roads the Border Patrol maintains."

Kade loved the light in her eyes when she was obviously in journalist mode, wholly focused on what he was saying.

"What types of sign?" she asked.

"Sign can be footprints, a scrap of clothing," he said, "or garbage that's been discarded."

Kelsey scrawled a note on her pad of paper. "How do you maintain the roads?"

"By pulling tires behind the vehicle." Kade raised his arms and laced his fingers behind his head. "That makes a relatively smooth surface to help us more easily see footprints. Even if the UDAs try to eliminate their sign by walking backward, or by using other methods, we can usually determine where they've crossed."

"When you locate sign, how do you know how old it is?" she asked.

"By a variety of factors." He found himself studying Kelsey's soft lips and had to make himself get back on topic. "We look to see what effect the weather may have had on the tracks, such as raindrops and wind. If it's been awhile, detail will diminish. We can even tell if the UDAs are walking in daylight or after dark."

Kelsey glanced from the note she'd written on her pad. "How on earth would you do that?"

"If the tracks head up to a bush, even though the person could've walked around it, more than likely they were walking at night."

She chewed the end of her pencil, staring at her notes. "Any other methods?"

"Animal tracks assist in aging the trail. Most desert animals move around at night, so if we find animal sign on the trail at five o'clock in the afternoon, it may not be fresh."

He wanted to grin because her expression was so serious. "What happens once you find a trail?"

"We have to describe it to other trackers who haven't seen it." He shifted and put his arm on the back of the seat. "Rather than relaying several types over the radio, we locate the most distinct tracks and describe them."

Kade pushed off with one foot and the swing started to rock. "Other agents work ahead to find the trail on roads that intersect the path. If an agent picks up the trail, he'll attempt to match the sign described by the agent who originally cut the sign. We continue until we catch the UDAs, or until we can't follow the tracks any longer."

She paused while she made a note. "How large are groups that come across the border?"

"These days twenty to thirty UDAs at a time is normal."

For quite a while, Kade continued answering Kelsey's questions, giving her a better idea of what the Border Patrol was about.

Somehow the interview itself faded away, and they moved on to other topics. He shared information with her about the Southwest and his family, and she chatted about her job and living in San Francisco. She was amazed at how easy it was to talk with Kade, and how much she enjoyed his company.

A door slammed and then Trent tore around the corner of the house, waving a piece of paper. "Kelsey Kelsey Kelsey," he yelled, then skidded to a stop. "Look what I drew."

She smiled and caught the paper Trent thrust in her lap.

"It's a picture of you and Dad that I drew all by myself. Do you like it?" He hopped up and down on one foot, blue eyes flashing and brown hair flying in time with his movements. "Do you, do you?"

With one finger Kelsey traced the crayon figures, surprised at the detail the almost-nine-year-old had drawn. In the picture, Kade wore a blue shirt and jeans, with Kelsey in pink, and they stood side by side. "It's wonderful." She looked from the drawing to the boy. "You're very talented."

Trent grinned from ear to ear. "You really like it?"

"Love it."

Kade reached for the picture. "Let me see, son." He studied it with the seriousness of a true connoisseur. "A fine work of art."

"I drew it for Kelsey." Trent's grin broadened, obviously happy with his dad's appreciation. "I can make you one, too."

"When you do, I'll hang it on my wall." Kade wrapped his arms around Trent and brought his son onto his lap.

After giving his dad a quick hug, Trent wriggled free. "Can we get everything ready for tomorrow?"

Kade nodded and ruffled his son's hair. "Sure."

A lump formed in Kelsey's throat as she observed the affection between father and son. What she wouldn't give to have a son like Trent and the kind of relationship he had with his father.

"We're going fishing for my birthday." Trent jumped up and down in front of Kelsey like a jack-in-the-box on an overdose of caffeine. "Wanna come? It'd be so cool if you'd go with us. Please?"

She glanced at Kade and then back to Trent. "Sure, if it's okay with everyone else."

"Fine by me," Kade said.

"All right." Trent spun in circles, and Kelsey wondered how he managed to maintain his balance. "That's so cool. I'm gonna go tell Grandma to pack a lunch for three."

As the boy dashed away, Kelsey's stomach flipped. "Sadie and Chuck aren't going?"

Kade gave her his slow, sensual smile that sent tingles from her head to her toes. "Mom and Chuck have friends from out of town visiting for the day, so it'll just be the three of us."

"Oh." She tried to sound casual, not to let on that the prospect of spending the day with Kade, without Sadie and Chuck around, made her more than a little nervous.

"We'll have Trent to chaperone, if you're worried about us being alone," he said as he studied her.

"I'm not worried." She shook her head. "But will I be interfering? Did you intend for tomorrow to be a father/son day?"

He smiled, his eyes warm and welcoming. "You're not interfering. Trent wants you to come and so do I."

"Thanks." She took a deep breath and smiled in return. "It sounds like fun."

Kade stood and looked down at her. "It's about time for dinner. You coming?"

"Sadie made lasagna." Kelsey shut off her phone's recording device, grabbed her notepad, and got to her feet. "Can your mother ever cook."

"You've got that right." Kade patted his stomach. "I might have to start counting calories like my sister."

"Ha. You don't have an ounce of fat anywhere on your body," Kelsey retorted.

He grinned. "I guess you'd know that now, wouldn't you?"

"Oh, God." She hid her face with her notepad, trying to cover her furious blush. "That wasn't what I meant, and you know it."

But yes, she knew for a fact that Kade was solid muscle. Everywhere.

"Great dinner, Mom," Kade said after he took the last bite of his third helping of lasagna.

He loved watching Kelsey's lips as she wiped her mouth with a cloth napkin. "It was wonderful," she said. "And I loved the spicy dressing you made for the tossed salad."

"Glad you liked it." The telephone rang just as Sadie spoke. "I'll get the phone." She pushed back her chair, and left the room.

"How long will you be staying here, Kelsey?" Trent asked.

She gave Kade's son a warm smile. "My flight is scheduled to leave the eighteenth."

Trent took a drink of his apple juice, slurping it through a straw. Then he asked, "How many days is that?"

"A little over two weeks away," Kelsey replied.

"Oh." The boy cocked his head. "That's not very long, is it?"

She stood and started gathering dirty dishes to take to the sink. "Fifteen days."

"Kade." His mother appeared in the doorway holding the phone. "It's your sister."

"All right." Kade stood, took the phone from Sadie, and headed into the study. "Hi, Sis."

"Hey there, big bro," Dara replied. "So, Mom tells me there's a woman staying with you all at the ranch."

Knowing what was coming next, he stared at the ceiling. "Yeah."

"Mom says Kelsey is intelligent, attractive, and nice, and Trent really likes her."

He rolled his eyes. "Uh-huh."

"And Mom says you have the hots for this woman."

Well, hell. Kade shook his head. "Can't believe everything you hear."

Dara giggled and he could picture her impish grin. "Mr. Confirmed Bachelor is having second thoughts, isn't he?"

Kade glanced through the door and saw Kelsey talking with Trent. He liked how she crouched down to his son's level so that they were eye to eye when they talked, and she focused on him like he was the only person in the room.

"Don't get carried away," he said.

"Ha." Dara laughed, and then lowered her voice as if someone might overhear. "So, tell me, have you laid one on her yet? A big ol' smack?"

"Never kiss and tell," Kade said, still watching Kelsey talking with Trent. "Did you just want to bug me or do you have anything else to say?"

"Nah, just wanted to gloat." Dara laughed. "Gotta get the twins to bed. Give Trent a kiss for me, and love to Dad."

After he said his good-byes and sent his love to his niece and nephew, Kade punched the off button and set the phone into its cradle. He sauntered into the kitchen to where Kelsey was chatting with Trent. She was sitting in a chair now, her back to Kade.

"Yeah, Dad takes me fishing lots," Trent was saying. "He always does stuff with me, like playing catch, and games and trucks."

Kade stood behind Kelsey, breathing in her incredible scent. He wanted to run his hands in her honey-blond hair, to feel the silken strands sliding through his fingers.

She stiffened and turned to look up at him. "Kade."

"Don't let me interrupt." He grabbed the back of Kelsey's chair and leaned forward. He sensed the tension in her as if his presence unnerved her.

Trent flipped his hair out of his eyes. "I was telling Kelsey what a cool dad you are and how you're always doing stuff with me. You're lots cooler than Bobbie's dad."

"Is that so?" Kade released the chair and walked around Kelsey to ruffle his son's hair. He could feel the difference in her as soon as he moved, as audible as a sigh.

"Yup." Trent gave an enthusiastic nod.

Kade crouched beside his son. "I was just on the phone with your aunt Dara. She said to give you a big ol' smack on the cheek for her."

Trent screwed up his face. "Ewwwww."

Kade laughed. "How about a bear hug? And we'll just tell her that I gave you a kiss."

"Okay." Trent threw his arms around his dad and squeezed him tight.

God, being hugged by his son was one of the greatest feelings on earth. Trent smelled of dirt, sweat, and dog, and Kade couldn't imagine anything better.

When Trent pulled away, Kade said, "It's bedtime and we need to get up early to go fishing. You'd better take your bath and brush your teeth. And don't forget to wash your face."

Trent groaned and pouted. "Aw, Daaaaad. I wanna play a video game."

"No." Kade stood and forced himself to look stern. "In the bathroom. Pronto."

"But—"

"Now."

Trent glared at Kade, stomped off to the bathroom, and shut the door. Hard.

Smiling, Kelsey got to her feet. "I'd better get to bed before I get into trouble."

He caught her wrist and pulled her close to him. "If you're not good, I might have to turn you over my knee."

"Just try it, cowboy," Kelsey murmured, but her cheeks turned red and he was sure she was imagining him following through with his threat.

Damn, she's cute.

He held back a grin as she dodged past him and escaped into her room.

Chapter 10

"Dad Dad Dad *Dad.*" Trent's voice shattered Kade's sleep. "Wake up, Dad. It's my birthday. Wake uuuuup."

Kade pretended to remain asleep as Trent shook him. Finally, he opened one eye. "Son, are you sure today's your birthday? I could swear—"

"Daaaaad. It's July fourth, my birthday, and you promised to take me to the lake today, remember?" Trent jumped on the bed and bounced on Kade's chest, the boy's brown hair flying in all directions. "Come oooon, Dad. Get uuuuup."

Kade glanced at the clock. "It's barely five. Don't you think that's a little early? Why don't we just go back to bed?"

Trent rolled his eyes and bounced on his dad. "Come on, come on, come on. You promised to take me fishing. You promised."

"Oh, yeah?" Kade tickled Trent in his most ticklish spots until the boy squealed with laughter, flopping around like a fish out of water.

Trent squirmed out of Kade's reach, tumbled off the bed, and shot out the door. "Kelsey Kelsey Kelsey Keeelseeeyyy. It's time to go fishing." He opened her door and darted in.

Kade raised an eyebrow. After the first night, he figured she'd kept her door locked to keep him out. Not that he'd invite himself in. She'd have to do the inviting.

"Happy birthday." Kelsey's sleepy voice came from her room, and then Trent was pulling her through the door. Kade saw she wore the same pink T-shirt and shorts he'd seen her in at the hotel.

"Good mornin'," Kade said, noting all her sensual curves that the clothes couldn't hide.

"Too early to tell." She ruffled Trent's hair. "Hey, Taz, how about a shower first?"

"You look great." He shook his head under her hand. "Just go like that. Come on."

Kade caressed her with his gaze. "You look beautiful."

Kelsey blushed, and Trent said, "How come you're turning all red?"

"Never mind. Give me ten minutes to shower." Kelsey ducked back into her room.

Once everyone was ready and the truck loaded, the trio headed to Parker Lake in the Huachuca Mountains, the sun barely rising over the horizon.

The night before, Sadie had packed a picnic basket brimming with ham and cheese sandwiches for Kelsey and Kade, peanut butter and jelly for Trent, and large slices of her Polish coffee cake. Kade had loaded the fishing poles and tackle. They made good time, and when they arrived, found they had the lake to themselves for a while.

After they'd caught a stringer full of fish, and Trent had broken his line for the third time, Kade sat down to re-string the line. Kelsey settled next to him on the picnic blanket and wrapped her arms around her bare knees.

Pink. She always wears pink, and it suits her, he thought. She wore a button-up shirt and blue shorts, showing off her long legs. A thick scar ran along her upper thigh, partially hidden by her shorts.

She inhaled and turned her face to the sky. "Mmmm, it smells wonderful out here. I love the fragrance of pine and fresh mountain air."

He forced himself to look away to check on his son, who was busy skipping stones across the lake, surely scaring all the fish away. But what the heck. The kid was having fun and it was his birthday.

Trent was a strong swimmer, and he knew the rules about not entering the lake without an adult, but Kade didn't want to take chances. He started re-stringing Trent's line, glancing at the boy every now and then as he and Kelsey talked.

"You've done a wonderful job as a single dad," Kelsey said as she watched his son.

"He's one hell of a kid." Kade smiled. "I've always worried about him not having a mom around, but he seems to be doing great."

"That must have been difficult, to lose somebody you loved when you were so young." Her voice was soft and thoughtful.

Kade didn't know what possessed him. He never discussed Lorraine, but talking with Kelsey was easy. Natural.

He shrugged and said, "It was sad, but sadder yet that it was her own damn fault. She was drunk and almost took other lives along with her."

Kelsey put her hand on his arm, concern in her eyes. "You don't have to tell me this."

"It's all right." Kade took a deep breath and rubbed at his neck, releasing tension in his muscles. "Thank God, Trent and those other folks lived. It's a real shame Lorraine died, but what's done is done."

"I'm so sorry." Kelsey squeezed Kade's arm, and to his surprise, he could see tears glittering in her eyes. His throat tightened, and he regretted spilling his guts.

"There's nothing to be sorry for," he said softly. "I have Trent, and he means the world to me."

He decided he'd better change the subject. "Have you gone fishing before?"

"Years and years ago."

Kade glanced from Trent to Kelsey and saw a haunted look in her eyes.

"With my sister, mother, and even my father." Her voice was as distant as her gaze. "We loved to go."

"Where do your folks live now?"

Kelsey was silent, and then she said, "They all died five years ago." Her voice caught. "I keep thinking I'll get over it, but not a day goes by that I don't miss Mother and Naya. That I . . . that I don't wonder why I survived the plane crash, and they didn't. Why wasn't it me instead of them?"

"I'm sorry, honey." Kade set the fishing pole down, put his arm around Kelsey, and brought her close, holding her head against his chest. Ice chilled his veins at the thought of her being in such a tragic accident, and the knowledge that she could've died.

As he stroked her hair, he breathed in her scent of honeysuckle and sunshine, and felt her tears through his shirt. He watched Trent as he rocked Kelsey, thankful that his son had survived the collision that had taken Lorraine but wishing Kelsey's family had been as fortunate as his son.

"I'm sorry for crying all over you." She tried to pull away, but he held on to her, and she relaxed against him again.

It all made sense. "That's why you're afraid to fly."

"Especially small planes." She sounded like in a way she was exorcising her demons as she spoke. "I'll never go in one again. The charter we'd taken on a sightseeing tour lost power and slammed onto the runway. I can still smell the smoke . . . and feel the flames . . . and hear the screams."

She turned her tear-streaked face to Kade. "I still don't understand why they died and I lived. Why I walked away with only this scar." She rubbed her leg as if trying to scrub away the memories of the accident.

He kissed her forehead and glanced at his son playing at the water's edge. "You were meant to survive. Like Trent. I'm sure your family would want you to live. To get on with your life."

"I know you're right, but it's so hard." She was quiet, as if searching through her feelings, trying to understand the reality she had to face when everything was over.

When she finally spoke, her voice was soft and full of regret. "That's why I fell into a relationship with Davis. Why he fooled me so well." She sighed and shook her head. "I put up with his abuse for so long because I was too devastated to lose again. In truth I was stupid not to realize that leaving Davis would be the best thing I could do to get on with living."

Kade hooked a finger under her chin with one hand and wiped away her tears with his other hand. "You're not stupid, Kelsey. You're intelligent and beautiful. It sounds like this bastard took advantage of you at a fragile time in your life. And if I meet the SOB, I'd like to make him pay."

The corner of her mouth twitched. "I can just picture you, dressed in white and riding to my rescue."

"I wear mostly blue." Kade gave a gentle smile. But that smile faded as he searched her eyes and the next question came to his lips. "Did he hit you?"

Kelsey stiffened and looked away. "Davis punched with words. He knew exactly how to rip me to shreds without laying a finger on me." A shuddering sigh rolled over her. "He attempted to control every aspect of my life. I was an idiot to not come to my senses sooner."

It was an effort for Kade to control the anger burning in him. He swore under his breath and pulled her closer. "So help me, that bastard better never stray across my path."

"Why did I just tell you my life story?" She drew away and met his gaze. "Why do I trust you?"

He brushed his lips across her hair, breathing her scent. So beautiful, so sensual, so sweet.

"What do you want from me?" Kelsey's voice had a slight tremble to it, saying more than her words, telling him of her fear of loss and betrayal. Her fear of repeating past mistakes.

Kade ran his thumb over her forearm, to the inside of her elbow and back, feeling the softness of her skin against his calluses. "What do I want from you? Nothing. Everything. Whatever you'll give me."

Kelsey caught her breath as his words gripped her heart. *Nothing. Everything. Whatever you'll give me.*

Trent darted up from the lake. "Is my line fixed, Dad? I want to catch more fish."

Kade squeezed her hand, sending dangerous sensations through her belly. He scooped up Trent's fishing pole and stood. "Hold your horses, kiddo."

The moment Kade left, Kelsey felt alone. Like a part of her was missing. His scent had been so intoxicating, his touch so sensual, surrounding her with his masculinity. She'd bared her soul, and just by telling him she felt lighter, as though she truly were alive again.

But did she dare trust him with her heart?

As she watched Kade with Trent, she couldn't believe that voice inside her that said all men were like Davis and her father. She couldn't believe Kade would intentionally hurt anyone.

She watched as Kade cast Trent's line, then worked with his son with such patience. Why did she feel like she could talk to him so easily? Perhaps it was the day. The intimacy of spending time together with just the three of them. Yet they'd probably spent a good hour chatting yesterday, long after the interview had ended.

While he settled Trent on a log to wait for fish to nibble, she took the opportunity to study Kade. His blue shirt accented his vivid blue eyes, and when he laughed at something his son said, that adorable dimple appeared in his cheek. Jeans molded his muscular thighs, and even though he was a big man, tall and muscled, his movements were as fluid as a mountain lion's.

And those hands. Strong, large. She thought of the texture of his skin against hers, how it felt when he'd held her face in his hands and kissed her, his calluses rough against her cheeks.

Kelsey glanced from Kade's hands to his face and froze. He was watching her with the same hunger in his eyes that must have been apparent in hers. Yearning curled in her abdomen like molten fire, and for endless seconds, she couldn't tear her gaze from his. Then a fish tugged on Trent's line, and Kade turned back to his son.

God help her, but she wanted him. Needed him.

It took all her effort to stop staring at Kade. She fought to compose herself, gazing out at the midnight blue of the lake, listening to the soft lap of the water against the shore. His husky voice washed over her as he spoke to Trent in a low, even tone. The boy's answering voice, so high and sweet, took hold of her heart, never to let go.

With her eyes closed, she focused on the wind whispering through pine and juniper trees and drank deep of the scents of rich loam and pine. The breeze caressed her face as softly as Kade's touch, and she ached for him, wanting his fingers sliding over her skin.

Kelsey opened her eyes, forced the thoughts away, and scooted to her feet. After brushing stray pine needles from the seat of her shorts, she strolled to the edge of the lake just as Kade helped Trent reel in a fish.

"It's a big one, Kelsey." The boy hopped along the water's edge while Kade added the fish to the stringer. "It's really, really big. It almost pulled me in. It's a catfish. Do you like catfish?"

"Love 'em." Kelsey put her hand on Trent's shoulder.

"I think that's enough." Kade pulled the stringer out of the lake and tossed it into the ice chest they'd brought for that purpose. "We need to get back for cake, ice cream, and fireworks."

"Okay. But first I wanna show Kelsey how to make a wish in the lake." Trent scooped up a small rock and held it up to her. "You take a rock and squeeze it real tight." The boy wrapped his fist around the stone. "Close your eyes, make a wish, and throw the rock into the lake. But you can't tell nobody what you wished for or it won't come true."

Kelsey laughed, delighted in the boy's enthusiastic instructions.

Trent gripped the rock in his hand and shut his eyes even tighter.

His lips moved, then he leaned back and threw the rock into the water. He opened his eyes and pointed to the ripples. "I threw it really, really far, and I made a great wish. Your turn."

She knelt and selected a flat round stone, then stood. Trent bounced up and down on the shore with unbridled energy. "Come on, Kelsey. Close your eyes and make a wish."

What did she wish for? She shut her eyes, feeling the smoothness of the stone against her palm.

Kade. His name popped unbidden into her mind, and a flush heated her body. But then the thought of Davis chased away the warmth, leaving only cold. Reminding her that she shouldn't make herself vulnerable again.

"Kelsey," came Trent's sweet voice. "Are you going to make a wish?"

"Yes," she replied, her voice too hoarse, filled with the pain of longing and the emptiness of regret.

And then it came to her, as clear as that July summer sky. She wanted a child as wonderful as Trent to call her own. With her eyes still squeezed tight, she brought the stone to her mouth and kissed it, feeling its smooth contours with her lips, then pitched the rock into the lake.

"Wow, you can throw far," Trent shouted.

Kelsey opened her eyes to see Kade beside her, his intense blue gaze boring into her as if he could see her dreams and know her thoughts. She shivered, longing to ease her arms around him and feel the comfort of his body next to hers.

Trent bounded between them and crinkled his freckled nose. "Why'd you kiss the rock? Do you think it'll make your wish come true?"

She shrugged and tried not to look at Kade. "With all my heart, I hope so."

Trent tugged on his dad's sleeve. "Dad, your turn. Make a wish before we go."

Kade scooped up a rock and gazed at Kelsey. Her stomach somersaulted again, and she wanted to touch him, to be near him. He closed his eyes, brought the stone to his lips, and kissed it. For a moment, Kelsey had the wildest thought, that she was the stone, and that he had his lips pressed against hers. He leaned back, the muscles in his arm rippling as he flung the stone into the lake.

"Cool." Trent grinned at his dad. "You threw it even farther than Kelsey. How come you kissed your rock like she did? You've never done that before. Do you think your wish will come true?"

Kelsey's gaze met Kade's and her throat grew too dry to swallow.

Kade tousled Trent's hair and smiled, but never took his eyes from Kelsey's. "I hope so, Trent. I hope so."

By the time they reached the ranch, it was late afternoon and Kade was starving. "We'll head on up to Bisbee for fireworks after dinner," he said as they piled out of the truck. "And, of course, after birthday cake for the birthday boy."

"All right." Trent clutched pinecones in his hands that he'd gathered in the forest. "Grandma makes the best cakes in the whole world," he said to Kelsey. "She always bakes a red velvet cake for my birthday with blue and white frosting on account of it's the Fourth of July, and it's my favorite."

The boy dashed off, then stopped. "What about presents, Dad? Do I get presents, too?"

Kade rubbed his chin. "Hmmm, presents? I knew there was something I forgot."

"Daaaad."

With a grin, Kade pointed toward the house. "Why don't you go inside and see."

Trent whirled and tore off like a mini tornado.

Kelsey grabbed the picnic basket and thermos while Kade took the ice chest full of catfish, and they walked together in companionable silence. The house smelled wonderful when they walked in, of fried chicken and hot biscuits.

"No catfish for dinner tonight," Sadie was saying to Trent when they walked in. "We'll have it tomorrow."

"Ahhh, Grandma, why not?" Trent pouted, his lower lip thrust out, and Kelsey almost laughed aloud.

"Not enough time to clean the fish and fry it up before the fireworks. That's why." Sadie turned back to the stove. "Besides, I made your favorite. Fried chicken."

"It looks awesome, Grandma." Trent peeked under foil covering a plate mounded with fried chicken. "Mashed potatoes and gravy and corn on the cob, too?"

Sadie nodded. "That's right."

Trent hugged her. "Thanks, Grandma."

She waved him off to the bathroom. "Go on and wash your hands."

Holding out his palms, Trent said, "They're clean. I cleaned them in the lake."

Sadie planted her hands on her hips. "Get into that bathroom and wash with soap and clean water. Do it before I cloud up and rain all over you."

"Yes, ma'am." Trent spun like a little whirlwind and headed for the hall bathroom.

Kade laughed and Kelsey snickered. Sadie brandished her spatula at the two of them, but with a smile. "That's enough out of you kids. Go clean up."

Chapter 11

Before dinner, Kelsey took a quick shower and put on a button-up pink blouse with a short jean skirt. After cake and presents, Kelsey and the whole family headed to town.

They reached the park in Bisbee just before dark and crowds had already gathered. Kade parked in their favorite spot near the old ballpark where years ago he used to play Little League, and they set up lawn chairs around the SUV. Trent settled between Chuck and Sadie. It was no surprise that he was so excited he could hardly sit still.

"When'll the fireworks start?" Trent was like a Mexican jumping bean in his seat. "I can't wait."

"As soon as it gets dark." Chuck patted Trent's knee. "Can you hold your horses that long, pardner?"

Trent wiggled out from under his grandpa's hand and stood. "I hope it hurries up and gets dark really soon."

"How about a walk in the park while we're waiting for the fireworks?" Kade asked Kelsey, hoping he would have some time alone with her.

She smiled and said, "Sure."

After Kade let everyone know what they were doing, he and Kelsey strolled across the street into the park, the way lit by an occasional streetlight. The night smelled of fresh-cut grass, charcoal, and barbeque, and the air was filled with chatter and dogs barking.

As they walked past folks sitting on picnic blankets and lawn chairs, they dodged the occasional beer cooler and avoided being trampled as laughing children raced past them. Kade noticed how Kelsey's gaze followed the kids, a soft smile on her face. He remembered when Kelsey had told him how she'd always wanted children, but how her bastard of a husband had been so cruel in his response.

A mutt streaked by, almost tripping Kelsey. Kade caught her hand, helping her balance, then laced her fingers with his. She stopped and studied him, emotions flickering across her features.

Fear? Longing?

Kade squeezed her hand. "I'm not going to hurt you."

She paused as if considering his response and then said, "I don't know about that, Kade Owen."

They walked farther into the park, as far away from the crowds as he could take her. Finally Kade pulled Kelsey under the shadows of a huge old oak tree and brought her close, resting his back against the tree, shifting so that his second handgun didn't press into his spine. She hesitated, then leaned closer and wrapped her arms around his neck.

Desire stirred in him as her warm body pressed to his. He brushed his lips over her hair, drinking in her honeysuckle scent. His cock hardened even more, and he was afraid she would draw away if she felt how much he wanted her.

He'd just have to take that chance, because right now, he wasn't letting go.

The sound of voices and laughter in the distance dimmed as the world narrowed, focused, and Kade's only thoughts were of Kelsey. She stirred against him, and he sucked in his breath as her innocent movement hardened him even more.

"Kelsey," he said against her forehead. "Do you have any idea what you do to me?" She lifted her face, and he stroked a soft wave of hair away from her eyes.

She smiled. "Tell me."

He pressed her closer to him. "You can't feel it?" It was too dark to tell if she blushed, but he would've bet she did.

Kelsey bit her lip and then said, "Um, yes. Hard to miss."

"It certainly is." Kade raised his eyebrows at the double meaning of her words.

She groaned. "I didn't mean that. What am I going to do with you?"

"Whatever you want, darlin', I'm yours." He cupped her face with his hand, her skin soft and smooth against his palm. The thought of kissing her, holding her, loving her, stoked the fire that burned for her, that heat he knew could consume them both. "It's been too long since I've tasted you."

Her lips trembled against his thumb as he ran it over her mouth. "Not that long, cowboy."

"Definitely too long." Kade moved his thumb from her lips, trailing it over her chin, then along her jaw to her earlobe. She shivered and moved her mouth to his palm, the caress of her lips shooting liquid fire through his veins.

He moved his lips to her ear. "You're like honey on my tongue."

Kelsey made a sound that could've been an answer, or a groan.

There was no doubt she'd been hurt in the past, no doubt she was scared of becoming involved in any kind of relationship. Hell, it almost scared him how badly he wanted her. But there was one thing he did know, one thing that was absolutely clear in his mind.

He wanted her for keeps.

Kade kissed the tip of her nose. "Tell me what you want," he murmured, his voice hoarse with all his pent-up desire for this woman. His woman.

"Kiss me," she whispered. "Please."

In a slow, tantalizing movement, he brushed her forehead with his mouth, then trailed kisses over the elegant arch of her eyebrow, down to the tip of her nose again. She trembled as Kade traced her lips with his tongue, teasing one corner until she moaned and parted her lips.

His tongue darted inside, lightly running along the serrated edge of her teeth before slipping deeper into her mouth. Her tongue met his in a tentative movement, as if she was afraid to show him how much she wanted him.

"You taste even better than I remembered," he rumbled against her lips, then pulled away so that he could look at her.

She moved her palm to his face, and for an endless moment she stroked his cheek and gazed into his eyes. "I lose my head with you. I can't afford that—I can't afford to lose myself again."

Kade kissed the corner of her mouth and moved to her earlobe. "If you get lost, I'll help you find your way back." He nipped at her lobe. "I need you, Kelsey. I'm not whole without you."

"You don't really know me," she said, her voice husky. "I barely know you."

"Give it a chance. That's all I'm asking." Kade brought his mouth back to Kelsey's, kissing her with a fierceness that surprised even him.

This time when she pulled away, she said, "I'll only be here a short time. That's not long enough to give anything a chance."

"Pretend we have all the time in the world." He brought up one hand and slipped it into her silken blond hair. "Just let go, darlin'."

"It's so hard." She lightly bit her lip and then added, "I've only been with one man. And he was the biggest mistake of my life."

"You were with the wrong man." Kade clenched his hand in her hair, lightly pulling on it as if that would draw her away from the bad memories and bring her into the present. "What I want you to think about is you and me. Right here, right at this moment in time."

The moon shone through the oak leaves, shadows and silver beams of light dancing across Kelsey's features. She gave a tentative smile and whispered, "All right."

He cupped the back of her head, feeling entirely possessive, and brought her mouth to his. This time she took him with no hesitation, surprising him with how intensely she returned his kiss. This time it was her demanding, her needing, her wanting.

And he wanted to give her everything.

His cock ached and he longed to bury himself deep within her core. To feel her naked body beneath him, to taste her silken skin.

When he drew away, Kelsey gasped for air, her eyes bright in the silvery light. He clenched his hand in her hair and pulled lightly. She moved with him, tilting her head back and exposing the pale flesh of her neck.

With one hand still in her hair, he slipped his other hand below her rib cage, holding her as he nibbled a path down her neck to the V of her blouse to the gentle swell of her breasts and flicked his tongue along her cleavage until she moaned.

Every touch burned like fire, searing her with every stroke of his fingers and tongue.

Kade slipped his hand from her hair and with deft fingers he unbuttoned the top two buttons of her blouse and settled his fingers at the front clasp of her bra. He paused, waiting for her to tell him to stop, but instead she slid her fingers into his hair and whimpered.

When Kelsey didn't stop him, he unhooked it and freed her breasts, exposing them to the cool evening air and to his intent gaze.

"Damn but you're beautiful, woman," he said, and then traced lazy trails with his tongue from her cleavage toward one nipple.

Kelsey didn't know what she was doing and why she was encouraging Kade to go as far as he was. She just knew that she needed a man's touch—no, his touch.

God, but he knew how to touch her. The fire he had started within her burned hotter and brighter. Her nipples tightened and her body ached. She could think of nothing but wanting him and how it would feel to have nothing between them . . . his chest rubbing against her breasts, his hips between her thighs. . . .

"What if someone sees us?" she asked, feeling dazed, remembering they were in a park.

"We're alone, far from the crowd, in the dark," he murmured, his warm breath causing her nipples to ache even more.

When his tongue circled her nipple, she gripped his hair even tighter, holding on to him. She knew she shouldn't be allowing this, virtually in public, but it felt wonderful to turn loose and just experience, just enjoy the feel of his hot mouth teasing and suckling her nipple.

That deep thrill she had every time she was around Kade intensified and headed down below her belly button to between her thighs. She ached so badly that she felt on the edge of an orgasm.

But she couldn't climax just from him sucking her nipples . . . could she?

"I want you so damned much," he said, and moved to her other nipple, lightly nipping at it and causing her to gasp and bringing her closer to that fine edge of losing control.

Her other nipple felt cool and moist from his mouth and achingly hard. Kade cupped both breasts in his big hands, and her breasts were large enough to fill his palms. He brought the pair up high, pressed them together, and flicked his tongue back and forth over both nipples.

"I don't know what you're doing to me," she started, "but I— oh, that feels good." Kelsey moved her hands to his shoulders and gripped him tight as her body started trembling. "What are you doing to me?"

"Come on, baby," he murmured in between licks, "just let yourself go."

Let go, Kelsey. Just let go.

Still holding on to Kade's arms, she leaned back and focused entirely on his mouth and his tongue as he went back and forth from one nipple to the other. She lost herself in the sensations, giving herself up to them, and to him.

Her entire body vibrated. She whimpered, so on edge she could just scream.

And then he pinched one nipple at the same time he nipped the other and she did cry out. Her entire being shuddered and shook. A powerful orgasm stormed within as he kept his hold on her nipples. She heard booming and saw brilliant flashes of color and the moment he released her nipples, she collapsed against his chest.

"Oh. My. God." She was stunned at what had just happened and shocked that she'd allowed it to. "I can't believe I just—I just cli-maxed like that."

He gave a low laugh. "Darlin', you have the most gorgeous and sensitive breasts. I could just eat you up."

She sighed and relaxed fully against Kade, her bare nipples press-ing against the roughness of his shirt. "You make me feel fireworks. I can even hear them."

Kade gave a low laugh. "I'd like to take credit for that, honey, but it looks like it's the Fourth of July fireworks you're hearing."

Kelsey opened her eyes as sparkling red, white, and blue fireworks exploded above them, filling the dark sky with twinkling lights. They winked out one by one, like hundreds of fireflies blinking through leaves of the oak. Several more fireworks burst above them all at once in an even more brilliant display.

She shook her head and looked back at Kade. "Those aren't the fireworks I'm talking about."

He drew her closer. "Just say when, and I'll give you all the fire-works you need."

Kelsey's nipples tingled as he hooked her bra, and it was hard to keep her voice from trembling with desire. "This is too fast for me. I can't even believe I went this far with you." She searched his fea-tures as he buttoned her blouse, but it was too hard to read his expression the way his Stetson shadowed his face. "You gave me an orgasm by just touching my breasts, for goodness sake."

When her blouse was buttoned, he raised his head and she could clearly see his sexy smile illuminated by the brilliant fireworks. "And I loved every minute of it." His expression grew serious as he con-tinued, "Don't be afraid of what's happening between us, Kelsey."

She stepped back and smoothed down her blouse, just for some-thing to do with her hands. "I need to slow down, okay?"

Kade gave a nod. "All right. We'll just take this one day at a time."

Kelsey sighed with relief mingled with regret that she couldn't just let herself go. "Thanks, Kade."

"Don't thank me." He moved so that his arm rested around her shoulders. He hugged her close as they started back across the park. "It's going to be hell keeping my hands off you, sweetheart."

Chapter 12

"Have lunch with me," Kade said to Kelsey at breakfast. "After your interview with Dee Carter, we could meet at the Monroe Café."

"Sounds like a wonderful idea." Sadie spooned scrambled eggs onto her plate. "If I didn't have to run errands in Tucson with Chuck and Trent, I'd drive to Dee's with Kelsey and join you."

Kelsey tried to hide the leap of excitement at the thought of spending time alone with Kade. "I probably won't get back to Douglas until one."

"Perfect." Kade stood and grabbed his empty plate. "Need directions?"

"I'll draw a map." Sadie poured a glass of orange juice. "You get on to work."

Kelsey couldn't help watching Kade as he headed to the kitchen to slip his plate into the dishwasher and then leave for work. Had she made a mistake with what had happened last night?

For crying out loud, she actually came from a man suckling her breasts.

And not just any man. Kade Owen, the sexiest cowboy on earth, the man who had already lassoed her libido.

She must be out of her mind. Kelsey rubbed her forehead with her fingertips and tried to shove away memories of Kade's kisses and the way he'd brought her to orgasm.

It was hopeless. She couldn't stop thinking about the way he'd held her, his earthy smell, his gentle touch, his sensual mouth.

After buttoning up her blouse last night, Kade had kept her close as they strolled back toward his family. Before they crossed the street Kelsey had pulled away, not ready for his family to see them together.

He'd simply given an earth-shattering, sexy smile that made her knees quiver, and she almost grabbed his hand to steady herself. She wasn't sure if she was disappointed or glad that he hadn't pressured her for more.

Who was she kidding? She could do nothing but think about the man and how somehow he'd managed to get so completely under her skin.

As Kelsey drove Sadie's SUV to the Carter ranch, the twenty-five miles to Douglas scrolled by, the sky overcast with the threat of a monsoon storm. She glanced at the hand-drawn map on the seat beside her and checked to make sure she'd taken the right exit.

Every few miles she passed a white-and-green Border Patrol vehicle. When she drove through Douglas, it seemed like it increased to about once every minute. Her heart beat a little faster as she thought about Kade, knowing that he was somewhere in that town.

"Get your head back to business, Kelsey," she muttered.

Another fifteen miles east of Douglas, Kelsey turned off on a dirt road leading to the ranch. She drove past the well-kept barbwire fence, over a cattle guard, and down the primitive dirt road that caused the SUV to rattle and shimmy every inch of the way.

Chuck had taught her some ranch terms the day before, so she actually knew what a cattle guard was. She even recognized the breed of cattle grazing on the northern pasture of the Carters' ranch as Black Angus, the same breed as the few head Chuck still kept on the JL Star.

Unlike at the JL Star, only a few mesquite bushes dotted the Flying C's expansive rangelands. Tawny mountains rose like earth-bound sentinels behind the sprawling ranch house, a stark contrast to the endless yellow fields of grass at its feet.

After Kelsey parked, she jogged up the steps to a porch with four large rocking chairs. Before she could knock, a willowy brunette opened the front door, a golden retriever at her side. "You must be Kelsey, Trace's friend." She held out her hand. "I'm Dee Carter-Reynolds."

"It's great to meet you." Kelsey smiled and shook Dee's hand, noticing her strong grip. "Trace shared a lot with me about growing up here on your ranch."

The woman gave a brilliant smile, and with her classic beauty, Kelsey could see that Dee must turn more than her fair share of heads. "Trace is in Texas with her husband, Jess, but she hopes to make it out to San Francisco to visit you."

"That's what she said." Kelsey smiled as the dog nuzzled her hand. "I hope she can. It would be great to see her and to meet her husband."

"Well, Apple certainly approves of you," Dee said with a laugh as she looked at the dog.

"You're beautiful, Apple." Kelsey allowed the golden to sniff her hand, then she rubbed his head. She smiled at the unusual name for the dog and the fact that the name reminded her of the scent of Kade's shampoo.

A man stepped through the front door, and Kelsey almost stumbled over Apple in surprise.

"Pardon," John Stevens said around the toothpick in his mouth, touching the brim of his cowboy hat as he paused in front of her.

"No problem." Kelsey smiled. "Are we still on for our interview?"

"Uh, yeah." He turned to Dee. "Gotta be on my way, Dee. Thanks for letting me use the john."

Dee smiled. "We'll talk later, Bull," she said as he headed down the steps, and he turned back just long enough to give a quick nod in acknowledgment.

"Hope I wasn't interrupting anything," Kelsey said as John Stevens climbed into his truck.

"Nah." Dee winked at Kelsey. "Bull only stopped by for a minute. He's off to the cattle auction, trying to rebuild his herd. Wanted to know if I'd like him to buy a few more cattle for our herd. Rustlers made away with a good number of them last fall."

Kelsey raised her eyebrows. "Rustlers?"

"We weren't hit nearly as hard as others." Dee gave a dismissive wave of her hand. "The bastards are in jail now, so it's old news."

Apple followed at Kelsey's heels as Dee led her into the sunny interior of the home and offered Kelsey a glass of ice water. She gladly accepted, taking a long draught to quench her thirst. She opened her laptop and booted it up at the kitchen table. After she adjusted the setting on her phone to record, she placed it on the table.

"So." Dee folded her arms on the table and leaned toward Kelsey as if sharing a secret, her ivy-green eyes sparkling. "Tell me how you're enjoying your stay with one of the most gorgeous eligible bachelors in these parts. In any parts, for that matter."

The question came just as Kelsey took another drink of water. She choked and came close to spraying a mouthful of water all over her laptop and the lovely Mrs. Carter-Reynolds. For at least the millionth time, Kelsey cursed the flood of red rushing to her face.

"Ah. Kade has charmed you, too." Dee grinned and sighed like a schoolgirl. "I had a crush on him from the time I was fourteen until I met Jake twelve years ago. No one would ever do for me again once I met Jake."

Kelsey managed to keep her tone casual. "So, Kade turns on the charm for all women?"

"Nah." Dee shook her head. "He was born with it. He doesn't have to do anything but walk into a room and you can just see the women drool. Part of his charm is that he doesn't even realize the effect he has on females."

A perverse desire to know more about him rose up in Kelsey, even if it shattered her illusions. "A lot of guys would take advantage of that."

With a little snort, Dee said, "Not Kade. I don't think he's dated more than a couple of women in the five years since his wife died."

Dee twirled a diamond wedding ring around her finger. "Sadie keeps thinking Kade will eventually find his soul mate." She smiled. "He may be a grown man, but his mama can't help but worry about him. She's hoping Kade might be more than a little interested in you."

"Yes. Well." Kelsey's face burned as she turned to her laptop and brought up the list of questions she'd prepared for the interview. "We'd better get started so that I don't swallow up too much of your day."

"Take your time." Dee leaned over and scratched her dog behind his ears. "It's another hour or so before Apple and I have to head off to feed the horses and check the stock tanks."

"Thanks." Kelsey glanced at the first question on her list. "Can you tell me how the traffic of illegal aliens affects ranchers?"

Dee ran her fingers through her dark hair and settled back in her chair. "In more ways than you might realize. Take Bull Stevens, for example. Illegals cut his fence and he lost thousands of dollars when his herd strayed through the fence and got into some bad feed and died."

Frowning, Kelsey said, "No wonder he hasn't looked pleased when I've mentioned talking to him about illegal immigrants."

The rancher gave Kelsey a wry smile. "That's putting it mildly." Dee jerked her thumb toward the window. "Then there's Kev Grand, who lives across the way from us. His loss has also been in the thousands."

Kelsey cocked her head as she remembered the name. "It's been some time, but I read an article in *The New York Times* that Mr. Grand is one of the vigilantes who took matters into his own hands."

Dee nodded. "You might say that, though he's really not the vigilante the papers have made him out to be. He just got tired of all the destruction to his property, as well as the drug traffic. So he set up sensors, started patrolling his own property, taking illegals into custody and calling the Border Patrol to escort them off his land."

"You mentioned destruction," Kelsey said. "What kind?"

"Like most ranchers around these parts, including the Flying C, Kev has had a lot of damage, with fences being cut in places the illegals passed through." Dee sighed. "This is a bigger problem than you'd think. Not only will cattle cross from one rancher's property to another, they could also end up in Mexico."

Kelsey's fingers flew over the laptop's keyboard as she took notes, questions flying even faster through her mind. "What other damage has been done?"

"Kev and other ranchers have had problems with *coyotes* shooting holes in fifty-thousand-dollar water tanks, as well as cutting water lines, just for the sake of getting drinking water." Dee clenched her jaw and shook her head. "What makes this even more frustrating is that they could find open stock tanks anywhere around here, every mile or so, where these people can drink without the *coyotes* destroying property."

Kelsey checked the next question on her list. "Do you have illegals cross your property or come up to your home?"

"Dozens of them cross our rangeland every night, and we've had groups of thirty to forty camp out in the pasture."

"Do you ever feel like you're in danger?"

Dee tilted her head. "Well, for the most part, no. These tend to be people coming to the U.S. to make a better life, and earning more money than they could in Mexico. But I've heard a few stories that have made me uncomfortable."

The rancher drummed her slender fingers on the table. "Now those *coyotes* are nasty. Real bad news. There's one in particular whose name keeps coming up. His name is Gordo, and from what little I've heard, he's a real SOB."

"Gordo? That means 'fat' in Spanish, correct?"

"Yes."

After Kelsey had interviewed Dee for a while longer, Apple bounded to the front door and back. He gave a low woof, nuzzled Dee's hand, then trotted back to the door with an expectant look on his expressive face.

Dee laughed. "Time to feed the horses. Any more questions?"

"I'm set." Kelsey shut down her laptop. "You've been terrific."

"No problem. Call me if you have more questions, or send me an e-mail." Dee gave Kelsey a business card, then walked her to the front door with Apple dancing at their heels.

As Kelsey turned to leave, Dee placed her hand on her arm. "I know it's none of my business, but if Kade is interested in you, don't let him slip through your fingers. He's a good man. One in a million."

Kelsey swallowed and attempted a smile. "Ah. Thanks."

Chapter 13

Butterflies invaded Kelsey's stomach while she drove down G Avenue, Douglas's main street, to the Monroe Café. She parked the SUV in front of the row of buildings crammed side by side along the street. Gold letters announced the café's name, along with the proclamation that it was the oldest restaurant in Douglas.

Wiping her sweaty palms on her jeans, Kelsey took a deep breath. It was only lunch with Kade, for goodness sake. Not a date.

Sheesh. She'd let the man give her an orgasm last night by sucking her nipples.

Then she saw him walking toward her on the sidewalk. His sexy smile. His walk, so fluid and powerful . . . No man should be allowed to be that gorgeous.

Lust. Pure and simple. She lusted after the man.

Another deep breath and then she grabbed her purse, got out of the SUV, and joined Kade where he waited in front of the café.

"Hello, darlin'." Kade smiled down at her, his azure eyes caressing her with a glance. He didn't even have to touch her, and she felt like she'd been kissed.

"Hi." Her voice was breathless and she couldn't think of anything else to say.

He opened the door to the café and motioned her in, his hand at her elbow. Delicious smells of barbeque and hot biscuits enveloped Kelsey as soon as she entered. It was a narrow room, one wall lined with floor-to-ceiling photos, posters, and playbills of Marilyn Monroe. The other wall was complete with a bar and glass-fronted display cases filled with pies and cakes.

They were silent as they waited for the host to seat them, but Kade's nearness drove Kelsey wild. All she could think about was last night, his kisses, his body pressed against hers, the way his mouth felt on her, and his promise of fireworks. No doubt in her mind that he could give her that and more.

She was so deep in thought about him that she almost jumped out of her skin when the host spoke, asking where they would like to sit. Warmth crept up her neck as she realized Kade was watching her, and she wondered how obvious her expression had been.

When they were seated in a booth, they took a few moments to examine the menu. Kelsey chose grilled chicken, and Kade ordered barbequed spareribs.

"How was your interview with Dee?" Kade asked when the waiter left.

Kelsey turned away from the picture of Marilyn that she'd been studying. "Dee's terrific."

"I've known her since I was a kid. We saw each other off and on at events around the county. She was into barrel racing and I was into calf roping."

"You were into rodeo?"

He smiled. "I owe a lot to the junior rodeo circuit for helping me get through my shyness when I was a boy."

"You? Shy?" Kelsey raised her eyebrows. "Never."

With a shrug, Kade said, "Let's just say that I could hardly look a person in the eye, but that club helped me to gain some confidence and believe in myself."

Kelsey rested her elbow on the table, her chin on her palm. "You surprise me."

"I'm full of 'em." He folded his arms and leaned forward. "Just try me."

The waiter arrived with their drinks, saving Kelsey from yet another blush. She squeezed lemon into her iced tea and added a packet of artificial sweetener.

"That stuff'll—"

"Kill me. I know." Kelsey smiled and met his gaze. "You told me the same thing on the plane about my diet soda."

By the look in his eyes, she was sure he was thinking about that first night they'd kissed. She still couldn't believe she'd kissed a man the same night she met him. But, well, it had been Kade. In her heart, she knew that dinner and kiss would never have happened with any other man.

Kelsey rested her chin on her hand again, studying Kade's handsome face and his brilliant blue eyes. "What was your childhood like?"

He shrugged. "Not much to tell. I grew up around here and had a pretty good time. My biological father took off when I was younger than Trent, so there were some tough years."

Kelsey's soul twisted at the thought of Kade, young and fatherless. "I'm sorry."

"Don't be." Kade smiled and squeezed her free hand. "He wasn't much of a father. Mom met Chuck a couple of years later, and when I saw how happy he made her, I was all right with it. As far as I'm concerned, Chuck is my dad."

"Did you play sports in school, other than calf roping?" Kelsey asked.

"In high school I was a decent linebacker," Kade said. "Also did pretty well in right field on our baseball team."

"I bet you were more than pretty good." Kelsey could just imagine him in those tight pants that football players wore. *Nice.* "After high school?"

"I headed off to the University of Arizona." Kade shifted in his seat and leaned one forearm on the table. "I wanted to go into law enforcement, and while I was in college I decided to get on with the Border Patrol. I trained at FLETC after graduation, and later was stationed along the Texas border. That's where I met Trent's mother."

"Your son is precious," Kelsey said. "You're fortunate to have such a great kid."

He smiled. "Yeah, I am."

Kelsey returned his smile. "And he's lucky to have you as a father."

The waiter served their lunch, and they ate while they talked. Kelsey told Kade what information she'd gathered so far on the problems with illegal immigration, and he ventured his opinion on a few issues.

As far as Kelsey was concerned, their lunch was over too soon and Kade had to get back to work. He walked her to the SUV, and as she opened the door he said, "Thanks for having lunch with me."

"Thanks for asking." Then, surprising even herself, Kelsey reached up and brushed her lips over his. "Later, cowboy."

Before he could react, she turned away, climbed into the vehicle, and shut the door, her lips tingling from the brief caress. He just smiled and watched her drive away.

Late-afternoon sun peeked through the monsoon-darkened sky as Kade reached the offices of *The Douglas Herald*. The newsroom occupied the bottom floor of one of the town's oldest buildings. Smells of ink, newspaper, and stale coffee overpowered the dingy lobby.

"Kade. Long time no see," said Patti Duarte, the paper's combination office manager/columnist. She stood up, her blond ponytail bobbing as she bounced toward the front counter. "Where ya been hiding out?"

He leaned against the counter. "Looks like you've been keeping this place above water. And looks like you're about to pop. I didn't even know you're expecting. Congratulations."

Patti, who had always reminded him of a pixie, patted her enormous belly. "Thanks. Twins, can ya believe it? I look like I'm about to explode, but we've got another two months."

Her blue eyes sparkled, and her cheeks seemed full and shiny. That old saying about pregnant women was true. They did have a special glow to their faces. For one strange minute, he pictured Kelsey, her belly large with his child, her features as radiant as Patti's.

He shook his head, pushing the vision to the back of his mind. "Twins. Bet Paul's as proud as a rooster at the crack of dawn."

Patti snorted. "He's scared shitless."

"Can't say that I blame the guy." With a laugh, Kade nodded to the back room. "That new reporter here? Gerald Spitz?"

"You mean you're not here to see little ol' me? Hold on, let me get him." Her ponytail bobbed as she disappeared through the door-way. Within a minute, she returned. "Come on back and meet God's gift to the newspaper business."

Kade raised his brows. "God's gift, huh?"

Patti rolled her eyes. "Thinks he is. Every time AP picks up one of his stories you'd think he won the Pulitzer."

"Miss working with Gerardo?" Kade asked.

"You betcha." Patti led Kade into the back room, past an an-cient printing press to a man sitting behind a computer at one of three metal desks. "Gerald, this is Border Patrol Agent Kade Owen. Kade, this is Gerald Spitz, editor-in-chief and reporter extraordinaire."

Patti winked at Kade as she left the room, and he held back a grin.

"Pleased to meet you, Agent Owen." Spitz didn't offer his hand. Instead, he made a show of tossing his head, flipping his dark hair from his face.

"Uh, yeah. My pleasure." Right off, Kade didn't like the guy. Something about the arrogant look in Spitz's brown eyes made him wary. Still, he had to get what he came for, so he stuck out his hand and forced a smile.

Spitz gave Kade a limp handshake. Soft and damp. No calluses, no weathering.

"Have a seat." Spitz pointed to one of two vinyl chairs in front of his desk. "What can I do for you?"

"Thanks." Kade settled into the chair. "Gerardo was a good friend of mine. Thought I'd come in and get acquainted with you."

Spitz gave Kade what amounted to a patient father-speaking-to-child smile. Only this father was about ten years younger than Kade. "But you have another reason for being here as well."

Might as well lay it on the table.

"No wonder you're such a good reporter, Spitz." Kade let his expression go serious. "Let's get to it. One of your sources gave you a big story on the life of an undocumented alien, and he mentioned a *coyote* named Gordo."

Spitz tossed his hair back again and smirked. "I don't reveal my sources, Agent Owen."

Kade nodded, trying to maintain his cool. "I understand what you're saying. Any source of yours that I might talk to would never be connected with you."

"I don't reveal my sources."

"Hold that thought, partner." Kade leaned forward in his chair. "While it's real good of you to stand up for your journalistic ethics, I want you to sit back and think for a moment. Think about all those good people crossing the border and dying. Dying 'cause some bastard *coyote* doesn't give a damn about them. Some bastard that's stealing from, beating, raping, and murdering these folks."

Spitz shifted in his chair. "I have my professional integrity to consider."

"It'll remain intact." Kade didn't blink as he stared the man down. "Give me a name and no one'll be the wiser."

"Like I said, my integrity is on the line." Spitz's eyes shifted to the doorway and back to Kade.

Kade spread his hands on Spitz's desk. "Consider this. How can a man look in the mirror and know he could've saved lives, but left them dangling for his own gain?"

Spitz's eyes narrowed, and his lips thinned. "Why do you give a rat's ass?"

Kade gave the reporter a level stare. "Tell you what, Spitz. I don't give a damn what you think of me. What does concern me is day after day these *coyotes* get away with murder. But my conscience is clear, and I don't lie awake at night, because I know I'm doing all I can to save lives. It's not enough, but I'm trying."

Kade got to his feet. "How well do you sleep at night?"

Spitz didn't move. "I sleep fine."

"Uh-huh. The next time you get to write a story about some poor man, woman, or child, dead at the hands of a *coyote,* you think real hard if something you can tell me might have saved their lives. Or many lives. And ask yourself if you're not just as bad as the man who killed them."

Spitz's lips thinned, but he said nothing.

Kade pulled his business card out of his wallet and tossed it on the reporter's desk. "Call me if your conscience gets the better of you. I can find my way out."

Chapter 14

A couple of hours later, after stopping at the station to shower in the locker room, Kade reached the ranch and his temper had cooled. He noticed Chuck's truck was gone, but Sadie's SUV was parked in the driveway.

When Kade walked in the door and kicked off his boots, he smelled something great, like Italian food. Tomatoes, basil, and oregano. He headed to the kitchen and smiled when he saw Kelsey. Her back was to him and she was wearing a pink blouse, a short little skirt, and was barefoot. She stood at the range lifting the lid off a pot, then turned off the flame beneath it. She looked good there, like she belonged.

He walked up behind her and slipped his hands around her waist. She gave a little yelp and whirled around, brandishing the pot lid.

She held her other hand to her heart. "Don't do that."

He took the lid from her and set it on the counter. "I should've learned by now that you're pretty dangerous to startle."

"You'd better watch yourself, cowboy." Her voice was low and breathless, her eyes wide.

"I'd rather watch you." Kade studied Kelsey's lips and braced his hands on either side of her, pinning her against the counter. "Where is everyone?"

"I think they'll be back from Tucson in an hour or so." She glanced at the stove, then back to him. "I'm making angel hair pasta for dinner. With garlic bread and steamed broccoli." She sounded a little nervous as fast as she was talking. "The sauce is done, and I've got everything else ready to throw together once they get here."

He didn't take his eyes off her lips. "I'm hungry."

She waved one hand, shooing him away. "Don't you have to take your shower or something?"

"Didn't do any fieldwork," he murmured. "But I took a shower in the locker room."

"Oh." She would have been happy to volunteer to soap his body all over. . . .

"Let's start with dessert," he said, his lips inches away from hers.

Kelsey caught her breath, then swallowed. "Dessert sounds good."

She gave a surprised yelp as Kade grabbed her around the waist and set her on the countertop, away from the range top.

Her pulse raced as he pushed her skirt up around her waist. Thank goodness she was wearing her nice silky pink panties and not cotton grannies. "What are you doing?"

"Sampling dessert." He hooked his fingers onto the sides of her panties and looked at her, waiting for her to tell him to stop.

Kelsey worried her lower lip as she stared at him. Why not? Why not enjoy what he was offering?

Yeah, when it came to Kade she was a total goner.

Instead of answering aloud, Kelsey braced her hands on the countertop and lifted her hips.

Kade gave her that slow, sexy smile that made her insides melt. He pulled her panties down her thighs, then gradually eased them over her legs and ankles, teasing her with every deliberate movement. Just the way his fingers caressed her legs as he brought the panties down was enough to make her ache from her nipples to the juncture of her thighs.

He stuffed the pair of pink panties into his back pocket, then pushed her thighs apart with his hands, totally exposing her to his gaze. The countertop was cool beneath her, but her body was already burning up. She was faintly aware of the pot of sauce bubbling on the range and the smell of garlic.

Everything faded as her world came to a pinpoint on the man between her thighs.

"You are so beautiful, darlin'," he murmured as he lightly brushed his fingers over the blond curls of her mound.

She trembled at the contact and her cheeks heated.

Kade set his Stetson on the counter beside Kelsey, then knelt on the tile floor between her legs. He gripped her thighs with his large hands as he brought his face to her folds. He paused and inhaled. "You smell like heaven."

Kelsey shivered and bit back a moan. This was right. This was good. . . . Feeling and experiencing what life had to offer and doing it with Kade.

Go for it, Kelsey. Live.

She couldn't hold back that inner voice that worried about the consequences. "What if everyone comes home early?" *What if I can never say no to you?*

He gave her a wicked grin. "Then I'll throw you over my shoulder and cart you off to my room and finish the job."

Before she could think of a suitable reply, Kade parted her folds with his fingers and licked her slit with a long, slow swipe of his tongue.

Kelsey moaned from the exquisite sensation and watched him sliding his tongue over her clit. She clenched the edge of the countertop as he pressed her thighs wider apart and licked and sucked her swollen nub.

His tongue swirled and tasted her as he slipped two fingers into her channel. Blood pounded in her veins and in her ears, so loud she could hear nothing else.

She'd never had a man do this to her before, and the feeling was incredible. Nothing on earth could replace the feel of a man's mouth on her folds, licking her slit, and his fingers thrusting inside her. She could just imagine him sliding into her channel, his rock-hard body pressed against hers.

She tilted back her head and felt her nipples, hard as stones beneath her blouse. Kade's stubble was rough against her folds and the insides of her thighs, driving her closer to that place inside her that was growing, budding, and blooming. She'd never felt anything like this and she was sailing so fast toward her climax that it fully blossomed inside her in a rush. She gave a little cry as heat burned her from head to toe and back again.

Kade slowed his movements but continued licking her until Kelsey's hips finally stopped rocking against his face. "No more," she begged, and shuddered with another aftershock.

He stood and moved between her thighs. Slowly he brought his face to hers and kissed her long and deep. It made another tremor go through her.

With a smile he moved back and caught her around the waist. He lifted her off the countertop and set her on her feet.

Kade tugged her skirt down over her hips while Kelsey tucked in her shirt. "I can't believe we just did that," she said.

His lips quirked as he dragged his hand over his mouth and chin. "I've been dying to taste you since I met you."

At that moment the front door crashed open and Trent's yell shattered the moment.

"Dad! We're home!"

Kelsey bolted out of his arms before Trent made it into the kitchen. Kade winked at her and then smiled at his son. "How's my favorite guy?"

After Trent had run off to his room and Kade greeted his mom and dad he excused himself and headed down the hallway.

Kelsey's gaze widened as she watched him walk away and she prayed that no one else had noticed.

Her bright pink silky panties were peeking out of his back pocket.

"Eduardo Montaño, please," Kelsey said to the courthouse's elegant receptionist. The nameplate on the woman's desk read PORTIA ZAPATA.

"Do you have an appointment with the mayor?" The receptionist wore a sleek black business suit, her voice smooth and professional. She seemed accustomed to heading off unwanted visitors.

"Yes. I'm Kale C. Nichols with San Francisco's *City by the Bay* magazine," Kelsey replied.

While the receptionist buzzed the mayor's office, Kelsey ignored the urge to fuss with her skirt and her press badge, doing her best to appear calm, cool, and collected despite the humidity. She'd spent the past week in casual clothing, and for the first time she could remember she felt confined wearing a silk suit. On top of that, the leather heels pinched her toes and she longed to be in her casual sandals or tennies. She'd arranged her hair in an elegant chignon at the nape of her neck, applied her makeup so that it gave her an air of elegance, and she wore diamond studs in her ears.

One of the most important things she'd learned early in her career was to dress as the natives do. When interviewing a rancher, dress comfortably in jeans and a blouse. When speaking with an office clerk, wear nice slacks or a pant outfit. When meeting with a politician, dress to kill.

A few moments later, the receptionist escorted Kelsey into the mayor's office. The news reports she'd seen of the mayor hadn't done him justice. He was almost beautiful with his long black eyelashes and aristocratic features. Not a speck of gray marred his ebony hair or his full mustache.

"Buenos días, Señorita Nichols," the mayor said with a small bow. "With the name Kale, I expected a man. Instead I find myself in the company of a most beautiful señorita. Or is it señora?" His voice was well modulated, his manner that of a true politician.

She smiled. "Thank you, Mayor Montaño. I appreciate you taking the time to meet with me. Is there a Spanish word that translates to Ms.?"

He took Kelsey's fingers lightly in his, lifted them to his mouth, and brushed his lips across her knuckles. His cologne was heavy, a cloying smell that reminded Kelsey of her ex-husband's cologne. "I'm afraid not. Call me Eduardo, please. May I call you Kale?"

She didn't share that her real name was Kelsey in situations that involved individuals in politics or certain other areas. As she withdrew from his grasp, Kelsey replied, "Of course."

"Have a seat, Kale." With a sweep of his arm, he gestured to one of two leather chairs in front of his desk. After Kelsey sat, the mayor hitched up his slacks and settled into the chair next to her.

"Mr. Montaño—"

"Eduardo, please."

"Ah, yes." Kelsey swallowed. "Eduardo. May I record our interview so that I can ensure my notes are accurate?"

He nodded and crossed his legs at his knees. "By all means."

After Kelsey pulled the cell phone out of her purse, she prepared it, then withdrew her notepad of questions. She glanced at the rich furnishings, trying to get a sense of the man she was about to interview.

Behind the desk was a large window, but the wooden blinds were drawn shut. Bookshelves lined one wall, filled with brass sculptures of bullfighters and bulls, as well as a few thick volumes. Oil paintings of matadors in vivid hues of reds, greens, blues, and yellows dominated the other two walls, the fighters waving traditional red capes before powerful black bulls.

"You have a lovely office," she said. "I see you have a penchant for bullfighting."

"Sí." Montaño's mustache twitched and he gave a ruthless smile. "The greatest of all sports."

Kelsey turned from looking at the sculptures and gave him her let's-get-down-to-business smile. "I understand you're running for United States Congress in this fall's election, and your campaign is on an immigration reform platform."

"Yes, that is correct." He placed his elbows on the arms of his chair and steepled his fingers. "I feel very strongly that something must be done to alleviate this ongoing problem."

"Will you explain?"

He nodded. "But of course. First, I believe we should grant amnesty to all Mexican nationals now living in the U.S." He ticked off the points on his fingers. "Second, I advocate free schooling for children of undocumented aliens in all states, and that we should not require these children to prove citizenship in order to go to school. Third, I believe that no one in any state should have to provide a Social Security number or proof of residency to obtain a driver's license."

Montaño continued in the manner of a politician practiced in outlining his views. "Fourth, I oppose mandatory reporting by employers of their employees' nationalities. Fifth, I do not believe we should fine employers who hire undocumented workers. And sixth, I do not agree with dragnets that round up immigrants from their homes or workplaces."

Kelsey made a note to herself on her notepad. "How do you feel this will help the problem with the numbers of people attempting to cross the border illegally every day?"

"I believe that we must ease the hardship of the suffering souls living in fear and despair on our side of the border," he replied. "Those poor people on the other side are in my thoughts and prayers. However, they must wait and cross into this country legally, as did my father, many years ago."

Typical politician. Talking in circles around her questions.

"I see. Now regarding the number of aliens crossing the border illegally, do you feel that going after the smugglers and *coyotes* would get to the root of the problem?"

"Of course we wish to find and prosecute these reprehensible beings." Montaño shrugged. "Let me express how much it saddens me that these smugglers of humans, these so-called *coyotes,* continue to cause the loss of so many lives. It's a terrible problem and something must be done about it."

She met his gaze head-on. "What do you propose?"

"First we must address the most important issues on immigrants already living in this country before we can tackle that obstacle."

Not going to get a straight answer.

Kelsey checked her list of questions and looked back to Montaño. "What do you know of a *coyote* named Gordo?"

For a fraction of a second, Kelsey thought she saw unease in the mayor's eyes, but a questioning look replaced it almost at once. "Gordo? I do not recall a *coyote* by that name. Where did you hear it?"

Was there something in his look? "Someone mentioned it to me," Kelsey said, and went to the next item on her list.

Montaño answered more of her questions in his carefully rehearsed manner, then glanced at his watch. "As much as I enjoy your company, señorita, I have another appointment I must attend to."

She gathered her belongings and thanked the mayor. He seemed like he was a nice enough man for a politician. As she left she wondered why the interview with him had made her feel so uneasy.

Chapter 15

It was going too fast. They would crash.

Screams filled the cramped cabin. Naya squeezed Kelsey's hand, crushing her fingers. "OhGodohGodohGodohGod," Naya cried over and over and over again.

"Head between your knees," Father yelled. Mother sobbed beside him.

Kelsey pushed Naya down. Naya was still praying. Kelsey's head filled with the chant, her heart pounding in desperate rhythm. "OhGodohGodoh-GodohGod, please. Let us live."

The plane slammed forward, nose down. Impact. The seat belt dug deep. Kelsey's head smashed into a seat back.

Spinning. They were spinning. Luggage burst from overhead compartments. Around and around they whipped. Back and forth. Suitcases battered her arms. Screams. Shrieks. The sound of metal grinding, tearing, as the plane ripped in half.

The caustic smell of electrical smoke filled the cabin. Sparks, then fire.

Whirling. They were spinning, screaming.

Slower, it moved slower, but Kelsey's head still reeled. The screech of metal against asphalt raked across her spine, like a giant hand scraping

*down an immense chalkboard. Finally, finally, the plane shuddered to a
stop.*

Were they really alive? Did they make it?

*Fire. Smoke. Screams. Sirens. The stench of burning flesh. Pain seared
Kelsey's thigh and she saw torn cloth, her flesh flayed open, blood covering
her lap.*

*Naya's hand still clutched Kelsey's in a death grip. Kelsey lifted her
head and looked at her sister. Blood shrouded Naya, and her mouth and
eyes were wide open, frozen with fear.*

"No!" Kelsey bolted upright in bed. Tears streamed down her face,
her clothes soaked with sweat, every inch of her body trembling.

The door burst open. Light from the hall silhouetted Kade's big
form, his hair rumpled. Through her tears she saw concern stamped
across his features.

"What happened?" He shut the door and in a couple of long
strides, he reached her. One look at her face and he slid onto the edge
of the bed and pulled her into his lap. "Honey. Are you all right?"

She sobbed against his strong shoulder. She couldn't speak.
Couldn't force the images from her mind of smoke, flames, twisted
metal, and her dead sister's face. Kelsey's leg throbbed, as if her
skin were still shredded, blood still pouring from the wound.

"A nightmare?" Kade's voice was soft and soothing.

She shuddered and nodded against his chest. "I—I dreamed about
the plane crash. Naya. Her face. It was so—so real."

For a long while he held her, gently rocking her, trying to soothe
the horror of her nightmare. Terror and grief raged within Kelsey. She
could barely think. Barely hold the screams trapped in her throat.

"Easy," came Kade's low murmur through the chaos. "I've got
you. You're safe."

Safe? How could anywhere be safe? Her swallowed screams turned to sobs. Nowhere on earth would ever be safe again. Father. Mother. Naya.

Dear God. Naya.

Hot tears streamed down Kelsey's cheeks, but Kade's embrace didn't falter. "Let it go. Let it out. I'll be here. Right here."

She let herself believe him, let herself relax in his powerful arms. The easy sigh of his breathing lulled her, and she smelled his earthy, grounding scent. So strong. He felt so strong. Her hand slid across his naked chest, through the patch of curling hair and the dampness of her tears against his flesh. Slowly, ever so slowly, the room returned to proper focus.

Kade. He was holding her still, his protective arms cradling her with more gentleness, more caring than she'd known from any man. Her heartbeat quickened, and once more, intense emotions stirred— but not fear. Not grief.

The antidote. Passion. Tenderness.

She turned her face to look into his eyes. Fathomless pools, midnight blue in the faint light. "You're always comforting me."

He brushed his lips across her forehead. "Do you need me to stay awhile longer?"

Closer. She wanted closer. She wanted his lips, wanted him to kiss her until there was no turning back. His body pressed to hers, nothing between them but a fine layer of perspiration. The intensity of her desire shocked her, but all she could think about was how much she wanted him. Now.

She turned her mouth to his chest, kissing the salty flesh, moving her lips to his collarbone and trailing her tongue along his skin. His breath hissed out, stirring the hair at her temple. She wanted him to kiss her the way he had at the park. So thorough, so exquisite that time meant nothing. Only the sound of his heartbeat against hers, the feel of his hands and lips on her body.

As Kelsey lifted her head, Kade pressed his fingertips to her mouth, stopping her from reaching his lips. She kissed his hand instead, moving her lips over each finger.

He groaned and shuddered. "Not now, not when your heart aches like this."

"But . . ." Disappointment swelled within Kelsey. He didn't want her.

"Yes, I do want you," he replied as if she'd spoken the words aloud. "More than you can imagine." His cock pressed against her hip like a rod made of steel, and she knew it was true.

"Tonight I'm your friend." He stroked her hair behind her ear. "Let your head clear, and if tomorrow, you still want that kiss . . ."

With a reluctant sigh, she snuggled closer, enjoying the feel of his hard body, his muscular arms wrapped around her. How different he was from Davis. Davis, who took advantage of her vulnerability.

As she shifted in his lap, Kade tensed. He gave a muffled oath, moved Kelsey to the bed, and stood. "You ought to sleep."

She could barely see him in what little light poured in from the hall, but it was enough to see the powerful muscles in his chest, the hard line of his body, the thrust of his cock outlined against the white of his boxers.

A moan caught in her throat. He was so beautiful.

He took a ragged breath. "Don't look at me like that, honey. Like you want to eat me whole. I can hardly think straight as it is."

She slid down her pillow and pulled the covers to her waist. "Okay."

" 'Night." He smiled, rakish yet wistful, and turned toward the door.

Kelsey sat up again. "Wait."

Kade stopped and looked back with hooded eyes.

Longing swelled within her, and something else. Something that made her want to tell him what his thoughtfulness did to her, how it made her desire him more than ever. But she only said, "Thanks."

"Get some sleep, honey." And then he was gone, closing the door behind him.

For a long time, Kelsey remained awake, but the nightmare didn't haunt her as she feared it would. All she could think about was Kade.

Chapter 16

Kade spent a frustrating day chasing dead-end leads, finding himself no closer to learning the identity of either Gordo or El Torero. By the time he'd exhausted his last resource, orange and pink streaked the western sky, the sun sinking behind the Mule Mountains.

And he was late. Marnie and Stan Perez had invited Kade's family and Kelsey to dinner. Marnie had promised to make her wicked chili con carne, homemade flour tortillas, and flan, a Mexican custard, for dessert. But Kade just wasn't up to socializing, even though he hated to miss the chance of being around Kelsey.

Dead tired, Kade stopped by the Perezes' ranch to make his appearance and his excuses. Sadie and Chuck were there when he arrived, but he didn't see Kelsey or Trent. Sadie let him know that Trent had come down with a stomach bug that afternoon, and Kelsey had volunteered to stay with him.

Only the porch light was on when Kade finally made it home, and the house was quiet, save for crickets chirping and Roxie sniffing her greeting. Absently, he scratched the dog behind her ears, feeling a surge of disappointment that Kelsey had apparently gone to bed. He'd hoped to spend a few moments with her—hell, more than a few moments.

Not that he was able to get to sleep right away after being near her. Warmth seeped into his blood when he remembered last night. He'd gone to Kelsey to comfort her, and when she'd calmed down, she'd reached for him with desire in her eyes and passion in her soul. Had he been a fool for turning away from her?

No, as much as he wanted her, he could never do that. When she came to him for more than petting and sexual play, it would be with a clear head. It would be because she wanted him. Last night could've just been a reaction to the adrenaline pumping through her body after her nightmare. No greater aphrodisiac than adrenaline.

Kade kicked off his dusty boots by the front door and tore off his socks, then put his Glock in the cabinet. He'd spent the day researching files, watching surveillance tapes, and talking on the phone, and hadn't come in contact with any UDAs, but he still wanted a shower.

In the kitchen, he washed his face and hands in the sink, before giving Roxie a bowl of dog food and water. He made himself a sandwich with Sadie's homemade bread and leftover ham, and scarfed it down along with a glass of orange juice.

When he finished eating, he went to the bathroom but found the door locked and heard water running in the tub. So, Kelsey wasn't asleep after all. What would she think if he slid into the bathroom and offered to join her? Would she welcome him? He shook his head and smiled. Just maybe.

He checked on Trent and found the boy fast asleep. He went to the laundry room and stripped off his clothes, then headed to Chuck and Sadie's bathroom to take his shower.

After a nice hot shower, Kade felt more than refreshed. His

blood boiled and his erection was obvious against the thick terry cloth towel around his waist. The tile felt cool under his bare feet as he headed toward his room. Should he knock on Kelsey's door?

When he reached the hallway, Kelsey was there. His pulse picked up and his gut tightened. She stood in the doorway of Trent's room, a soft smile on her face. Only light pouring from her bedroom lit the hall, but it was enough that he could study her.

Heat gathered in Kade's groin as he watched Kelsey, his arms aching to draw her close, aching to touch her face, aching to stroke her body. She was beautiful. Her skin pink, the ends of her hair damp. And of all things, she wore his faded bathrobe.

She turned away from Trent's room and froze.

"Hello, Kelsey," Kade said softly.

"Kade." She hugged the robe tighter. "I thought you'd be going to the Perezes'."

"Too tired." He smiled and leaned against the door frame of her room. "At least I was."

Kelsey wiped a tendril of damp hair from her face, her chocolate eyes drawing him closer. "I was checking on Trent."

Kade struggled to stay put, to keep his hands away from her. "How's he doing?"

"His fever's down." She glanced in the boy's room, then back to Kade. In the background, he heard country-western music playing on Trent's radio.

Her gaze darted to Kade's bare chest, as if she'd just noticed he wore only a towel. She blushed as she looked back to his face. "I'd better let you get to bed."

She brushed past him into her room. Her soft body slid by him as silken as a caress, the fragrance of her warming him like whiskey in his veins. And God help him, he followed her.

"Kelsey."

The Victorian lamp bathed her in a rose glow, her hair glittering in the gentle light like strands of finest gold. As she turned back to him, she made a soft sound and bit her lip.

"Are you all right?" Kade reached for Kelsey and pulled her to him. She buried her face against his bare chest and slid her arms around his waist. She fit against him perfectly, the top of her head just reaching his chin. He stroked her hair down to the damp ends, and then again.

A deep breath, and then she shuddered. "You smell so good." His chest muffled her voice.

"No, darlin', it's you. Honeysuckle and soap." He smiled. "You look sexy as hell in my robe."

Kelsey lifted her head and the sensual glitter in her eyes made him want to take her now. "When I took a bubble bath, I forgot to bring my clothes into the bathroom. So I borrowed your robe from off the door hook. Do you mind?"

"Never." He gave a wicked grin. "But I envy all those bubbles, touching you, covering every inch of your body. And right now I envy my bathrobe even more."

She caught her breath, her eyes growing wide and her lips parting.

Her mouth looked so inviting, so delectable. He lowered his head and brushed her lips with his. Kelsey wrapped her arms around his neck and kissed him. Long and tender, her tongue teasing him with timid strokes.

He deepened the kiss, delving into her until his head spun and she had completely intoxicated him. He was drunk with the taste of her, the smell of her, the feel of her. Dear God, this was a woman he could never get enough of.

Kade gritted his teeth, his body rock hard against her feminine softness. He felt the slight tremble of her body in his arms and he pulled away. "I'm finding it tough to control myself around you."

She drew him back and melded her body to his. "You taste like orange juice, and something more." She kissed him again, and trailed her lips over the stubble on his chin, down to the hollow of his throat. "Man. You're all man."

Fire burned within Kade, desire so fierce it shook him to the soles of his feet, nearly knocking him on his ass with its intensity.

His breathing grew ragged as he captured her mouth with his. God, but she tasted good. Her lips, so soft and sweet, tore away at his determination. "Kelsey. Honey. I don't know if I can take much more of this. I'm about to throw you on that bed and take all of you."

"Please," she whispered, nuzzling at his ear. "I want those fireworks you promised me."

He squeezed Kelsey to him, his heart nearly ceasing to beat. "Are you sure? Very sure?"

Kade's words made her even more confident in her decision. Like a light shining into a darkened room, she realized it was what she had wanted all along. She didn't just want kisses and almost-sex. She wanted all of him. She wanted him so deep inside her that she could feel him everywhere.

He wasn't Davis. Kade would never hurt her. And even if it didn't last, she needed Kade with a desperation that almost frightened her.

She nodded, her heart pounding, her throat tight. "I want to be with you more than anything."

"You're trembling." He stroked her cheek, then slid his fingers into her hair. "Are you afraid?"

"No. It's just that I . . . I've only been with one man." She brushed her lips against Kade's neck. "He never made me feel the way you do. Never."

"Kelsey," he whispered. "There hasn't been a woman I've cared more about than you."

"Please." She stroked his face, his stubble coarse against her palm. "Be with me."

Chapter 17

"Don't move."

Kade pulled away and left the room, and Kelsey felt alone. Naked. Like a part of her was missing. In moments, he was back. He tossed a box onto the nightstand and shut and locked the door.

"Condoms," she murmured as he brought her into his arms. Embarrassment burned her cheeks for not having thought of needing them. But at the same time she marveled at the man in her arms. After leaving Davis, she'd stopped taking the pill, not planning to have sex with any man. And there she was, wanting Kade so much she could hardly think straight.

He pressed his lips to her forehead. "Second thoughts?"

"No." She shook her head. "I want you so bad I'm shaking."

"Same here." He laughed, low and sensual. "And that's never happened to me before."

She sank against him, breathing in his male scent and running her hands through the hairs curling on his chest. He felt so solid, so good beneath her palms.

A flash of reality struck Kelsey and she tried to step away. "Oh, my God. What am I thinking? Trent is down the hall."

He kept her caged in his arms and nuzzled her hair. His laugh was soft. "Why? Do you make a lot of noise?"

She flushed. "No—I—"

Kade trapped her mouth in a slow, sensual kiss that burned Kelsey to her soul. Her knees gave out, but he was holding her tightly to him.

After devouring her lips, he lifted his head and gave her a lazy smile that sent heat flushing over her again. "You're warm, sweet, passionate, and sexy as hell."

Pleasure tingled within every nerve in her body. He made her feel so alive, so wanted, beautiful even. She glanced at the door. "What about Trent?"

"The kid sleeps like a rock. His radio is on, and his room is all the way down the hallway." Kade caressed her shoulders through the robe, the heat of his hands warming her. "As long as we're discreet and keep the door locked, I don't see a problem."

He hooked a finger under her chin and smiled. "Have you changed your mind?"

She shook her head. "No. I want you."

"Good, 'cause I sure wasn't looking forward to a cold shower." He wrapped his arms around her waist and lowered his head. "I've never tasted anything as good as you."

He traced his tongue along her bottom lip and then the top, a slow, sensual tease. A wave of dizziness swept over her, and she felt as if she would never breathe again. Their tongues met and she wanted more of him.

With a groan, he lifted his head and pulled at the neckline of her robe, baring her shoulder. He caressed the naked skin. "What're you wearing under there?"

His feather kisses continued from her neck down to the rounded softness of her shoulder, bringing another moan to her lips. She found it almost impossible to speak. "Absolutely nothing."

"Show me." Kade's voice was husky as he nuzzled her neck, and it sent thrills skittering in her belly.

"Wait." She put her hands on his chest and glanced at the Victorian lamp. "We need to turn off the light."

"No. I want to see you." His gaze searched her face. "Every last bit of you."

Kelsey's cheeks heated and she tried to push away. "But I—" She dropped her eyes. "I'm not thin and beautiful."

"How could you think that?" Puzzlement and wonder crossed Kade's features when he lifted her chin with his finger and forced her to look at him. "You're perfect."

He slid his hands down her, alongside the curve of her breasts to her waist, and over the flare of her hips. She gasped as he cupped her rear, his hands warm through the robe. "I love to look at you and your curvy body. You're so sensual. So gorgeous. I've been dying to touch you everywhere. Every inch of you."

When she opened her mouth to protest, he put a finger to her lips. That simple touch, the way he traced her lips, undid her. She shivered as Kade ran his finger over her chin down her neck, then between the swell of her breasts until he reached the tie.

All it took was one tug and the robe fell open. Kelsey's nipples tightened, the air cool, but her body burning hot for him. She wanted to pull the robe around her, to cover her body, but he pushed it down her arms to land at her feet.

"Beautiful. So incredibly beautiful." He caressed her with his gaze, taking in all of her from her swollen lips to her bare toes. She trembled, then caught her breath as he cupped her breasts and ran his thumbs over her nipples. "Tell me, Kelsey. Do you blush everywhere?"

She flushed with heat and he smiled, a sensual smile. "I knew it. Your entire body turns that pretty shade of pink."

Kelsey wrapped her arms around his neck. "Shut up and kiss me, cowboy."

Kade pulled her to him, his chest hair tickling her sensitive breasts. They kissed with such urgency and fervor that she was drunk with the taste of him, the smell of him, and she wanted more. But he teased her, slowly relishing her body. He trailed his tongue down her neck, settling in along her collarbone before beginning the leisurely descent to her breasts. She had to fight from crying out as he circled first one nipple, then the other. He took one in his mouth and tugged on it, driving Kelsey out of her mind with wanting him.

When he lifted his head, he gripped her buttocks with his hands, pressing his erection hard against her belly.

"Damn. What you do to me," he groaned as she moved her lips to his chest.

She licked his flat nipples as he'd done to hers, then nipped at him while running her hands over the soft hair of his muscled chest to his hard abs. She couldn't help herself—she wanted to eat him whole, to touch every inch of his body. He caught his breath as her hands neared his hips—a little too close to his cock right now to maintain control.

"Let me feel you." Her hands shaking, she pulled the towel away and let it drop to the floor. His breathing grew more ragged as she stroked his erection. "There's so much of you."

Kelsey knelt before him, running her hand from balls to tip, amazed at how big he was. She'd seen only one before and it wasn't nearly the size of Kade's.

She cupped his balls as she slid her mouth over his erection. With her free hand she stroked him at the same time that she swirled her tongue around the head of his cock, just feeling and getting lost in the moment. It was not something she'd enjoyed doing before now, but with Kade she wanted to experience everything. Wanted to do everything she could to give him pleasure.

And she loved it.

Kade groaned and slid one hand into her hair, clenching his fingers in the strands that were still damp from her bath. He wanted to thrust his hips, to slide himself in and out of Kelsey's hot mouth, but he let her control her motions.

Gritting his teeth, he kept a tight hold on her hair as she licked the length of his cock while stroking him at the same time. Her other hand caressed his balls and he had the feeling she was enjoying getting to know him so intimately.

His climax built up within him, his gut tightening and his balls drawing up. "I'm gonna come if you don't stop."

Her answer was a sigh that heated him, and then she took him deep, to the back of her throat. He tried to pull away, but she held on to him and sucked.

Kade came so hard he literally saw stars. Kelsey kept sucking on him even as she swallowed his fluid, drinking it down until he was spent.

When she slipped his cock out of her mouth, he couldn't believe that he was still semierect after what she'd just done to him. He brought her up, sliding her body against his. "You sexy little thing," he murmured as he bent down to kiss her.

Kelsey felt the heat of him, the hardness of his cock against her belly, and it amazed her that he was clearly ready and able even after he had just climaxed. His hands roamed over her as he kissed her, paying close attention to her breasts, then moving down to cup her butt cheeks. He moved one hand between them and slipped his fingers into her folds.

He lifted his lips away from hers. "Tell me what you want, darlin'."

Now wasn't the time to be coy. It was time to admit what she had wanted ever since she'd met him. How could she say it without using the F word and definitely not using *making love* because this was just sex?

"Tell me," he said as his lips brushed over her forehead. "You can say it."

Kelsey bit her lip, then took a deep breath. "I want you to . . . I want you."

Kade's gaze was entirely focused as he stroked her clit. "I want to fuck you, Kelsey." He plunged two fingers into her channel and she gave a soft cry. "I want you to tell me what you want, too."

She couldn't believe how much it excited her to hear him say it out loud like that. "I—I want you inside me, Kade."

With almost ferocious intensity, Kade kissed Kelsey, plunging his tongue into her mouth. He nearly growled as he lifted his head and took in Kelsey's dazed expression, her moist lips, and the way her chest rose and fell with every breath.

Kade took her hand and led her to the bed, then pulled her onto it beside him. He twined his long legs with hers and moved his thigh close to her mound. "I've wanted to make love to you since the moment I saw you in the airport," he said, and then traced her nipples with his tongue. She gasped as he slid his hand down her belly to the apex of her thighs and cupped her mound.

"I—I—Kade." Kelsey choked back a cry as his finger teased her clit and wild vibrations rocked her. She clenched her hands in his hair and arched her back as he slid his fingers inside her satin warmth.

"You're so perfect," he murmured as he moved his fingers in and out of her channel.

Slowly, agonizingly slowly, he moved his mouth from one nipple to the other, licking and sucking each one until they were so hard they ached. Continuing his tease, he worked his way between her breasts, down her belly, then licked her navel before moving on, but he bypassed her mound and went instead to her leg. With his lips, he caressed the scar on her thigh, softly kissing the length of it.

Kelsey brought her hands to her nipples and pinched them, needing to relieve the ache as Kade took his time exploring her body. He kissed a trail down her leg to her foot, then flicked his tongue against the sensitive spot at the arch. When he finished, he gently released her leg and moved to the other. He started the slow ascent, paying attention to her foot, the inside of her knee, and the soft skin of the inside of her upper thigh.

She trembled as he nuzzled the soft curls of her mound. He ran his tongue over the tops of her folds. He drove her wild when he again tasted that most intimate part of her, licking and sucking her swollen folds. Streamers of pure pleasure rippled through her as he flicked his tongue against her clit. She bit her lower lip to keep from screaming.

This time his tongue worked its magic at a much slower pace, as if he were attempting to drive her out of her mind. He slipped two fingers into her and drove them in and out the way she wanted him inside her. At the same time he pressed his face tight against her folds, licking her hard. Her thighs trembled and her breathing grew more ragged. "I'm going to come," she said, barely able to speak.

He only licked her harder until she climaxed with a jerk and a barely suppressed cry. Her body was still trembling, the muscles at her core still contracting so hard she could feel it from her mound to her breasts.

Kade worked his way back up as her body shuddered, slowly circling her navel and licking a path up to her breasts, where he licked and sucked them. When his mouth met with Kelsey's, his tongue made love to her, and she could taste herself on his lips. She enjoyed the feel of his weight on top of her, his hips between her thighs. She arched her back, wanting to be closer to him, wanting his cock inside her.

"Are you ready for me?" he murmured.

"Yes." She raked her nails softly across his back. "Definitely yes."

He leaned over to the nightstand and took a condom from the box, then knelt between her thighs as he tore open the package. She gazed into his gorgeous eyes and she wanted to lose herself in them.

No. With Kade, she wasn't losing herself. She was finding herself.

He sheathed his cock and tossed aside the wrapper. And then he braced himself above her, his weight partially against her. "I want to be a part of you."

"Now," she moaned. "Please, Kade. I want you inside of me."

He brought the head of his cock to the entrance of her channel and just stared down at her for a moment. "Kelsey," he murmured, the sound of his voice giving her raw pleasure.

She caught her breath, waiting for that moment when he would be inside her. Then he thrust deep. She gasped as he filled her so completely that she couldn't imagine ever being apart from him. It was like he belonged there. Right there. He remained motionless for a moment and she squirmed beneath him, wanting more.

Kade lowered his head and captured one of her nipples with his mouth and she bit back a cry of pleasure. She pushed her hips tight against his, wanting him to thrust inside her so deep the sensation would travel throughout her body.

"You feel so good wrapped around me, so snug and tight," he said as he stared down at her. In the faint light his blue eyes glittered with desire. "I'm going to take you now."

"Yes." Kelsey scraped her nails down his back to his ass and gripped his muscled buttocks. "Don't make me wait anymore."

"Damn." His strokes were slow and deliberate, but his jaw was clenched and his eyes wild. Sweat dripped down the side of his face and a droplet landed on her chest. "I want to take you hard and fast, honey."

"Then do it," she urged. "I want it. I want it all."

Kade began thrusting harder into her, his hips firm against the cradle of her thighs. Kelsey matched his rhythm, giving him everything she had and wanting to take more. She whimpered, needing as much of him as he could give.

He paused and hooked his arms around her knees, drawing her up and opened her wide. He plunged himself as deep as he could go and Kelsey felt his cock against her G-spot, that place she'd found only with her vibrator before. But oh, this was so much better, so incredible she could almost cry with the pleasure of it.

Kade plunged in and out of her, hitting that exquisite spot again and again. Ecstasy built within Kelsey—so great, so intense that she wanted to scream. Just as a scream was about to break loose, he kissed her hard, swallowing her cries before they could escape.

She wanted him harder and deeper, wanted all of him, until it built up to a crescendo, higher and higher, until she saw only colors and light, and felt a release unlike anything she'd known before.

Every thrust of his hips drove her beyond that pinnacle, taking her beyond this world and into a place filled with exquisite sensation. She climaxed yet again, and this time the pleasure was almost more than she could bear.

Kade's body grew tense and he gave a low growl as his cock throbbed within her. His thrusts slowed and her body rippled again and again. With one last thrust he held himself still, looking down at her with amazement in his eyes.

"You are beautiful, Kelsey," he murmured before kissing her, a soft, slow kiss. "So beautiful."

Chapter 18

Kade awoke before dawn, his arm numb, but he wouldn't move to shift Kelsey. He didn't want to wake her, not yet. He watched the gentle rise and fall of her naked breasts, her contented expression as she slept.

Last night amazement had filled him as he'd thought about what they'd shared. He'd never so thoroughly enjoyed a woman before, never in his life had wanted anyone like he wanted Kelsey. The realization of how deep that desire went hit him hard.

Too astonished to say anything, he drew Kelsey into the circle of his arms, and she cuddled next to him, looking like a princess who had enchanted him completely. If she wasn't asleep, he'd make love to her now in a heartbeat.

His cock was hard as granite this morning. Every time he was near Kelsey, he felt such a desire to be with her in every way. And now that he'd tasted her and enjoyed her so thoroughly, he knew he'd never get enough.

It was still dark outside, but they'd fallen asleep with the lamp on, and he could see her clearly in its soft light. The sheet had settled around her waist, and her breasts tempted him. They were full and high, the nipples a deep rose color and so soft. Kade shifted so that he could lean closer to the peaks. He kissed one and smiled as it grew taut beneath his lips.

"Mmmm," she murmured, and stirred.

He traced his tongue around the base of her hardened nub, then captured it in his mouth, gently nipping it. While he seduced her nipple, he watched her face.

Her eyes opened a slit and she smiled. "What a wonderful way to wake up." She stretched, then slid her hands into his hair, holding him close to her breast.

"Good morning, darlin'." He moved to her other nipple, gently raking his teeth over it. She gasped and arched her back. "I'm hungry. How 'bout you?" He scooted down, his tongue trailing to the hollow at her navel. He savored the taste of the salt on her skin, the smell of their sex.

"I— Yes," she moaned as his lips neared the fine curls between her thighs.

Kade wanted to slide into her velvet softness but fought for control. The thought of pleasuring Kelsey again filled him with intense desire. He watched her face as his tongue found her folds and he reveled in her soft moans. When his tongue met her clit, she covered her mouth with her arm, obviously holding back a cry.

He thrust two fingers inside her while he licked and sucked her pussy. She squirmed and bucked her hips against his face. He drove her toward completion until she finally shuddered long and hard before her body relaxed.

With a smile he moved up and braced himself over her. He watched her face, wanting to see the wildness in her eyes. She slid her hand between their bodies and grabbed his cock.

In a fast movement he flipped her onto her belly and Kelsey gasped. "Kade."

He positioned a pillow beneath her hips, raising her up so that he could penetrate her more deeply from behind. He paused to sheathe his erection with a condom. "God, you're beautiful," he whispered as he slid inside her.

Kade loved the way her ass looked and the feel of her soft flesh beneath his palms. He watched his cock moving in and out of her and he reveled in the soft cries she made against the bedsheets.

She fit perfectly. Everything about her did. She raised her hips back to meet him as he drove into her, the silky heat surrounding him. He plunged in and out, harder and faster than he had last night, and she took his every thrust.

Her body began to tremble and then she gave a broken cry and he felt her pulsating release gripping and releasing his cock over and over. Kade arched his back and pressed his hips tight to Kelsey's as searing pleasure shattered him to the center of his being.

When the sky lightened, Kade awoke again and stroked a strand of hair from Kelsey's face.

"I've got to get ready for work." He kissed the curve of her smile, breathing in her vibrant scent. "Have breakfast with me."

"Mmmm." She nuzzled his neck. "Too bad you can't play hooky."

"You tempt me." He laughed softly. "I work today and tomorrow, and then I'm off for the next two days. So don't make any plans that don't include me, all right?"

She kissed his ear and whispered, "Okay."

The doorknob rattled, and then a knock interrupted the morning quiet. Kelsey bolted upright, clutching the sheet to her chest, her eyes wide.

"Kelsey. Is Dad in there?" Trent's muffled voice came through the door. "He's not in his room and I can't find him in the house. His bed's already made up, too."

"Ah—" She bit her lip, a panicked look on her face.

Kade caressed her shoulder. "I'll be out in a minute, Trent. Kelsey and I are talking."

"How come the door's locked?"

"Never mind. Go eat breakfast and I'll be there after I take a shower."

"Okay, Dad."

Kelsey fell back on her pillow and covered her head with the sheet. "Oh, my God. What were we thinking?"

Kade traced her features through the cloth, and kissed her nose. "It's okay. As far as Trent knows, we're just talking. He's only nine." He peeled the sheet away from her face and kissed her lips. "Come on and get up."

"What about Sadie and Chuck?" She looked so worried that Kade had to struggle to hold back a smile.

"We're two consenting adults. Besides, Mom and Chuck like you."

Kelsey groaned. "I can't believe I did this. In their home."

Kade kissed her soundly. "It's my home, too. Don't regret what we shared last night. It was too special."

She smiled, the warmth coming back into her chocolate eyes. "You're right. It was wonderful. Incredible."

"Good." He sprinkled kisses over her face, eyes, and nose. "Now get up. I've gotta take a quick shower."

He grabbed his robe from where it had landed the night before and slipped into it. After he made sure the hallway was clear of nine-year-olds, he dodged into the bathroom.

Just thinking about Kelsey and her passionate lovemaking

made Kade's cock hard all over again. With a curse, he switched the water from warm to cold.

When he finished showering, he ducked into his room and pulled on jeans, his bulletproof vest, a T-shirt, and then a button-up shirt over that. As he headed to the kitchen, Kelsey came out of her room wearing shorts and a blouse, her hair back in a French braid.

"Ready to face the cavalry?" he asked.

She attempted a smile. "I think so," she murmured.

He kissed her, then followed her into the dining room, letting her get there a little ahead of him. He didn't care if Chuck and Sadie knew he and Kelsey were together, but he knew that she needed to get adjusted to it.

Kelsey slipped into a chair and scooted up to the table. "Looks like a gorgeous day out."

"Well don't you look fine," Chuck said as he put orange marmalade on a biscuit.

"Thanks." Kelsey smiled as she reached for a biscuit and started to butter it.

Sadie speared a sausage. "Did you get a good night's rest in spite of Trent being sick?"

Kelsey nodded, her eyes avoiding Kade's.

"'Morning." Kade ruffled his son's hair, then slid into the chair next to Kelsey and pressed his knee close to hers. "Feeling better, Trent?"

"Yeah. I could eat ten eggs." Trent grinned at his dad. "Hey, how come you were in Kelsey's room this morning? Did you sleep in there? What were you guys talking about?"

Kelsey dropped the butter knife, and it clattered on her plate. She blushed a deep pink and Kade had to hold back a grin.

"We were just talking." He turned to Sadie. "Please pass the sausage links, Mom."

Sadie raised her brows and glanced from Kade to Kelsey, who was intent on ladling scrambled eggs onto her plate. Sadie passed the platter of sausages to Kade, and he could see that she was trying to hide a smile.

"Well then." Chuck reached for the gravy. "Let's have us some breakfast."

Kelsey was mortified. Her palms tingled and her face flushed so hot she felt as if her cheeks were sunburned. As wonderful as the scrambled eggs, sausages, and biscuits smelled, the food tasted like rubber and sawdust.

But the night had been so wonderful. She blushed again at the turn of her thoughts, and avoided looking at anyone.

Trent's chatter rolled over her like the sound of a june bug buzzing on a summer day. He jabbered on as if he'd never been sick, telling anyone who'd listen about his plans for taming the new calf in the barn and starting a rock collection.

Kade squeezed Kelsey's knee beneath the table, and she almost jumped out of her skin. A slow burn invaded her belly when she looked at him. He was so sexy. And she had seen every charming inch of him. The thought of their passion sent another wave of heat over her skin.

He leaned close and whispered in her ear, "Don't be embarrassed, and don't regret anything. You're too special. We're too special together. All right?"

She nodded, unable to speak, feeling like a lump the size of a baseball had lodged in her throat.

"I've got to get to work." He grabbed his plate and headed to the kitchen. "Great breakfast, Mom."

Chapter 19

As Kade drove to work, his thoughts remained on last night and making love to Kelsey. It was better than he'd imagined. The woman was so warm and sensual. He wasn't sure he would be able to get his mind off her and onto his job.

When he arrived at the Border Patrol station, he forced himself to get a grip on his thoughts and get them back on the problems at hand. He had to track down Gordo and El Torero and he needed his usual single-minded focus to accomplish it.

Kade walked into the station and found a message from the *Herald* reporter, Gerald Spitz, waiting for him.

Maybe the worm had a conscience after all.

Kade sat at his desk and dialed the number.

"Spitz," a voice answered.

Kade grabbed a notepad and pen. "Owen here, returning your call."

A pause. "Can you meet me at Mario's at noon, Agent Owen?"

Kade set the pen on the desk. "I'll be there."

The line went dead. Real sociable guy. Probably killed Spitz to make the decision to talk to him.

Kade arrived at Mario's early to make sure he could snag a good booth and grab a bite to eat. The lunchtime boozer crowd was there, the air so thick with cigarette smoke it was like walking into a giant ashtray. The corner booth where he'd met with Jorge Juarez was open, and Kade eased into it, facing the door, and waited for Spitz.

His skin crawled at his nape, and he knew someone was watching him from the back room. He glanced over his shoulder and saw Mari, the waitress. Her full lips were painted in shimmering red. The color matched her low-cut dress that looked as if she'd been poured into it then tossed in a dryer for good measure.

She slunk up to Kade on spiked heels that must've been a good four inches high. "Have you come back to see me?" She leaned forward and her hair swept across his arm, her breasts almost spilling from her dress.

He forced a tight smile. "I'll have a plate of nachos supremos, and iced tea."

"Is that all?" She traced her red-tipped fingernail along his bicep.

Kade gave a slight nod. "That'll do it."

Mari gave a seductive pout and walked away with swaying hips.

He had little patience for women like Mari, but in his line of work, she could eventually make a good contact. That is if a man didn't have to sleep with her to get information.

Within a few minutes, Mari brought Kade the nachos and tea. She slipped her arm around his shoulders, her gold bangles scraping his neck, and probably would've slid onto his lap if the bartender hadn't called her away. Cheap perfume hung in the air along with the smell of sour beer. Wood-bladed fans spun overhead, but about all the good that did was recirculate the stench of sweat and smoke.

The nachos were tasty, and Kade had munched down half the platter by the time Spitz walked through the front door. The reporter strode to the bar and ordered, then looked around like a man checking to see if there was anyone he knew. He nodded to a couple of guys, then spotted Kade. With a beer in one hand, Spitz sauntered to Kade's table.

"Owen."

"Spitz. What's up?"

Mari brushed by Spitz, and he said loud enough for her to hear, "If you ever want to spill your guts, give me a call." He flipped a business card on the table and walked back to the bar. Kade heard Spitz order another beer and ask the bartender to turn on the Arizona Diamondbacks' game.

The side of the card facing up had Spitz's name and office information. Kade didn't bother to turn it over. He left the card where the reporter had dropped it, and finished eating his lunch.

Out of the corner of his eye, he saw Mari serving a patron on the other side of the bar, her gold bracelets glinting in the artificial light. When Kade stood, he dropped a ten on the table, slipped Spitz's card into his pocket, and walked out the front door.

The sky was hazy bright, like the morning after a good rain, but clouds were building over the mountains. They'd be getting a good storm that night, no doubt. He slid into the driver's seat and started his truck, then pulled Spitz's card out of his pocket and flipped it over. PEDRO RIOS, 123 AVENUE A was written in sharp black letters.

Kade radioed the station on a secure channel and informed his ASAC—Assistant Agent in Charge—that he had a lead, and gave

the name and location. Then he put the truck into gear and drove
to the address Spitz had given him.

Weeds and refuse choked the front yard of the small house. The
blue paint, likely vivid at one time, was now bleached ghostly pale
and crackled like a parched riverbed. Like most homes in the border town, iron scrollwork barred the windows.

The rusted gate creaked as Kade swung it open. As he walked
up the concrete steps, he saw the door standing open about an inch.
His gut clenched. He glanced up and down the street and pulled
out his Glock, shielding it. No cars were parked in front of the
house or the houses next door. The street was empty of people.

As soon as Kade crept up to the door, he smelled it. The heavy
miasma of decomposing flesh.

Bile rose. He leaned back, his head against the house, fighting
to keep his stomach from heaving up the nachos.

A rhythmic *whoosh-whoosh-whoosh* echoed from inside the house.
With his Glock in his right hand, Kade eased the door open with
his left.

No sign of anyone inside.

He knocked. "Police," he said, the universal word for law enforcement.

No answer. Not that he expected any.

Kade pushed the door wider with his boot, but remained out of
sight. When nothing moved and he heard no sound but the whoosh-
ing noise, he held his Glock in front of him and rounded the corner.

The overwhelming stench slammed into him, enough to damn
near drive him to his knees. His eyes and throat burned, and he
struggled to swallow. He pulled a handkerchief out of his pocket
and covered his nose.

The body hung on a rope. A rope tied to a meat hook. A man. His swollen head tilted at a bizarre angle, and his tongue . . . Kade closed his eyes for a moment, then made himself look again. That thick, engorged tongue—and the face, hideous purple-blue like the hands. His hands looked like surgical gloves blown up and painted black.

A ceiling fan churned next to the corpse, the blades skimming the top of his black hair and striking the rope, causing the *whoosh-whoosh-whoosh* noise. The room was trashed. Chairs smashed, garbage littering the floor, the couch on end.

Damn.

Kade listened for sounds inside the house and heard none. He headed back outside and jogged down the stairs, filling his lungs with clean air.

From the looks of the man, not to mention the smell, he'd been dead for a while, and Kade doubted if anyone had hung around to see what happened next. He kept his weapon drawn and went back to his truck to radio the Border Patrol headquarters and the police.

While he waited for the cops to arrive, he checked out the front room again. He didn't recognize the man, but the face was too bloated to be sure. The cadaver's body was at least two feet off the floor. No chair, or anything else he could've stood on, was close enough to the man for it to be a suicide. Plaster had chipped away from around the meat hook, exposing the beam it was screwed into.

Sirens screamed in the background as he glanced at the garbage around the room. Fast-food wrappers, a sock with a hole, a toothpick, a matchbook cover, and sunflower seed shells were scattered among the trash.

Kade noticed a torn piece of paper. He couldn't quite make out the word. Was that *Toro* scrawled across the top of the scrap?

Was it related to El Torero, meaning the matador? Or toro, meaning bull?

Red and blue lights flashed through the open doorway into the interior of the dim house as the first law enforcement vehicle arrived.

Two hours later Kade headed home, after giving his statement to the police about how he'd come across the body, and why he was there.

He'd hung around to gain information during the police investigation. Identification in the corpse's pockets said the man was indeed Pedro Rios. After examining the scene and the body, the homicide detective said he had no doubt Rios had been murdered but would have to complete a full examination.

Gerald Spitz would be in for a nasty surprise when he got hauled down to the police station for questioning. Protecting sources was one thing. Murder was another.

After she returned from her interview with another rancher, Kelsey headed out to relax beside Sadie's pond. She sank into the swing's cushions, slowly rocking back and forth in time with the sound of toads croaking by the pond.

The waterfall's gentle babble soothed her nerves, and a late afternoon breeze stirred and caressed her face. The air smelled of rain, the sky dark with pregnant storm clouds.

Pregnant. What would it be like to be pregnant with Kade's child? To have his baby? Kelsey stretched out on the swing and covered her face with her hands. How could she think of such a thing, when she'd known the man for such a short time?

What an incredible night they'd had, not to mention the hours before dawn. She never knew it could be like that. So fulfilling. So incredibly good.

That's what Theresa and Calinda had always talked about. Now, after her night with Kade, she believed them.

And yes, he was right. No matter what happened next, she couldn't regret what they had shared last night.

She relaxed, imagining all the tension in her body seeping through the cushion of the swing, swirling into the ground, deeper and deeper, until everything around her faded and she slid into a deep sleep.

The sun warmed Kelsey's face, caressing her lips, her eyelids, her brow. A heady sense of pleasure enveloped her and she sighed, content to bask in the gentle, loving heat.

"Kelsey," the sun called to her in a throaty whisper.

"Mmmm," she murmured, then opened her eyes to see that it was dark outside and Kade was bent over her. "Kade."

He balanced on the edge of the swing, his arms propped on either side of her hips. He shifted and ran his finger down her nose. "Wake up, sleepyhead."

She smiled. "I dreamed the sun was kissing me."

"Not the sun." He bent and brushed his lips over hers. "Me. I kissed you here." Her lips. "And here." Her nose. "And here." Her eyelids. "And I want to kiss you in places the sun can't reach. In places that only I can touch you."

Kelsey flushed and wrapped her arms around his neck. "I want to kiss every inch of you, too."

Kade gave her his sexy grin that made her stomach flutter. "I'll consider that a promise."

She noticed his hair was wet and he smelled of apple shampoo. "You've taken your shower."

He ran his hand down her neck and over the curve of her breast, and she gasped, her nipples tightening at the sensual touch.

"It was one of those days," he murmured. "I knew if I came near you first, I couldn't control myself." He nuzzled her ear, then kissed it. "See? I can't even keep my hands or my mouth off you."

"Mmmm." She loved what he was doing to her, how he was making her feel. "Let me sit up."

"Why?" Kade nipped at her chin and then her lips. "I like you where you are. Beneath me. But if you want to be on top that's all right with me, too."

Kelsey grinned. "Maybe."

He helped her up, then drew her onto his lap. She didn't protest. The strength of his arms made her feel safe and secure, and wanted, something she hadn't felt since her parents and sister had died.

"Are you ready to tell me what your ex did to you?" Kade murmured, surprising her with the directness of his question that seemed to come out of nowhere.

She slipped one arm behind him and the other across his hard stomach. The scent of Sadie's roses mingled with the smell of impending rain. A chorus of crickets filled the night and in the distance a coyote howled. The only light came from the windows of the house, and stars had begun to appear through patches of clouds in the evening sky.

Kelsey gave a deep shuddering sigh as Kade caressed her shoulder, down her arm and back again. "Do we have to talk about him?"

"I think it'll be good to realize that he was just a bastard who didn't deserve you." Kade gently massaged the nape of her neck. "How did someone as sweet as you ever hook up with a son of a bitch like that?"

She tensed at the thought of her ex-husband's so-called courtship. "We started dating during my junior year of college. Davis was charming, attentive, and handsome. And I was young and naïve."

A raindrop landed on Kelsey's ankle and soft splatters hit the canopy above. When she started talking again, her voice was flat. "After the accident he was always around. A few months after I lost my family Davis stopped by my apartment and found me crying. He fixed me a glass of wine and said it would relax me. Next thing I knew it was morning, and we were in bed, naked."

Kade made a sound like a low growl. Rain pattered harder, but Kelsey continued, knowing she needed to tell him everything. "I couldn't remember a thing. I freaked out, but Davis said I drank the entire bottle of wine on my own, then pleaded with him to stay."

Memories twisted in her gut like a serrated blade. "He insisted that I begged him for sex and told him I didn't want to be a virgin any longer. He said we should get married because he loved me, and in case I was pregnant.

"I thought I was in love with him. I trusted him." She curled her fist. "I was so stupid. I really thought he loved me."

Kade caught her chin in his hand and made her look at him. "Stop beating yourself up over the guy. You were young and innocent, and the bastard took advantage of you."

She reached up and kissed him. "You're so good to me."

"You're so good for me." He brushed his lips over hers and she shuddered, every nerve in her body raw with desire. "Think anyone would notice . . ."

"Out here?" She gave him a horrified look.

"I'm just teasing you." He kissed her again. "Though I find the idea appetizing."

Rain began pouring down and a barrage of lightning split the sky. Thunder rumbled, an unearthly sound that made her heart pound.

"We'd better get inside." Kade scooted her off his lap. "We're sitting on a metal swing, and that's not a smart thing in a thunderstorm."

He grabbed her hand and they raced in the rain to the house. They reached the porch just as brilliant lightning flashed again, the crash of thunder immediately following. They were still laughing, still holding hands, when they walked into the house.

When she saw Trent, Chuck, and Sadie, she tried to pull away, but Kade wouldn't let go.

"How come you're holding Kelsey's hand, Dad?" Trent's face twisted as if in thought. "Is she your girlfriend?"

Kelsey blushed, but Kade nodded, his face solemn. "Yes, she's my girlfriend."

Trent bounced up and down. "Cool. Can I have a little brother or sister?"

Chuck and Sadie burst out laughing, and Kelsey wanted to hide.

Kade smiled and looked at her. "One step at a time, Trent. One step at a time."

Chapter 20

"Damn straight I'm upset about what those illegals did." John Stevens scowled around his toothpick in response to Kelsey's question.

They were sitting in the office of the former sheriff's sprawling ranch home. After asking the rancher's permission, Kelsey had gotten out her cell phone that was, as usual, set on record. She checked her list of questions as they talked.

"Exactly what happened?" Kelsey kept her expression professional, but her pulse beat a little faster at the heat in Stevens's words.

He narrowed his hazel eyes, his scowl deepening. "A group of 'em passed through the east pasture. Instead of climbing through the barbwire fence, they cut it with wire cutters. Hundreds of my cattle got out." Stevens clenched his fists and his face reddened. "My herd got into some bad feed and it killed 'em all. We're talking thousands of dollars gone to hell."

Before Kelsey could reply, a phone rang. Stevens withdrew a cell phone from the breast pocket of his plaid shirt and checked the display.

"'Scuse me, ma'am." He shifted in his seat and glanced toward the doorway. "I've got to take this call."

"I'll wait in the hall until you're done." Kelsey stood and wandered out of the ranch office as she heard Stevens answer the phone, speaking fluent Spanish.

As she waited for him, she studied framed photographs and newspaper articles on the man's walls. Apparently the rancher was active in local politics. He and Mayor Montaño shook hands in one shot. In other clippings, Stevens had posed with men and women who were local politicians and businessmen, according to the various captions.

A few minutes later, Stevens came out to the hall to let her know he was done with his phone conversation, but he'd have to cut their interview short. Kelsey followed him into the office, sat down, and hurried through the remainder of her questions. In some ways she was glad for the earlier interruption. The rancher seemed more relaxed, even jovial, after the phone call, as if he'd received good news.

When she finished the interview, Kelsey gathered her cell phone and laptop, and thanked the rancher. The phone rang again as she was leaving, and she told Stevens she'd see herself out.

As she drove the SUV along the dirt road leading from the ranch, she passed a vanload of people heading toward Sweetwater. The van was traveling so fast that a cloud of dust rose around it, and the driver almost swerved into Kelsey's vehicle. She bit her lip as she gripped the steering wheel.

The man driving the van barely spared Kelsey a glance, even though he'd almost run her off the road. She clenched her teeth. Some people shouldn't be allowed to have a license.

* * *

In the Turners' study, Kelsey sat before her laptop computer. She typed in John Stevens's responses to her questions as she transcribed the recorded conversation.

When she came to the part where she'd left the room and the rancher began to speak in Spanish, she started to fast-forward. She hadn't even thought about the fact she'd left the phone on record when he took the call. She paused when she recognized one word.

Not a word—a name. *Gordo*. The same name Dee Carter-Reynolds had mentioned.

Was Stevens speaking to or about someone named Gordo? Or was he talking about something else altogether?

Kelsey's cell phone rang, indicating a call was coming in and interrupting Kelsey's train of thought. When she glanced at the display, she saw that it was her editor and put the phone to her ear. "Hey, Theresa."

"How's my favorite reporter and shopping bud?" Theresa's pleasant voice flowed over Kelsey, making her homesick for her friend.

"Wonderful." Kelsey smiled and sighed. "Couldn't be better."

"Mmmm-hmm. You sound awfully satisfied. Does that mean you've found yourself a decent man?"

Warmth crept up Kelsey's neck, and she tried to keep her voice from betraying her. "What in the world makes you say that?"

Theresa snickered. "You can't fool me."

No use trying to keep anything from Theresa—talk about an investigative reporter. She'd been one of the best. The woman definitely could scent anything out of the ordinary.

Kelsey settled in the office chair and eyed the door of the den. "His name is Kade and he's the most incredible man I've ever met."

"Way to go." Kelsey could picture Theresa's devilish grin. "So, how's he in bed?"

A wave of embarrassment swept over Kelsey. "Theresa."

"I want details. Come on, give it up."

"Well." Kelsey glanced at the door again and lowered her voice. "The man is amazing."

Theresa's throaty laugh was so loud that Kelsey had to pull the phone away from her ear. " 'Bout time you found a real man. You deserve better than that loser you were married to."

Kelsey picked at a loose thread on the hem of her blouse. "I'll only be here a short time more."

"You're having fun, aren't you?"

Smiling, Kelsey said, "He makes me feel beautiful."

"You are beautiful," Theresa said. "I've been telling you that for ages. You should never have listened to a damn word the jerk ever said."

"Yeah, yeah." Even though Theresa couldn't see her, Kelsey brushed off the comment with a wave of her hand. "How's Calinda? Keeping you company since I'm not there?"

A phone rang in the background as Theresa spoke. "We're having lunch tomorrow."

"Tell her hello for me." Kelsey spun around in the chair. "Did you call just to chat?"

"Of course." The sound of crinkling paper came over the line, probably Theresa shifting one of the many piles on her desk. "Well, that and I thought I'd check to see how your feature is coming along."

Kelsey stuck out her tongue as she would have if Theresa were there. "Knew it—you had an ulterior motive."

"That and to see if you'd found a man," Theresa said with a laugh.

"Ha." Kelsey rattled off a summary of what she'd learned so far.

"You rock, girl." Theresa's voice sounded more than pleased. "I've got one more question."

Kelsey raised her eyebrows. "What's that, dare I ask?"

"Even though you hopped in the sack with that hunk named Kade," Theresa said with obvious mock-seriousness in her voice, "you're still coming home on the eighteenth."

Kelsey rolled her eyes. "What do you think I'm going to do? Park myself here permanently just because I met a man who's incredible in bed?"

"I think that's as good a reason as any," Theresa said.

Letting out an exaggerated sigh, Kelsey said, "You're incorrigible."

Theresa gave a wicked laugh. "Before you return home, just come up for air every now and then, okay?"

After Kelsey said good-bye, she punched off the phone, set it aside, and wandered into the kitchen. She was still smiling when she saw Kade's mother. "Need help with anything, Sadie?"

"If you'd like, you can help me with dinner, but I won't be starting it for at least an hour." Sadie grabbed her gardening gloves off the counter. "I'm going to gather a few squash, tomatoes, and onions out of the garden."

Trent tore into the room and almost smacked into Kelsey. "Hey, Kelsey. Wanna come outside and play with me in my hideout?"

Kelsey looked from Trent to Sadie. "Sure, if your grandmother doesn't need me in the garden."

"You two go ahead." Sadie picked up a wicker basket from the table. "It'll give my ears some rest."

Trent took Kelsey by the hand and dragged her through the orchard to where his hideout was hidden in the windbreak. His hand felt small and warm in hers.

Through the trees, Kelsey could see the dirt landing strip where

Kade kept his plane, and she shivered. Beyond that, stubby mesquite bushes seemed to go on endlessly to the foot of the mountains. One thing she'd noticed about this part of Arizona was how she could see for miles and miles in the valley. No trees or hills blocked the view, other than those planted around the ranch house.

When they reached the playhouse, she scooted in after Trent and sat cross-legged on the floor.

"Wanna play chess or checkers?" Trent snatched a game board from a pile beside the toy box. "Dad and Grandpa taught me how to play both of those games and I'm really good."

Kelsey laughed. "You'd probably destroy me at chess, so how about checkers?"

Trent set up the board in record time, and proved to be a great checkers player. She was amazed at the mature strategy he used to beat her.

When it became too dark to play anymore, they packed up the game and went back to the house. As soon as they walked through the door Kelsey saw Kade, his hair wet from his shower. Her pulse picked up and butterflies filled her belly.

"Dad." Trent ran up to Kade and hugged him. "I beat Kelsey three times at checkers and she only won two times and then it got too dark and we had to come back into the house."

Kade ruffled his son's hair. "You'll have to challenge her to chess next."

"I did but she said I'd destroy her, so we played checkers." Trent whirled and headed for the kitchen. "I'm so hungry I could eat ten peanut butter and jelly sandwiches. I'm gonna ask Grandma what's for dinner."

When Trent raced around the corner, Kade grasped Kelsey's

waist and kissed her long and hard. "I've been wanting to do that all day long."

"I've missed you." She settled her head against his chest, her hands resting on his shoulders, allowing herself to feel wanted in his embrace. "How was your day?"

"Great, now that I'm home, and you're in my arms."

Chapter 21

When the house was quiet, and after Kade was sure Trent was asleep, he went to Kelsey again. Rain fell from the eaves outside her bedroom window in soft patters.

She was waiting in one of his western shirts, the snaps undone to where he could see the curve of her breasts. After he locked the door, he turned to her and she slid her arms around his waist.

"About time." She tilted her head up to smile at him. "I've been dying to get my hands on you."

He kissed her hard, letting her feel all the passion built up inside him. When he pulled away, his breathing was already ragged. "I almost said to hell with waiting."

Kelsey led him to the bed. "Yesterday I promised to kiss you all over, but we were a little, ah, rushed last night," she said, remembering how they could hardly wait to tear off each other's clothes once everyone went to bed. This time she wanted it slow, wanted to pleasure him in the ways that he had pleasured her.

Kade helped her pull his T-shirt over his head and his lips quirked into a grin. "You were quite the little wild thing. Not sure I can wait, though."

She ran her fingers through the hair on his chest and smiled at the teasing note in his voice. "Well, you're just going to sit back because it's my turn," she said as she ran her fingernails lightly over his flat nipples.

Kelsey skated her fingers down his hard abs to the waistband of his jeans. She unbuttoned them, her knuckles brushing his cock with every movement. His erection seemed to grow harder and longer, and she smiled when she saw Kade grit his teeth and clench his hands at his sides.

She took her sweet time as she pushed the jeans to the floor and then he stepped out of them. Before she pulled down his boxers, she ran her hand over the length of his erection, tracing the outline with her fingertips, teasing and taunting him.

"I can't get over how big you are," she murmured.

Flames roared in Kade's gut at her every touch, her every word. The approval in her eyes was obvious as she gazed at his naked body and especially his cock, which jutted toward her.

She pulled his boxers slowly down to his feet. "I plan to kiss you everywhere."

"Everywhere, huh?" He kicked off the boxers, then sat on the bed. He settled on his back, his hands behind his head. "I'm all yours, darlin'."

Kelsey traced an outline on the skin around his cock. "That's what I want." A rumble rose in his chest when Kelsey eased onto the bed and straddled him.

"I want all of you," she said in a voice that sounded like a purr.

His shirt looked so damn good on her, and he could see the dark circles of her nipples through the opening.

He groaned, wanting to roll her onto her back and thrust into her hard and fast. To hell with it. He wanted to take her now. "You're gonna torture me, aren't you, woman?"

"Yeah." She trailed her fingers through the hair on his chest to his waist and back, but avoided his cock. "I love your body."

Another rumble rose within his chest and he ached to stroke her. He slid his hands under the shirt and felt nothing but the satin skin of her hips. Blood gathered in his groin and he gritted his teeth.

Honey-gold hair fell across his face as she brushed her mouth against his. She ran the tip of her tongue over his lips, then slipped into his mouth. She tasted of mint from her toothpaste. He clenched her hips in his hands as he drank her honeysuckle scent.

Her lips met his nose in a kiss as light and fleeting as a butterfly. Slowly she moved her lips to each eyelid, softly kissing each one. When she trailed her tongue to his ear, she murmured, "I love how you sound like a rumbling mountain lion when we're together."

He reached under the shirt and captured her breasts, then traced her nipples with his thumbs. With a small gasp she arched her back, pressing her hips closer to his. She pulled at the snaps of the shirt until it was completely undone, and then let it slide from her shoulders.

Rain continued to pound on the rooftop in time with the beating of his heart. In the low lighting of the Victorian lamp, Kade could clearly see every curve, the way Kelsey's breasts rose firm and high and the way her nipples jutted toward him. She was silk and satin, heat and fire, and he wanted her in ways he'd never imagined wanting any woman.

Kelsey lowered her head and scooted farther down his body. She flicked her tongue over his Adam's apple, then kissed the hollow at the base of his throat. With slow strokes of her tongue, she worked her way over his collarbone and down to his pecs.

She bit softly at one of his nipples before trailing her way across his muscular chest to his other nipple. Lower and lower she moved, licking, biting, and kissing until she reached the curling hair between his thighs.

His breath hissed out. "You're about to make me lose my mind, woman."

"Good." She looked up at him, a wicked glint in her eyes. "That's what you do to me."

The corner of his mouth curved into a sensual smile. "Witch."

She gave a soft laugh. "I want to taste you again, like you've tasted me." He groaned as she licked his cock like an ice cream cone, swirling her tongue over the head. Then she slid him into her mouth, raking him softly with her teeth. He grabbed her head between his palms and clenched his hands in her silken hair.

Her head bobbed up and down as she slid her mouth along his erection and Kade guided her. He raised his hips to meet her, enjoying the sight of his cock thrusting in and out of her hot mouth.

When Kade couldn't take any more without climaxing, he grabbed a foil package from the top of the nightstand. "I've got to be inside you, honey."

Kelsey smiled and took the condom from him. She eased it onto his cock, her tongue leading the way, like fire licking at his soul. After the protection covered him, she moved up to straddle his hips. She grasped his cock with one hand and placed it at the entrance to her core. She slid down on him, taking him deep, as deep as it could reach, until it hit her G-spot.

"Yes, there." She moaned as he filled her, as he thrust up to meet her. She wriggled her body and rode his cock, her breasts swaying as she rocked her hips. "I want all of you, Kade. Deeper. Harder."

He grasped her hips, raising her up and down the length of his cock.

Keeping their bodies joined, he rolled over and brought her under him so that she was pinned beneath him. He plunged into her as she started to close her eyes.

"Look at me." His voice was a demanding growl.

He wanted to see her passion, wanted to see her release. The need in her eyes nearly sent him over, but he held back, watching her as he rocked his hips against hers.

She gasped and her eyes rolled to the ceiling and he could see her losing herself to the sensations. Her body jerked hard beneath him and she bit her lip to hold back her cries. She trembled, her body quaking with the force of her orgasm.

Kade pounded into her, harder and harder yet. He loved to watch her, to see her face flushed with desire for him. He braced his hands to either side of her and held off as long as he could, wanting to draw out her orgasm.

His own orgasm wouldn't wait any longer and he had to bite back a shout. Just as a powerful climax stormed his body and his cock released his seed, he felt the condom tear.

Shit.

His muscles clenched as his body pulsated. He held himself still, unable to withdraw from Kelsey's body. It was too late.

He closed his eyes and relaxed between Kelsey's thighs, not wanting to separate from her.

What was done was done. It was too important to be with her.

Kelsey could get pregnant.

The idea of Kelsey carrying his child gave him a heady feeling. But he wasn't sure how she would take it.

"Mmmm," she said, easing her hands into his hair. "This could be addicting."

"I'm already addicted to you." Kade propped his head on one hand and ran his other over her silky skin, drawing circles around her nipples. "What if I told you the condom tore?" he asked, not taking his gaze from her face.

Kelsey's eyes widened and her body tensed beneath him. She dropped her hands to his shoulders. "Did it?"

He studied her expression, her reaction. "I'm almost positive."

"Oh. My. God." She closed her eyes, and he wished he knew what she was thinking.

"If you're pregnant," Kade trailed his finger down the tip of her nose to her lips, "we could get married."

"No—I—no." Her eyes flew open. "We barely know each other. I can't marry you just because I might be pregnant." Her voice trembled as if she was about to cry.

"We know each other pretty well." Kade rained kisses on her face, hoping to calm her fears.

She remained silent, not meeting his eyes.

And then it occurred to him how eerily familiar the situation was, and he cursed himself for his stupidity for suggesting they could get married.

Kelsey's SOB ex had convinced her to marry him in case she became pregnant after he raped her. And that's what Kade thought of it. Rape. She hadn't given herself to that bastard with her consent. The son of a bitch had taken her virginity and used her.

Kade eased out of Kelsey, and sure enough, the condom hadn't made it. He disposed of it and pulled her into his arms. "Don't worry. Everything'll be fine."

"How can you say that?" She covered her face with her hands. "It never occurred to me the condom could tear." Her voice was muffled behind her palms. "What if it happens again?"

"The odds are you won't get pregnant from one time. And the odds are definitely against a condom breaking a second time." He pulled her hands away from her face and kissed her. She stiffened, then gradually melted against him again.

She sighed and slid her hands around his waist. "You shouldn't be here when Trent wakes."

"I'll be back in my own bed when the sun rises." He kissed her forehead. "And when my son rises."

Kelsey smiled faintly and snuggled into the curve of his arm. Rain pattered on the roof as he held her. It felt so good holding her. Like he'd just come home from a long journey to find her there, waiting for him.

Kade didn't fall asleep until her breathing was soft and even and she'd completely relaxed. He finally fell into a light sleep, dreaming of babies with sun-kissed hair and chocolate-brown eyes.

Kelsey woke alone, the bed cold and empty without Kade. As she stretched, she thought about their lovemaking last night and smiled.

Then she remembered. The condom tore. Her smile vanished as she slid her hand to her belly. What if she was pregnant?

The thought heated her, a slow flush of pleasure that eased over her body like warm rain on a summer day.

A baby. Their baby.

Kelsey curled into a ball and hugged herself. Last night Kade had mentioned marriage—probably wanting to do "the honorable thing." But she'd never marry him because he felt he had to.

A knock jarred Kelsey from her thoughts. She pulled the sheet up to her neck. "Yes?"

Kade slipped in the door and locked it behind him. He was dressed in jeans and a blue shirt that intensified the color of his eyes. The bed sank under his weight when he sat beside her and gave her a light kiss. His lips were warm and firm, and she couldn't help remember how it felt having those lips all over her body.

He nuzzled her ear. "Are you planning to sleep all morning?"

Smiling, she slid her arms around his neck. "I missed waking up with you next to me."

"I'd like nothing more than to wake up with you every single day." He smiled and gave a lock of her hair a light tug. "Now get up, before I decide to pull off my clothes and join you."

She lowered her lashes and gave him a coy look. "Best idea you've had yet."

He started to pull back the sheet when they heard Trent's frenetic chatter in the hallway. He sighed and kissed her forehead. "I'll head off Taz. You get dressed."

She threw the pillow at his back. "Slave driver."

After he closed the door, Kelsey put on his robe, grabbed her clothing, and then dodged into the bathroom for a quick shower. For some reason she felt utterly feminine that morning, and instead of dressing in jeans, she wore a silk blouse and a short skirt that flattered her curves.

When she walked into the living room, Kade's low whistle caused a thrill in Kelsey's belly. She thought he was going to kiss her in front of his family, so she dodged away, not ready for that kind of demonstration of affection in front of everyone.

"Your calendar clear?" he asked after breakfast, when they were alone in the kitchen. Sadie and Trent were gardening and Chuck was feeding the calves.

Kelsey slipped her arms around Kade's waist and hugged him. "I'm all yours."

"I have something I want to show you." He slid his knuckles across her cheek. "Then I'd like to take you to dinner afterward."

She smiled and brushed his lips with hers. "Take me away, cowboy."

Late in the afternoon, they left in Kade's truck and drove a few miles, past fields of cotton, corn, and alfalfa, past rangeland dotted with red cattle, to empty acreage that butted up to the low mountain range.

After crossing a cattle guard, they traveled down a dirt road that was little more than a pair of tracks through grass and mesquite bushes. At the end of the road, they parked and climbed out of the vehicle. Kade took her hand and brought her around to the front of the truck.

He watched her expression. "What do you think?"

Kelsey took in the rugged mountain that hugged the edge of the property and the high desert terrain. Mesquite bushes were green from summer rains, the earth dark brown from last night's storm.

A family of quail skittered into the bushes, their nervous calls a gentle sound in the desert quiet. The air smelled clean and fresh. The sky was a brilliant blue, but outlined by clouds building up over the mountaintops.

The desert beauty was astounding. "It's wonderful."

"This is my land." Kade released her hand and went back to his side of the truck. He reached in and pulled out a brown tube from behind the seat, then came back to where Kelsey was waiting. He withdrew a set of blueprints, unrolled and spread them on the hood of his vehicle. "These are the prints for the house I'm having built here."

He put his arm around her as she leaned closer to get a better look. "I bet it'll be incredible." She traced a line with her fingertip.

"A split-level house." Kade pointed to the blueprint with his free hand. "Here, on the bottom floor, is where the kitchen will be, the living room, study, guest room, and family room." He moved the top page aside and showed her the one under it. "This is upstairs. Trent's room will be here, a couple more bedrooms here and here, and this is the master bedroom. The master has a covered balcony that faces the mountain."

"Perfect for enjoying summer rainstorms." She smiled up at him.

He trailed his finger down her nose to her lips, and held her gaze with his intense blue eyes. "Perfect for raising a family."

Chapter 22

Kelsey stopped breathing. The way he looked at her. The way he mentioned raising a family. Like he was asking a question with his eyes. Nervousness rose within her like a flock of panicked birds.

"The builder's scheduled to break ground in August." He took his arm from her shoulders and focused his attention on rolling the blueprints and shoving them into the tube.

She took a deep breath and tried to calm the tremors in her hands. No, he wasn't asking her anything. He was just sharing his plans.

"What does Trent think of it?" she asked.

Kade shrugged. "I haven't told him yet. He'll miss living with his grandparents, but he's old enough now, and they don't need him underfoot all the time. Mom wants to continue watching him when I'm at work. They love that kid."

Kelsey nodded. "He's a wonderful little guy."

"Yeah, he is." Kade returned the tube to the truck. "You ready for dinner?"

"Absolutely. Where are we headed?" she asked as they climbed into the vehicle.

Kade started his truck and the powerful engine roared. "There's a popular place in Douglas that serves excellent Mexican food."

Kelsey smiled. "My favorite. Anytime. Anyplace."

He raised an eyebrow. "With anyone?"

She laughed and buckled her seat belt. "Especially blue-eyed cowboys."

When they arrived at the restaurant, it was almost dark. Most of the parking was taken, but they managed to find a space not too far away. The restaurant was located in one of the older buildings in downtown Douglas. "Downtown" consisted of a single street lined with ancient two-story buildings and a historic hotel.

"Los Dos Hermanos means 'the two brothers' in Spanish," Kade explained as they walked to the door, his large hand engulfing Kelsey's. "The García brothers opened the restaurant twenty years ago, and then sold it to Montaño a few years back."

"Montaño?" That same sense of unease tickled at her belly. She held her purse a little tighter to her chest. "The mayor?"

Kade stopped at the door, his hand resting on the wooden handle. "You've met him?"

She nodded. "I interviewed him a few days ago. I didn't realize he owned this restaurant."

Kade pulled open the door and guided her inside. As they entered the cool interior, smells of Mexican food and sounds of voices, clinking plates, and mariachi music swept over Kelsey.

The interior was dimly lit, but decorated in splashes of vivid colors. Serapes and sombreros graced the walls, and baskets of colorful gourds were arranged artistically around the room. Piñatas in red, green, and white hung from big metal hooks anchored into the ceiling's exposed beams. Wood-bladed fans stirred the air, the pi-ñatas dancing in the breeze they made.

To the right of the hostess station was a larger-than-life plaster statue of a matador, the color chipped and peeling. It stared ahead with sightless eyes where the paint had apparently flaked off.

"The man sure likes matadors." She glanced from the statue to Kade. "Has tons of them in his office, too."

Kade studied the old matador. "He does?"

She shrugged. "I saw his collection when I interviewed him."

A trio approached them from inside the restaurant, and Kelsey saw that it was John Stevens, Dee Carter-Reynolds, and a good-looking man she didn't recognize.

Seeing Stevens reminded Kelsey of the interview she hadn't finished transcribing yesterday, and she wondered if she should mention to Kade the phone conversation she'd inadvertently re-corded.

"Kelsey, Kade. It's wonderful to see you both." Dee smiled and gestured toward the handsome man beside her. "Kelsey, this is my husband, Jake."

"Hope Kade's treating you well." Jake squeezed Kelsey's hand in a firm grip.

"His whole family is great." Kelsey smiled.

John Stevens tipped his hat at Kelsey. "Ma'am."

"Thanks again for the interview for the feature," Kelsey said to Stevens, and he gave a shrug of his massive shoulders.

He turned to Kade. "Haven't seen you around much lately."

Kade nodded. "Busy as hell."

"Saw your folks and your kid at the dance." John chewed on his toothpick. "That kid of yours looks like he'll be quite a hellion when he's older."

"Can't imagine Trent ever being a hellion," Kelsey rushed to say as Kade's expression went flat. "He's just full of energy."

"How's your feature?" Dee asked Kelsey, her green eyes sparkling.

"Terrific." Kelsey smiled. She couldn't help like Dee. "The information you provided has been invaluable."

"You just missed Sal," Dee said to Kade. "John was bullshitting with him at the bar when we got here."

"I'll catch up with him at the station," Kade said.

After Stevens and the Reynoldses said their good-byes, the hostess arrived. She was beautiful, with high cheekbones, dark hair, and skin like flawless beige silk. Her name tag read ISABEL.

As they followed the hostess through an archway to a nearby booth, Kelsey wondered if Kade noticed the woman's beauty and how slender she was. The insecurity that had developed during the five years of Davis's emotional abuse crawled up her throat, threatening to surface. Threatening to suffocate her. Why couldn't she let those old feelings go?

When they reached the booth, Kade slid next to Kelsey on the padded bench. Isabel left them with two menus. "Buenas noches," she said in a lilting Hispanic accent.

Kelsey watched the hostess leave. She was so elegant, the gentle sway of her hips probably as natural to her as breathing. *She's gorgeous,* Kelsey thought, and then realized she'd spoken the words aloud.

"Who?" Kade glanced up from his menu.

"The hostess." She picked up her own menu and chanced a look at him.

He gave her that slow, sexy smile that made her knees tremble. "You're the most beautiful woman here, and I bet you don't even realize it."

Warmth eased through her, but she shook her head. "You're a good liar, cowboy. But I think I'll keep you around."

He took the menu from her and captured her hands in a movement so fast she caught her breath in surprise. "Kelsey, I've never lied to you and I never will. That's one thing you can count on." The intensity of his gaze trapped her, and she didn't know how to reply. He brushed his lips over hers, and then released her hands. "Don't ever forget that."

"Okay," she whispered.

They decided what they wanted, and then Kade ordered in Spanish from Dora, their waitress, who wore a flowing red skirt and a white peasant blouse with colored ribbons woven around the neckline and sleeves.

Dora left, then returned minutes later with their iced teas and a basket of tortilla chips that were so hot they burned Kelsey's fingers when she put a few on her plate. This time she didn't make the mistake of dipping one into salsa before asking for the mild version.

When the platters of food arrived, they were heaped with beef tacos, cheese enchiladas, Mexican rice, refried beans, guacamole, and sour cream. Kade's food vanished, while Kelsey managed to eat less than half the contents of her plate.

"No, I'm stuffed," she said when Kade said she needed to eat more. "If you're still hungry, you finish it."

She grabbed her purse and excused herself to go to the ladies' room. Her sandals clicked on the tile as she walked through the archway, past the matador at the front entrance, and through a door marked BAÑOS.

The hallway was dark, and she blinked to adjust to the dimness. There were three more doors, and she went into the one labeled

SEÑORITAS. After using the facilities, she washed her hands and touched up her pink lipstick.

When she finished she stared at her reflection in the mirror. Her brown eyes were warm and expressive, her honey-blond hair flowing in soft waves to her shoulders. Maybe Kade was right, she was pretty. She'd let Davis's verbal assaults eat at her for far too long, and it was time she let them go.

When she returned to the table, Kade had paid the bill and was ready to head out into the night.

With his arm around Kelsey, Kade opened the front door and led her out of the restaurant. As soon as they stepped into the warm night, she stopped and wound her arms around his waist. Her fingers brushed the gun at his side and she froze.

"Why do you have your gun?" she asked, her voice muffled against his shirt.

"Just my line of work, honey." He nuzzled her hair. "I always carry it and usually a spare."

"Oh." She tilted her head and gave him a worried look. "I keep forgetting what a dangerous job you have."

"Don't worry so much." He rubbed her shoulders and all he could think about was getting her alone. "What do you think about heading up to Bisbee? There's a nice bed-and-breakfast we can stay at. A good friend of mine, Nicole, owns it."

"Yes." She looked up and smiled. "I'd love to."

On the way to Bisbee, Kade used his cell phone to call Nicole to see if she had an available room. Fortunately she did have one left, and said it was all theirs.

He also called Sadie and let her know that he and Kelsey wouldn't be back until the following night. He could hear the smile in his mom's voice when she told him to have a good time.

Sadie was more than delighted with Kade's interest in Kelsey, and if he knew his mom she was probably working hard to finish that wedding ring quilt. More and more, Kade was finding he hoped she would need to.

Chapter 23

"We're lucky Nicole had an available room," Kade said as they walked into the bed-and-breakfast. "Couldn't get into this place normally. We're in historic Old Bisbee. A real tourist magnet. Tomorrow, I can show you the sights—all two of 'em."

He signed the old-fashioned guest register with the plumed pen provided by a man who looked like he came straight from the sixties. He wore a faded tie-dyed T-shirt and frayed jeans, had a flowing beard, and long blond hair held back with a leather strap.

"All we have is the honeymoon suite." The clerk handed them a set of brass keys, rather than a modern key card.

"Where's Nicole?" Kade asked. "I'd like to introduce her to Kelsey."

The clerk shrugged. "She's out with her cousins."

"Maybe we'll catch her in the morning," Kade said as he took Kelsey's hand and led her up the stairs.

A paisley carpet runner covered the polished wooden staircase, and every step creaked. Old-fashioned gas lamps lit the stairwell and hallways, and the walls were painted a deep mulberry. At the top of the staircase, their room was the first to the left.

When he opened the door, Kade thought it was a nice room, as far as rooms went. But Kelsey seemed enchanted.

"Incredible. All the furniture is at least 1800s, and this pitcher and washbasin are fabulous." Kelsey tossed her purse on the bed and then dodged into the bathroom. "This is so wonderful. And the tub is enormous."

She peeked around the corner and gave him a sexy smile that made him hard in a rush. "Big enough for two." She went back into the bathroom. "Oooh, and champagne bubble bath, too." He heard the pop of a cork and then running water.

"Right behind you." After he pulled a foil package out of his wallet, Kade tossed the wallet into the top drawer of the dresser, slid his Glock next to it, then peeled off his clothes. An ice bucket with a chilled bottle of champagne sat on the vanity, along with two crystal glasses and a note that read *Compliments of the staff on your honeymoon.*

Kade smiled at what he was sure was Nicole's mischievousness. He had dated her a couple of times, but they'd decided they enjoyed being friends more than they liked dating each other.

He opened the bottle, poured two glasses full, and managed to carry both along with the bottle to the bathroom. By the time he joined her, Kelsey was chest-deep in bubbles. She was leaning back in the tub with her eyes closed and a look of total relaxation on her face. He set the champagne bottle on the vanity beside the tub before he climbed in.

Water and bubbles rose and splashed over the side as he settled next to Kelsey, his naked body sliding along hers. He pressed one of the chilled glasses against her left nipple and her eyes flew open.

"That's cold," she murmured as the nub grew taut and he brushed the glass across the other nipple, making sure it had equal attention. "You naughty boy."

He winked and handed her the glass. "How about a toast?"

"Mmmm, champagne." She took the crystal stem and held it up. "To what?"

"To us." Kade brushed his lips over hers. "And to first times."

"First times?" Her breath was warm on his mouth.

He took his glass and slid it to the sensitive spot between her breasts. "First time making love in bubbles."

Kelsey gasped and shivered at the feel of the crystal sliding over her skin. "I'll toast to that."

Kade clinked his glass to hers, the sound like the sweet chime of a bell. Feeling utterly content, Kelsey took a single swallow of the golden fluid, the bubbles tickling her nose and her throat.

He drained his glass and set it on the vanity beside the tub. "Drink up, sweetheart," he said with a glint in his blue eyes. "I want to take as much advantage of you as I possibly can."

Kelsey couldn't help a giggle. "All right." She raised her glass. "Here's to being taken advantage of by the hottest cowboy in the West."

The corner of Kade's mouth quirked as he watched her sip from the champagne. "Come on now, down it, honey."

She took the challenge and tilted her head back and swallowed the rest in one long draught. When she handed him the glass, she was amazed at how she already felt woozy from the champagne.

He set her glass on the vanity with his, then grabbed the bottle of champagne. When he brought it toward Kelsey, she raised her eyebrow. "What are you going to do with that?"

"I like dessert with my champagne." Kade tipped the bottle and

Kelsey gasped as he poured some of the sparkling fluid over one of her nipples, washing away the soap bubbles from the hard pink nub and her breast. He lowered his head and licked the champagne with long strokes of his tongue.

With a moan Kelsey arched up to him, reveling in the contrast of the cold champagne and now his hot mouth licking and sucking her nipple. He poured more of the bubbly over her other breast and proceeded to lick it all away, too.

Kelsey could only feel, could only give herself up to the sensations. The champagne affected her senses and she felt so relaxed yet so hot for Kade.

"Hold on, honey," he said as he set the champagne bottle aside again.

Kade settled on his haunches between her thighs. He positioned Kelsey so that her back rested against the side of the tub and she was in his lap, against his cock. She slid down a bit in the bubbles but braced her hands to either side of her. Her head was still above water as he hooked her legs above his shoulders, raising her ass up in his palms so that she was wide and exposed to him.

Somehow he managed to hold on to her and grab the champagne bottle, and then poured more of the fluid over the soft curls on her mound.

Kelsey cried out at the incredible feel of champagne bubbling over her. When he set the bottle aside, he raised her up while lowering his head and began licking and sucking her.

The tipsy feeling from the champagne, combined with the sensation of Kade's warm mouth on her, was almost more than she could bear. Her arms trembled as heat rushed over her, expanding to every pore in her body. It was like fire, fire licking her from her toes to her thighs, her belly, and on up over her breasts and her cheeks to the roots of her hair. She gave a choked cry and almost slipped under the bubbles as her climax hit her.

Kade released her long enough to catch her to him and pull her up out of the water and onto his lap. She faced him so that her legs straddled his. His jaw tensed, his eyes sparking with blue fire as he cupped her head and brought her to him and kissed her. With her dazed senses she could swear he tasted of fire as well as champagne.

"I've got to take you." His expression was fierce as he pulled away. "Now."

Kelsey was burning up as he grabbed a foil packet that he'd apparently left on the vanity. He tore into it and in no time he tossed aside the wrapper and covered his erection.

"I want to fill you up," he said. "I want to take you rough and hard. Is that how you want me to take you?"

"Yes." Kelsey nodded, wanting this wildness, this freeness that she'd never before experienced. "Please, Kade."

She gripped his powerful shoulders as he raised her up and brought her down on his cock, deep and fast. God, how he stretched her wide and filled her so, so deep. She let herself go and rode him hard, raising herself up and down his length. Her breasts bounced and her nipples ached as she gripped his shoulders.

He had a tight hold on her and he moved her even faster. "That's it, sweetheart. Ride me just like that."

Kelsey watched his face, his intent expression, the fire in his blue eyes, and the way he gritted his teeth as if holding back with everything he had. She pressed her hands on his shoulders and rose up and down on his shaft, slamming down on his cock so that it reached her G-spot again and again. Water splashed and blood roared in her head as he took her like he never had before.

All the sensations were too much. Kade's tongue flicking against her nipples, his cock deep within her, water sliding over her body. Kelsey came in a rush, her body so hot that this time she thought she'd burn into cinders. Her channel contracted around his cock, gripping and releasing him in wild flares as her body continued to tremble. Several more thrusts and Kade's growl told her he'd climaxed. He gripped her hips tightly and she collapsed against him, their bodies melding together completely.

Sunlight spilled through sheer curtains at the bay window and onto their bed, caressing Kelsey's face with its gentle warmth. Kade had molded his body to her back, his arm snug around her waist, and she could feel his cock, hard against her. She smiled, loving the feel of him against her, not wanting the moment to end.

His breath tickled her neck, and she shivered. He moved his hand to her shoulder and traced a pattern on her back with his finger.

"What are you doing?" Her voice was husky with sleep.

"Playing connect the dots," he murmured. "You have the cutest freckles across your shoulders."

She rolled over in Kade's arms to face him. "Oh, yeah?"

"Mm-hmm." He ran his finger along her collarbone, then down to the swell of her breasts. "More freckles here. And here. And here."

Kelsey stroked his cheek with her palm, his stubble coarse to her touch yet somehow erotic, inflaming her desire for him. He slid his thigh between her legs and she felt his erection hard against her stomach.

She wiggled so that his thigh was higher, pressing against her mound. "We'll be late for breakfast, cowboy."

"It's a bed-and-breakfast. Bed comes first, then breakfast." He lowered his mouth to hers, his kiss waking every nerve in her body. "Or breakfast in bed, which is what I'm interested in."

With a teasing grin she slid her palm down his muscled chest, his tight abs, and down to his cock. "Can I have seconds?"

His mouth quirked into that drop-dead sexy grin of his. "And thirds."

Kelsey kissed his chest, flicking her tongue and tasting the salt of his skin and breathing in his masculine scent. She didn't care if they ever got out of bed. She couldn't imagine a more perfect moment than this.

A rumble rose up in Kade's chest and he worked hard at regaining his self-control. He intended to make love to Kelsey this morning, not hard and fast like they had last night. The way she was kissing and touching him, he was finding it harder and harder to hold back, but he was a man with a mission.

A mission to make her his . . . forever.

He loved her slow and easy, taking his time to taste and touch every inch of her. And when he finally slid his cock into her silky heat, it was like everything around them slowed to that one point in time.

He rocked his hips against hers, feeling a sense of satisfaction welling up inside him in tune with his building climax. This was his woman, and there was no way on earth she was getting away from him.

Chapter 24

They barely made it to breakfast in time. Kelsey let out a sigh of contentment as the desk clerk escorted them to a garden courtyard with a fountain splashing in the midst, a sheer rock wall hugging one side of the patio.

Sunlight filtered through leaves of oak and mulberry trees, their shadows dappling the white patio furniture. A hodgepodge of geraniums and roses in brilliant hues of reds and pinks crowded the tables. Because she and Kade had arrived during the night, Kelsey hadn't realized that the B & B was nestled against a mountain.

A breeze caressed her skin, as soft as a newborn's breath, the perfume of roses light in the air. Kelsey wore her hair in a French braid but felt grungy wearing the same clothes she had the day before. Kade promised to take her shopping after they ate, but once Kelsey got a look at the casual clothing of the hotel staff, she didn't feel a bit out of place.

Kade introduced Kelsey to his friend Nicole, who owned the B & B.

"You've got a real cutie here," Nicole said to Kade with a good-natured grin as she ushered them to a table for two and set out a menu for each of them.

Heat reddened Kelsey's cheeks, but Kade said, "Don't I know it."

Once they had ordered, the vivacious Nicole stayed and chatted for a few moments, then went to greet more guests.

In no time at all, the waiter brought plates heaped with toast, scrambled eggs, sausages, and Danish pastries, then poured glasses of fresh-squeezed orange juice. Kelsey looked at the mounds of food and her appetite vanished.

"Is that all you're going to eat?" Kade asked as she finished a piece of buttered toast and pushed her plate away.

She gave him a smile. "I'm full."

Kade's vivid blue eyes bored into her. "Sure you're okay?"

"You worry too much." Smiling, she reached down to squeeze his knee under the table. "When I'm with you, everything's all right.

"So, tell me about this town," Kelsey said, changing the subject before the moment got too serious.

Kade shrugged and reached for a cheese Danish. "Bisbee does have a pretty interesting history. Back in the late 1800s until the mid 1970s, it was a major copper mining community. It was called 'Queen of the Copper Camps.'" He took a bite of his Danish.

Kelsey smiled, enjoying watching him. "Bisbee is an unusual name."

He nodded and finished chewing. "It was named for a guy that never even set foot in this town. DeWitt Bisbee, a judge and investor from San Francisco." Kade drank his orange juice, then set the empty glass next to his plate. "When I was a kid, I'd wonder how a guy could never bother to go see a town named after him."

"Hey, he was from San Francisco. Can't beat some of the snobs in

my home city." Her smile faded as she thought of Davis, the epitome
of a successful elitist.

After breakfast, they strolled onto Main, a narrow street that
snaked its way down Tombstone Canyon. Homes and trees clung to
the steep sides of red canyon walls.

"Reminds me a little of home," Kelsey said. "Though in San
Francisco you don't usually see houses that look like they're going
to slide off the side of a mountain at any moment."

"A lot of people compare it to Frisco," Kade replied. "But the
weather here beats the hell out of your hometown. When I was in
San Francisco a couple of weeks ago, I almost froze my ass off, and
it's the middle of the summer."

Kelsey nodded and laughed. "My favorite quote about the city is
one by Mark Twain. I think it goes, 'The coldest winter I ever spent
was a summer in San Francisco.' "

Kade laughed. "Twain also said that in Arizona the temperature
'remains a constant hundred and twenty degrees in the shade, except when it varies and goes higher.' "

She leaned against his arm, feeling relaxed. And wanted. Something she hadn't felt since her parents and sister had died. She didn't
care to think about how limited their time together was. Too soon
the magic would end. Only in fairy tales could anyone be as happy
as Kade made her. It couldn't last. But today she would pretend that
it would last forever.

Hand in hand they walked down the sloping sidewalk, from Castle
Rock to the century-old masonry buildings along Main Street. Art
galleries, potters, and antique stores filled the buildings that Kade
said used to house department stores, jewelers, and banks when he
was a kid.

They found an eclectic clothing store where Kelsey bought a

filmy skirt and blouse that had been hand-dyed a soft rose. The skirt swirled around her ankles, just above her silver sandals, and the peasant blouse rested off her shoulders. And she wasn't wearing a bra or panties, which made her feel both sexy and naughty.

Kade smiled when she came out of the changing room wearing the new outfit. "Beautiful."

Kelsey warmed at his approval, and they paid for the purchase, the clerk giving Kelsey a bag to carry her other clothes in.

They spent the morning exploring shops along Main. At a pottery store, she fell in love with handmade dinnerware in an unusual pattern of soft mauve, sea green, and butter yellow.

"Think this would go good in the kitchen when our new home is built?" Kade asked as she ran her hand over one of the glazed plates.

For a second her heart stopped when he said *our* home.

Stop it. He meant his and Trent's.

Kelsey collected herself and replied, "Absolutely." She pointed to the price tag. "It costs a small fortune, though."

He nuzzled the top of her head. "I like it. Let's get it."

Let's?

Their conversation with the potter was an experience. Half the time Kelsey thought the woman was in another discussion altogether. The potter wore a clay-streaked T-shirt and jeans, her long black hair tied back with yarn away from her thin face, and her hazel eyes seemed vague, as if she was thinking about something else the entire time.

Kade ordered the entire dinnerware collection and arranged to have it shipped to Sadie and Chuck's home.

Kade glanced at his watch when they left the shop. "It's after twelve. Ready for lunch?"

"Sure." Kelsey hadn't regained her appetite but didn't want him worrying.

They chose a small sidewalk café where she was able to look out the picture window as they ate and observe shoppers and tourists. A sense of contentment filled her and she sighed.

"What?" Kade asked as he looked up from his menu.

She smiled and shook her head. "This day is too perfect."

Her stomach flip-flopped as he gave her his slow, sexy grin. "If you could travel anywhere in the world, where would you go?"

"I'm happy right here." She tilted her head. "But I've always wanted to go to Kauai. It seems so wild and beautiful from all the pictures I've seen."

"Not as beautiful as you." He took her hand in his and studied her fingers, then placed his palm against hers. "Your hand is so small."

"Next to yours, maybe. But for a woman they're not small."

"Oh they're small all right. Your ring finger is only the size of my pinkie." He turned her hand over and placed his lips to her palm. "And your skin is much softer than mine."

Kelsey gasped at the sensual contact, the feel of his lips against her skin. Her eyes locked with his and she couldn't move. Couldn't think.

She knew only that she was truly lost.

When they finished eating, Kade and Kelsey walked outside the café and ran into Sal Valenzuela.

The Border Patrol agent slapped Kade on the back. "Buenas tardes, amigo." He turned to Kelsey and held out his hand. "Hello, Kelsey. You look beautiful. Kade's a lucky man."

She blushed and returned Sal's friendly smile. "Get out of here."

Sal slid his hands into his pockets. "Coming to CP tomorrow night, Kade?"

Kade shook his head.

"What's CP?" Kelsey asked.

"Choir practice." Sal's mustache twitched and mischief sparked in his dark eyes.

Kelsey folded her arms and looked from one smirking man to the next. "Uh-huh."

Kade ran his hand over his head. "Well, it's CP if we're referring to our Check Points, like the one where you met Sal."

Sal laughed. "But it's also the term for an after-shift party to relieve stress—usually involving beer."

Kelsey raised her brows.

Kade slipped his arm around Kelsey's shoulders. "The guys refer to it as Choir Practice to give the tongue-in-cheek illusion to our spouses and significant others that we are not drinking, not smoking, and not swearing."

Sal wiggled his eyebrows. "And not talking about past sexual conquests."

Kelsey's eyes widened.

"You can get lost now, Sal. See you at work tomorrow," Kade said with a grin, then steered Kelsey down the sidewalk.

"Past sexual conquests, huh?" she said as they walked.

He hugged her closer. "Sal's full of it, so don't listen to him."

It was midafternoon when he took her to the Bisbee Mining and Historical Museum.

"The brochure says this museum was the first rural Smithsonian affiliate in the country," Kelsey said, just as the guide started speaking.

Their tour guide was a middle-aged woman who spoke with a soft lilt, the movement of her hands like butterflies floating in the wind. She wore a velvet patchwork skirt that reminded Kelsey of a crazy quilt, and heavy silver-and-turquoise jewelry blossomed at her neck and wrists.

"In the early 1900s, Bisbee sported a population of around twenty thousand, and it was the largest city between St. Louis and San Francisco," the guide said. "The town burned down three times, survived outbreaks of typhoid, annual floods, labor strikes, and the closing of most of the mining operations in the mid-1970s.

"Our population hovers right around six thousand now," the guide continued, "and the town has reinvented itself as an artists' colony and retirement community. Travelers come from all over the world to drink in the history and enjoy the culture.

"You may want to visit our Romanesque-style Copper Queen Hotel," she went on, waving her hand toward one window, in the direction of the hotel. "It was once considered one of the grandest in the West. Even Teddy Roosevelt stayed there."

The guide waved her hand again in another direction. "Just around the corner from the Copper Queen is Brewery Gulch, an infamous part of our history, which was home to almost fifty saloons and bordellos around the turn of the century."

Her butterfly hands fluttered in a different direction. "Another of our attractions is the Lavendar Pit Mine. It's three-quarters of a mile wide, nearly a thousand feet deep, and one of the largest surface mines in the world. It was named for a man whose last name was Lavendar, with an *ar* at the end, not *er*. It wasn't named for the color and the lavender hues as many people think."

"Amazing," Kelsey said as they left the museum. "Fifty saloons on one street?"

"Don't forget the bordellos." Kade kissed the top of her head.

"The history of this town has never been so interesting to me before coming here with you."

The sun was low over the mountains and the streetlights flickered on. Kelsey sighed, wishing they could stay forever in this perfect time, this perfect place. Of course, they couldn't. Fairy tales came true only for children, not grown women with too many scars and mileage.

Hand in hand, they strolled toward the bed-and-breakfast, toward Kade's truck, and toward a reality Kelsey wished she could escape for another day. Even another hour. She knew that was impossible, but the dream felt pleasant even as they drew closer to the truck.

She leaned against his shoulder, feeling tired but content. And happy. She'd never felt so happy in all her life, even though she only had a short time longer with Kade. "Thanks for a wonderful day."

He eased his arm around Kelsey and squeezed her to him. "Darlin', every day that I'm with you is wonderful."

Kelsey had nodded off on the drive home, her head resting against the window. She looked pale, and Kade was concerned that she wasn't feeling well. But when they arrived at the ranch and he woke her, she insisted she was all right.

"Dad. You're home!" Trent bounded into Kade's arms when they walked in the door and gave his father a hug and a sticky kiss on his cheek. The boy wriggled free and then wrapped his arms around Kelsey's waist and hugged her. "I'm glad you're back."

To Kade's surprise, she gave Trent a kiss on his dirty cheek, and the boy gave her a big smack in return.

"You're just in time for dinner," Sadie said as they entered the kitchen. "I made a big batch of spaghetti and a tossed salad. And a fresh pitcher of iced tea."

Kade sniffed the air and his stomach grumbled in appreciation.

"Breadsticks with garlic and butter, too." Trent pointed to a basket on the counter covered with a gingham cloth. "Can I have one now?"

"You hold on till we all sit down to dinner." Sadie slapped playfully at Trent's hand as he lifted up the edge of the cloth. "Go on and wash up."

"All right, Grandma," he grumbled, and ran off toward the bathroom.

"I bet the spaghetti is wonderful," Kelsey told Sadie. "But I'm not hungry and I'm tired. I think I'll lie down."

Sadie patted Kelsey's hand. "You go rest up, and if you get hungry there'll be plenty of leftovers in the fridge."

Kade walked Kelsey down the hall and into her room. "You okay?"

She nodded and smiled. "Just tired."

He drew her close and she sighed, leaning against him and sliding her arms around his waist. For several minutes they stood in each other's embrace, until he thought she'd fallen asleep standing up. With more than a little reluctance, he parted from her and she opened her eyes. Her lids drooped as if she could hardly keep them open.

"I think I plumb wore you out." He ran his finger down her nose to the tip.

"Feel free to wear me out anytime," she murmured.

He kissed her, then closed the door behind him when he left her room.

Chapter 25

Kelsey had only intended to take a nap when they returned home from Bisbee, but she didn't wake until just before dawn the next morning. Apparently, Kade had slipped into bed without disturbing her and held her all night.

Her head was tucked under his chin and she was facing him, his arms tightly around her. He smelled so wonderful, felt so great in her arms . . . and he was good and naked, his early-morning erection pressing against her belly. She wished she were as bare as he was, but she was still wearing the skirt and peasant blouse they'd bought yesterday, and no panties.

Kelsey sighed. A girl could get used to this.

Fascinated by the hair curling on his chest, the powerful muscles of his arms, the scent of him, the taste of him—she slid her hands across his skin and kissed his warm flesh until he stirred and woke.

Kade gave her a sleepy grin. "Now this is one hell of a way to wake up."

"Mmmm-hmmm." Kelsey's tongue circled his nipple and the

tiny nub tightened. She smiled and moved her mouth to his other nipple and she teased it just as slowly and deliberately.

He rolled her onto her back in a swift movement that took her breath away. He braced himself above her, his hands to either side of her breasts. For a moment she just stared up at him, his sleep-tousled hair and morning stubble making him even sexier.

"You're so beautiful." His face was intent as his gaze raked over her. "Waking up with you is the best thing I can imagine."

Before Kelsey could respond, he pulled down the rumpled peasant blouse and dipped his head to lick first one nipple and then the other. She gave a little moan as she reached for his cock, needing to feel its rigid warmth in her hand. In her.

Still bracing himself on one arm, Kade reached for her skirt and she released his cock to move her hands to his shoulders. He pulled up her skirt around her waist and his eyebrows rose when he saw she wasn't wearing any panties. "If I'd known you were naked beneath your skirt, I'd have taken advantage of you yesterday."

Kelsey gave a soft laugh. "Well, take advantage of me now, cowboy."

In moments he had sheathed his cock with a condom from the nightstand.

"Spread your legs wider for me, honey." Kade held his cock, ready to penetrate her, as she opened her legs as wide as possible.

In a single thrust he buried himself deep within her. Kelsey gasped and slipped her hands beneath his arms to hold on to his back. As he moved in and out of her, she dug her nails into his flesh and it seemed to spur him on. Harder. Faster.

Her senses whirled and everything blurred around her. Warmth pooled in her abdomen and grew, larger and larger until her orgasm exploded within her. Kade continued pumping in and out of her and then he came with a low rumble that sent aftershocks through her.

With a sigh of contentment, he rolled onto his side, still locked with Kelsey, her leg hooked over his thigh.

Kelsey snuggled against him, feeling as if she had the world in her hands.

After Kade got up to get ready for work, Kelsey dressed and joined him and his family at breakfast. As she was picking at her slice of French toast, Kelsey's thoughts turned toward her feature, and to her interview with John Stevens.

Should she mention the recording to Kade? Or was it nothing?

Maybe he'd think she was overreacting, but her gut told her differently. She trusted her instincts—at least when it came to reporting.

When he carried his empty plate to the kitchen, she followed.

She slipped her own plate into the dishwasher beside his. "Have a second?"

Smiling, he tweaked a strand of her hair. "Always for you, darlin'."

"I interviewed John Stevens at his ranch a couple of days ago."

Kade wrapped the strand of her hair around his finger. "I'll bet Bull had something to say. He lost a big chunk of cash due to illegal immigrants."

Kelsey explained how she'd left the room when Stevens took a call, but she'd left her phone on record, and how she'd transcribed her notes afterward. "His conversation was in Spanish, but I understood a name. At least I think it was a name."

As Kade raised one eyebrow, she continued, "I'm sure he was talking to someone named Gordo."

She winced as his finger tugged a bit too hard on her hair.

"Sorry," he murmured, and caressed her scalp. But he looked distracted, like wheels were churning in his mind.

He moved his hand from her hair and settled it on her shoulder. "Where's the recording?"

Kelsey led him to the office and passed him the phone. While he listened to the one-sided conversation, she chewed the inside of her cheek, wishing she'd taken Spanish instead of French in high school.

"Mind if I borrow your phone to get the recording?" he asked when the recording stopped.

Kelsey hated to be without her phone, but she nodded. "Sure." By the look in his eyes, she didn't think it would have mattered if she'd refused. He was taking it regardless, so it had to be important. Very important.

"I'll get it back to you this afternoon." He slid the phone into his shirt pocket. "See anything or anyone out of the ordinary while you were there?"

"No." Kelsey started to shake her head, then paused. "Wait— when I was leaving, this guy was driving a van loaded with people up to the ranch and he almost ran me off the road."

Kade narrowed his gaze. "What did he look like?"

"Early forties, Hispanic, handlebar mustache. Big guy." The man's image came easily to her. "I remember because he swerved so close and I was angry that he almost hit me."

"Fits," Kade muttered. "On the tape Bull was talking to someone on a cell phone who was on his way to the ranch." He gave Kelsey a quick kiss and headed out the door. "Don't mention this to anyone, all right?"

"Okay."

But he was already gone.

* * *

When Kade made it to the Border Patrol station, he found his ASAC, Miguel Martinez, at the water cooler. "Hey, Mikey. Got a minute?"

Miguel waved Kade to his office, then shut the door behind them. The man was below average in height and had a slim build, but he had a presence that filled a room and commanded respect. "What's on your mind?"

Kade paced around the cramped office. "As you know, a couple of names keep popping up. One is Gordo, the other El Torero. From the information I've gathered, Gordo is head *coyote,* but Torero runs the show."

Miguel scrubbed a hand over the stubble on his chin. "Just got in some surveillance today. We think we've made Gordo—a guy named José Hernandez."

Miguel gave Kade the description and Kade whistled through his teeth. "Good news and matches what I came across."

"As far as Torero . . ." Miguel shrugged. "Nothing solid."

"I think I have a line on Torero." Kade dragged his hand over his face and through his hair. "I need surveillance set up on John Stevens."

"The cattle baron and former sheriff?" Miguel dropped into his chair and looked at Kade as if he'd lost a cog. "He's funding the campaign for Eduardo Montaño, the man most likely to win the election for U.S. Congress. And Montaño's running heavily on his immigrant platform."

"I've got proof." Kade sat down heavily in the seat across from Miguel.

Miguel frowned.

Kade ran over the recorded conversation. "The recording only has his side of the conversation, but it was enough to convince me that Gordo was on his way across Sweetwater. And when Kelsey Nichols was leaving the property, she saw a man who fits the description you just gave me."

With a sigh, Miguel said, "Doesn't make sense. Stevens hates smugglers for what they've done to his herd."

"He's been pretty bitter about it. Maybe he's found a way to recoup some of that cash."

Miguel shook his head. "What else have you got?"

Kade rattled off the rest of the information he'd gathered, including the scrap of paper with *Toro* written across it and the toothpick among the garbage he'd noticed when he found the dead informant. "Stevens's nickname is Bull, so Toro could refer to him. And the man's always chewing on a toothpick." He paused. "I've got a gut feeling about this, Mikey."

Miguel stared at the ceiling before returning his gaze to Kade. "I trust your instincts—they've never failed you before. But we'll need to keep this quiet. If it gets out that the mayor's being backed by a smuggler, all hell will break loose."

Miguel pushed a frog paperweight along the edge of his desk. "Montaño's probably the most popular man in this town. Hell, one of the most popular men in the whole damn state. Loads of connections. Running for Congress."

"Yeah, I know." Kade stood and hooked his thumb in his belt loop. "But if Stevens is our man, we need to put him away."

Nodding, Miguel shoved the paperweight to the back of his desk. "No shit."

Kade turned and walked out of the office, and almost ran into Sal.

"What's up, compadre?" Sal asked, falling into step beside Kade. "You don't look like a guy who just spent the weekend with one gorgeous woman."

Pushing open the front door of the station, Kade stepped into the hot July sunshine. "I think I've made El Torero."

"Yeah?" Sal nudged the brim of his hat up and scratched his head. "Who?"

"John Stevens."

Sal narrowed his gaze. "You gotta be kidding."

"Nope."

"Think we need to talk." Sal checked his watch. "You up for some dinner?"

Kade shook his head. "Thanks, but I've got something I need to take care of."

Chapter 26

After he visited a jeweler in Douglas, Kade headed home, smiling as he thought about Kelsey. He'd found the perfect ring to give her, and had left it at the jeweler's to be sized. He'd compared her ring finger to his pinkie, so he had a pretty good idea of the right size. Now he just had to find the perfect time to propose.

Kelsey was still away at an interview when he arrived at the ranch. Kade took a quick shower, then went in search of Trent and found his son in the windbreak. The boy was digging in the rich soil beside the playhouse.

"Dad." Trent jumped up and hugged Kade with his dirt-covered arms before going back to his Tonka trucks and a giant mound of earth. "I'm building a city around a mountain made of gold, and digging a swimming pool with the backhoe behind this stick house that's really made of gold, too. Wanna help?"

Kade crouched beside his son. "What do you want me to do?"

Trent pushed a bright yellow truck over to his dad. "You run the dump truck and I'll fill it with dirt that I dig up with the backhoe."

Memories of his own childhood came back in waves as he spent time with his son. When he was a kid, he would dig in the dirt, build forts in the mesquite bushes, or ride his bike. His biological father had never taken the time to play with him, and by the time Kade was Trent's age, his dad was long gone.

The day Kade had learned Lorraine was pregnant, he vowed he would be there for his child. As often as possible, he would attend Trent's Little League games, school recitals, 4-H competitions, and birthdays. He would take him to the county fair, play catch, and play in the dirt. He'd hoped to have more children—brothers and sisters for Trent—but he'd never found a woman he wanted to spend the rest of his life with.

Until Kelsey.

"Say, Taz. What do you think of Kelsey?" Kade asked as he guided the truck to the mountain of dirt and dumped its load.

"She's cool and lots of fun." Trent used the little backhoe to dig more earth and lifted it into the back of the dump truck when Kade pushed it into place. "When you're not here, sometimes she plays games with me and I show her all kinds of stuff." He looked up at Kade and squinted. "Can we keep her?"

Kade chuckled. "That's a great idea. But I think that'll be up to Kelsey."

Trent jumped up and brushed his dirty hands on his even dirtier jeans. "Let's ask her."

"Now hold on." Kade grabbed the boy's arms. "Don't say anything to Kelsey, okay?"

"Why not?" Trent frowned. "I want her to stay here, with us."

Kade paused, trying to think of a way to explain it to his son. "She lives where Aunt Dara does, which is far away."

Trent scrunched his eyebrows as he thought about that. "In Sanfrisco?"

"Yes, San Francisco. That's Kelsey's home," Kade said, "and she may want to go back there when she's finished with her job here."

Trent screwed up his face in thought. "We could ask her to stay with us."

"What if she misses where she lives?" Kade pushed the dump truck toward a mound Trent had piled up. "She might not like living here, so far from her home."

"Oh." Trent eased off his dad's lap and stood. "What should we do?"

"Leave that up to me." Kade patted Trent's shoulder. "Kelsey's supposed to be here another week, so for now, promise that you won't say anything about keeping her, yet. Okay?"

His son had a dejected look. "If she leaves I'm gonna really, really, really miss her."

Kade stood and hugged his son. "Yeah. Same here."

With the aid of Marnie Perez as interpreter, Kelsey spent the afternoon interviewing two illegal migrant farmworkers. The men explained how poor their families in Mexico were and how the money they earned in the United States helped to keep their relatives from starvation.

Kelsey learned from their point of view how badly the smugglers treated them, yet the men were willing to accept it as a means to sneak into the United States and better their families' lives.

When she finished the interview, Kelsey thanked the men and Marnie and headed back to the ranch in the waning light. The sun was setting low behind the mountains, crimson and tangerine streaking across the western sky. Her customary energy had vanished and she felt so tired that all she wanted to do was crawl into bed and sleep. Hugging Kade.

While she drove, gentle warmth filled her as she recalled waking up in Kade's arms that morning. She couldn't get enough of the man.

That was going to make it all the harder when it was time to go back to San Francisco.

Kelsey sighed and tried not to think about leaving him, but it was impossible. Less than a week now. Just days until her flight was scheduled to depart from Tucson. Originally, she'd considered changing her flight to stay and interview for a position with the Tucson magazine. But now she wasn't sure she could be that close to Kade and not be with him.

One day at a time. She would cherish whatever time she had with him and then get on with her life, no matter how lonely that life would be without him. It took some effort, but she reminded herself again that she wasn't ready for a permanent relationship. Her heart and soul had been so badly bruised by her ex-husband and her hardhearted father that she couldn't help think that Kade was too good to be true.

It was dark when she drove up to the ranch. Her pulse picked up when she saw Kade's truck parked in the driveway. A feeling twisted through her belly, as if she were home. And that these people were family. The thought surprised her. No place had truly felt like home since her family was taken from her.

Thinking that way was only going to make things harder when she left.

Roxie bounded up and greeted Kelsey when she climbed out of the SUV, and she scratched the dog behind her ears. Roxie proceeded to slobber all over Kelsey's shoes and jeans as she returned the greeting. There was just enough light from the porch that she could make her way to the house.

Kelsey caught her breath as a shadowy figure stepped out from behind the vehicle. When she realized it was Kade, her muscles went limp with relief.

"Kade," she murmured, hand to her pounding heart.

"I missed you," he said as he drew her close. His arms felt so good around her, she never wanted to leave his embrace.

"You scared me," she said against his chest, her heart still pounding. She poked him in the ribs with one finger. "Don't do that."

Chuckling against her hair, he said, "I came outside so that I'd be able to kiss you without an audience."

"I'm glad you did." Kelsey reached up and brushed her lips over Kade's. "Just don't sneak up on me again. Got that, cowboy?"

"Uh-huh." He grinned against her mouth. "What do you say to a little walk in the dark?"

She cocked an eyebrow. "Oh, and what do you have in mind, mister?"

With a roguish grin, Kade took her hand. "I want to take advantage of you."

A low thrill skipped within her belly as he led her into the dark windbreak and past Trent's playhouse.

Excitement flowed in her veins at just the thought of what Kade had in mind. Before she realized it, they were approaching his plane. She tried to stop, fear overwhelming her and replacing her arousal. "I can't." She shook her head. "Not in there."

Kade gently pulled her toward the plane. "We're not going to fly anywhere, honey. I just want someplace where I can have you all to myself."

Taking a deep breath, Kelsey forced herself to go forward, telling herself it was all right since they were going to remain on the ground. Just the warmth of Kade's big hand covering hers helped to calm the fear churning in her belly.

When they got to the plane, Kelsey's heart was pounding like mad, but she let Kade help her into the back and she settled herself on the edge of the seat as if she might bolt at any moment. It was a little four-seater, not a six like—

No. Don't think about it, Kelsey.

When Kade climbed in he shut the door behind him. He sat in one of the back seats and pulled Kelsey onto his lap. For a long time he held her, just kissing her hair and hugging her close. She smelled that peculiar odor that small planes had along with dust, as well as night air and Kade's comforting scent.

Gradually the fear eased and Kelsey relaxed. Instead she focused on Kade. He felt solid and real next to her and he smelled so good, like testosterone and his own elemental scent. The fact that they were in a small plane didn't seem to matter any longer as she focused on the man who held her so tightly to his chest. She felt safe and secure and she knew that he would never let anything happen to her.

Kade felt Kelsey's body relax, and he squeezed her tighter to him.

She turned her face to his and lightly kissed his mouth. "I'm all right now," she murmured as her lips brushed his cheek. "And I want you. Right here in the plane. I want you."

He trailed his thumb across her lower lip and smiled. "Let's get you out of those jeans."

After she kicked off her shoes, Kelsey sat on the floor and Kade helped her shimmy out of her jeans and panties. She tugged off her blouse and tossed her bra aside. In the dim light from the half-moon he could see her voluptuous shape and he couldn't wait to get inside her.

Kade unzipped his jeans, releasing his erection. He was still sitting on his seat and Kelsey rose up, sliding between his thighs and grasping his cock in her small hand. She lowered her head and gave a little sigh as she slipped her lips over the head of his cock. She clenched one hand in his jeans and used the other to stroke his erection while she applied light suction with her mouth.

A groan rose up from Kade as he slid his hands into her silky hair. "You go down on me so good."

Kelsey merely replied with, "Mmmmm."

Kade groaned again and clenched his hands tighter in her hair. "Your mouth feels so hot and wet on my cock. And what you do with that tongue of yours . . . damn."

He was so close to coming that he almost lost control. He held her head still as he pulled a condom out of his pocket. In the dim light pouring into the plane, he could see her satisfied smile.

He sheathed his cock and grabbed her around the waist, pulling her up and over his erection. She sank down on him, his cock sliding into her.

"You feel incredible." Kelsey couldn't believe how she just couldn't get enough of this man. She braced her hands on his shoulders as he gripped her hips and moved her up and down. "I love it when you're wearing all your clothes—your jeans and cowboy hat—and I'm naked and you're—you're . . ."

"Fucking you?" Kade said with a teasing sound to his voice.

Heat rose to her cheeks and she nodded. "Yeah."

"What about making love to you?" he murmured, and more heat flushed over her.

She didn't know how to respond, so she just rode him harder.

Her breasts bounced and Kade licked her nipples and gripped her ass, guiding her along even faster.

Everything around Kelsey blurred until she felt as though she were flying—that the airplane was gliding and she was riding it out in a storm. But she wasn't afraid, she was safe with Kade.

Higher and higher she soared until she came with a shuddering cry that echoed in the small plane. Kade continued to raise her up and down on his cock and she held on to his shoulders for support, too boneless to guide her own moments.

Several more thrusts and Kade groaned and climaxed, his cock throbbing in her channel. He held her still for a few moments, riding out his orgasm until he was spent.

With a soul-deep sigh Kelsey relaxed, her naked breasts pressed against his chest, his cock still deep within her. "Ready for another round?" she murmured, and Kade laughed.

"Anytime, sweetheart." He kissed the top of her head. "Anyplace."

Chapter 27

The next day, after her interview with Kev Grand, Kelsey drove back to the JL Star. She felt exhausted, although Kev certainly wasn't the reason she was feeling so poorly. The rancher was sexy in a hard and dangerous kind of way. No doubt it would take a hell of a woman to tame that man.

Chickens scattered in front of the SUV as Kelsey pulled up to the ranch, and thoughts of Kade washed over her. How did she manage to fall so completely for his charm? To fall so completely . . .

No. She wasn't even going there. She pushed the thought to the back of her mind as she noticed Chuck's truck was gone and that Kade wasn't home yet.

Late-afternoon shadows stretched across the driveway, and when Kelsey checked the dashboard clock, she saw it was after three. Kade could be home soon, or might come in as late as seven at night, depending on how his day went. She parked, grabbed her belongings, and headed for the front door.

Roxie gave Kelsey her usual greeting, slobbering all over

Kelsey's pants. She'd come to love the rottweiler as much as every person in the family.

The house was locked, and she opened the door with the key the Turners had loaned her. A note on the fridge said that Sadie, Chuck, and Trent were at the Perez home for a surprise birthday party for Jamie and would be gone through dinner, and that Kelsey was invited.

After tossing her purse and laptop onto her bed, Kelsey changed into shorts and a T-shirt, and wandered into the kitchen, barefoot. The house was eerily quiet, save for the tick of the kitchen clock. She missed Trent's chatter, Chuck's dry wit, and Sadie's musical laughter.

And Kade. His presence that filled the room. His touch. His teasing grin.

Kelsey couldn't hold back a smile, thinking about the time they'd spent together last night in his plane. She now had at least one positive thing to think about when it came to small planes.

A sound like a car door slamming came from outside, interrupting her thoughts.

Kade. Kelsey hurried to the bathroom, ran a brush through her hair, and touched up her lipstick. She smelled Kade's apple shampoo from the shower, the scent reminding her of him, the feel of his hair under her fingers. She ached to touch him.

The front door opened and shut, the sound reverberating through the house. She couldn't help smile as she walked back to the living room.

He was kicking off his boots and when he saw her he gave her a weary smile. "Damn but it's good to see you when I get home."

Kelsey's heart skipped a beat. "I'll bet. You just want some good hard sex."

Kade's lips quirked into a grin. "I'd have to say that's an added bonus."

She laughed and went to him, but he held her off with an upraised hand. "Gotta take my shower, sweetheart. Been one of those days."

Kelsey gave him a teasing smile. "How about I lather you up real good, cowboy?"

Kade raised an eyebrow. "I could live with that."

After he threw his clothes into the washing machine and he grabbed a condom, they slipped into the bathroom. Kelsey stripped out of her clothes while Kade climbed in under the spray. She followed him and took the bar of soap he was holding.

She began lathering his whole body, starting with his muscled chest and shoulders and working her way on down. The soap had a clean outdoorsy scent that she identified with Kade. Water streamed over her as she soaped his thighs and ignored his erection.

"Turn around," she ordered him after she soaped him all the way down to his feet. He looked a little disappointed that she'd ignored his package, but he faced the spray so that his back was to her.

Still on her knees, Kelsey was now staring at his tight butt cheeks. She sighed. Yeah, an ass you could just bite.

A bit of mischievousness rose up inside her and she leaned forward so that her lips were against his wet skin. And then she bit.

"Hey." Kade turned his upper torso and pulled lightly on her hair so that she was looking up at him. He had an eyebrow cocked and a spark in his eyes. "Who said you could bite my ass?"

She grinned. "I did. Now turn around and let me finish the job."

"Ass-biting wench," Kade grumbled in a teasing tone.

"Now brace your hands on the wall while I take care of you, mister."

He obliged and she proceeded to soap the back of his body, up his legs to that fine ass that she was tempted to bite again. She continued on up to the broad expanse of his back and his shoulders. Soap and water streamed down his back and shoulders and water pelted her face and hair.

"Face me," she demanded, doing her best to sound forceful.

Kade turned with his hands up and a stern look, as if he were being arrested.

Kelsey laughed and started soaping the fine curls around his cock and he lowered his hands, closed his eyes, and tipped his head back in the spray. She sighed at the sight of her wonderful man, his power, his masculine beauty.

Her man.

Kelsey shook away the thought and washed his cock, then let the water rinse away the soap. She set the bar aside in the soap dish. "I want you to stroke yourself now. I want to see how you pleasure yourself."

"You mean jack off?" he said, opening his eyes and raising his eyebrows.

She narrowed her gaze. "Do it, cowboy."

An amused expression crossed his face and he gripped his cock in his big hand. Kelsey watched in fascination as he worked his erection from his balls to the head, his thumb rubbing over the tiny hole at the top before sliding back down his length. He studied her while he did it, and she wondered where her sudden confidence had come from, the way she was ordering him to do things she'd fantasized about.

She felt so comfortable with him now, like she knew him better than anyone she'd ever known.

Could he feel the same way?

She lowered her head to lick the top of his cock. Kade released his erection and moved his hands into her wet hair as she slid her mouth over him, taking him deep.

She loved the way he felt in her mouth, the way he felt in her hand as she licked and sucked his cock. She loved the way he gripped his hands in her hair and guided her up and down.

Just as she thought he was about to come, he commanded her, "Stop." When she looked up at him, he said, "It's my turn now."

Kelsey let his wet cock slide out of her mouth. "Oh?"

"Yeah." He took her by her shoulders and raised her, then grabbed the condom he'd left open on the edge of the tub and rolled it over his cock.

"Put your arms around my neck," he said as he brought her flush against him. Her folds ached and excitement skittered throughout her when Kade gripped her ass and said, "Hold on."

She squealed in surprise as he lifted her up and drove his cock inside her. Kelsey clenched her legs around his hips and hung on tight as he raised her up and down, thrusting in and out of her. Water from the shower poured over her head and face, and it was so like her fantasy that it made her all the more excited.

The power in his arms, his muscles flexing, and the concentration in his expression undid her. She came so fast it made her head spin.

Kade climaxed moments later and hugged her tightly to him as his cock continued to throb within her.

Chapter 28

Early the next day, when Kade reached the station, Miguel waylaid him in the hallway. "Owen."

Kade ran a hand over his stubbled cheeks. "What's up, Mikey?"

"I've got something you'll want to hear," Miguel said as he motioned to his office. Kade followed his ASAC.

After Miguel shut his office door behind them, he motioned to a chair and Kade seated himself. Miguel eased back in his own chair and said, "Thought you might be interested in hearing about the surveillance we set up on Stevens."

"Yeah?" Kade leaned forward.

"I put a couple of undercover agents on Stevens's tail last night." Miguel spun the frog paperweight on his desk. "He had an interesting visitor drop by his ranch, around midnight."

"Who?"

"José Hernandez." Miguel smiled. "Gordo."

Satisfaction gripped Kade and he hit his thigh with his fist. "I knew it."

Miguel held up his hand. "Of course that's not enough, but it's a start. We've got a helluva lot of work to do."

"Damn straight," Kade said, feeling a thread of satisfaction. "We'll nail that SOB."

He got to his feet and took his leave from Miguel. *Gordo.* Yes, that bastard was the key to everything. Daryl Jones, who manned the front desk, waylaid him in the reception area.

"Got a call for you, Kade."

Kade took the phone. "Owen here."

"This is Juarez." The informant's voice shook. "Meet me at Mario's at one."

"Sí, amigo," Kade replied and hung up.

Kelsey would be at the station to interview Miguel at ten. Kade was tempted to hang around, but he had work to do. He spent the morning tracking down surveillance info on Gordo and Stevens, and worked over a couple of other leads.

At one o'clock sharp Kade arrived at Mario's Cantina. As soon as he slipped into his customary booth, Juarez appeared and slid onto the seat across from him. The informant smelled of sweat and like he hadn't taken a bath in days. Something in the man's eyes made Kade's gut tighten.

Glancing around the bar, Juarez licked his lips. "Your life is in danger, amigo."

Kade's muscles tensed and he leaned forward. "What do you mean?"

Juarez's eyes shifted from Kade to the bar and back. "El Torero wants you dead. He suspects you know more than you should. He will do anything—take anything from you he can. Kill you. Kill your whole family. Back off, amigo. Hear me. Back off."

A chill crept over Kade's skin. Before he could ask Juarez for more information, the informant slid out of the booth and vanished out the front door.

When it was time for her to leave for her interview, Kelsey dressed in navy slacks, low heels, and a pink silk blouse, her press badge attached to her belt loop. She smiled and waved good-bye to Sadie and Trent, who were working in the garden, and headed for Douglas.

Due to the increase in the number of Border Patrol agents, the agency had recently built an enormous facility on the outskirts of the Douglas city limits. Kade had explained that the old station, near the county fairgrounds, was originally designed for a staff of only fifty agents.

The new station was sleek, modern, and efficient in appearance, and smelled of paint and new carpet. A man with red hair, freckles, and a million-dollar grin manned the front desk. His ID badge read DARYL JONES. He reminded Kelsey of a kid she'd had a crush on in the third grade, and she smiled.

"Hello, Mr. Jones." Kelsey's voice was smooth and professional as she switched into journalist mode. "My name is Kale C. Nichols, and I'm a reporter with *City by the Bay* magazine. I have an appointment with Miguel Martinez."

"Hold a sec." Daryl dialed the phone. A moment later he said, "He'll be right up."

As Kelsey waited for Miguel Martinez, her gaze wandered around the busy station. A picture of the president of the United States graced one wall, next to the American flag. Dirt and scuffs marred the polished linoleum floor, attesting to the volume of human traffic in the building.

Male and female agents walked in and out of the reception area, some clothed in spruce green "rough duty" uniforms, and others wearing jumpsuits of the same color. She noticed agents in shirts and jeans, not unlike Kade. At the thought of him, a nervous tingle spread in her midsection, and she wondered if he was somewhere nearby.

A man in full uniform approached Kelsey. He was her height, clean-shaven, and smelled faintly of aftershave. He had dark brown hair, green eyes, and a deep cleft in his chin. "I'm Miguel Martinez. You must be Ms. Nichols."

"Agent Martinez." She extended her hand and smiled. He had a strong grip, and his pleasant, comfortable manner set her at ease.

"Let's sit in my office," he said as he turned to walk down the hall. Kelsey followed him through the station, noticing the constant flow of traffic, the hum of conversation.

He closed the door and motioned to a chair, then sat down, his manner relaxed and confident. As she took her seat, she pulled out her laptop and turned it on, wishing she had her cell phone to record.

As always when she interviewed, the outside world slipped away.

After the interview, Martinez had Kelsey sign a waiver form, then took her in one of the Border Patrol SUVs and drove several miles along the border. She was amazed at the sheer number of vehicles positioned along its length.

Once they completed the drive, Martinez gave her a tour of the station, including the areas where the UDAs were detained and processed. When he took her to the control room, he had the agents shut down visuals on cameras where sensors were located. He explained it was standard procedure as no unauthorized individuals were allowed to see the locations of sensors on the remote desert locations.

When Kelsey concluded the interview with Martinez, he shook

her hand and she thanked him, then headed out to the parking lot.

A dull pain throbbed behind Kelsey's eyes when she slid into Sadie's SUV. Her stomach churned and she felt as if she would throw up. Kelsey leaned back in the seat and closed her eyes. She'd been so nauseated since . . .

Her eyes flew open and a cold chill swept over her. No. It couldn't be.

Instead of heading back to the ranch, Kelsey drove into Douglas, straight to a grocery store.

By the time Kade finished following up on a few leads and made it back to the office, he was burned out and ready to head home. Not to mention concerned by Juarez's statement about danger to his family and himself.

"Hey, Owen. Take a call before you book on out of here." Daryl Jones held up the phone as Kade started to leave the station.

Kade took the receiver and dragged a hand over his hair. "Owen here."

"We know where you live," a deep male voice said.

An iron fist clamped Kade's gut. "Who is this?" He barely had the presence of mind to motion to Daryl to have the call traced.

"We know you live with your mother and stepfather. And you have a handsome young son. He is nine, no?"

Rage filled Kade, a wave so powerful that his entire body shook. "Listen, you son of a bitch, you so much as come near my family and you're a dead man."

"Tch—tch. Such anger. Ah, and we must not forget the lovely señorita staying with you."

Kade clenched his fist. "What the hell do you want?"

"Turn in your resignation by tomorrow morning and walk away, Agent Owen."

The line went dead.

"Oh, my God," Kelsey whispered while she stared at the blue plus sign on the test stick. "I'm pregnant."

Kelsey's head spun and for a moment darkness closed in on her. The stick clattered into the bathroom sink as she grabbed the rim to steady herself. When the feeling passed, she made sure the toilet lid was down and collapsed onto it.

If Theresa hadn't gone through a pregnancy while Kelsey worked at the magazine, she would have had no idea that it was possible to get morning sickness so fast. But Theresa had been ill almost from the moment she'd conceived. And thanks to modern-day tests, it was possible to detect pregnancies within days.

So many feelings surged through Kelsey. Intense joy that she'd never known before filled her, and she almost laughed. She felt giddy and light-headed.

She was going to be a mother. A mother.

It didn't seem real. A life was growing inside her. She did the math, and realized she would be giving birth in April.

Giving birth. A baby.

She was having Kade's baby.

The thought filled Kelsey with sheer pleasure. Kade's baby. Her baby. Their baby.

Did Kade love her . . . like she loved him?

And there it was. How she'd struggled to deny it.

I love Kade.

What a realization to come to, sitting on the toilet seat in the bathroom, just having found out she was pregnant with his child.

Kade was such a good father. Sadie and Chuck—what would they think about having another grandchild? And Trent. Would he really like to have a kid brother or sister?

Kelsey sighed and pulled the clip out of her hair. She couldn't deal with it, not at that moment. She needed time to absorb it all. Even if she really was in love with Kade, and even if he did love her, did she want to get married? Hadn't she already learned her lesson?

More doubt crept in, stealing her joy. She didn't have the slightest idea what to do as a parent. How could she be a good mother? And could she make it on her own as a single parent?

After a few moments, she got a grip on her emotions, took a deep breath, and forced herself to stand. She knew she would do whatever it took to give her baby the best home possible.

And maybe it would be with Kade.

As soon as the line went dead, Kade dialed home. "Mom," he said when Sadie answered. "Is everyone okay?"

"Fine," Sadie replied with a question in her voice. "Why?"

Kade ran his hand over his head. "I don't have time to explain. Is everyone home now? Kelsey, too?"

"We're all here."

"Good. Make sure everyone stays inside, and keep the doors locked. Don't open the door for anyone."

Sadie hesitated. "What's wrong?"

"I'll explain when I get there. I'll see if a unit can get to the ranch and sit out front until I make it."

After he hung up with Sadie, Kade asked Daryl to radio for an agent to stay at the ranch, and had a quick conversation with Miguel Martinez.

Before Kade left the station, he asked Daryl to book four seats out of Tucson to San Francisco for late that evening. Kade gave him the passengers' names and his credit card number.

The thirty-minute drive home seemed more like an hour. He pounded the wheel in frustration. Sal radioed in that he'd reached the ranch, and reported that all appeared to be fine.

When Kade drove up to the house, Roxie bounded out to greet him. Sal was sitting inside the cab of an agency green-and-white SUV.

Kade climbed out of his truck and walked up to Sal. "See anything?"

"Nada." Sal nodded toward the house. "I called from the car and told them to sit tight."

"Thanks, compadre."

"Want me to hang around for a while?"

"I don't expect anything to come down until tomorrow."

Sal whistled and shook his head. "I don't have a good feeling about this. Maybe you should do as they said, and resign. For now."

Kade glared at his friend. "No way in hell I'm going to tuck my tail between my legs."

Sal glanced around the yard. "Sure you don't want me to hang around?"

"I'm going to get my family out of here," Kade said. "Then take care of business tomorrow."

"I understand." Sal nodded. "I would do the same. Mañana, then."

Kade didn't wait to watch Sal leave. He hurried to the house and Sadie opened the door at once.

He locked the door behind him. "You all need to get packed."

Sadie's face creased with concern. "What are you talking about?"

"I'm sending you to Dara's." Kade raked his hand through his hair. "Daryl booked seats out of Tucson to SFO for eight o'clock tonight. That gives you four hours to get packed, drive to Tucson, and get to the airport."

Sadie frowned. "You still haven't told me what this is all about."

"Let's get Dad," Kade said, and Sadie hurried to find Chuck and returned with him.

After Kade explained the threat, Chuck nodded. "I think a trip to see your sister'll do us some good."

"Where's Kelsey?" Kade asked.

"She went into the bathroom right before you called," Sadie replied. "I just heard the shower start up. I haven't had a chance to tell her anything."

Kade kicked off his boots. "I'm gonna take a quick shower in your bathroom, while you're packing. Then I'll tell Kelsey she needs to get her things together."

Chapter 29

While thinking about her pregnancy, Kelsey continued to vacillate between joy and sheer terror as she showered. She wasn't ready to be around anyone, and a shower was as good an excuse as any to have some time to herself. It had the added benefit of relaxing her and helping bring everything into focus.

All she could think of was the baby. Every other thought had dissipated. Would it be a boy or a girl? Should she find out beforehand, or let it be a surprise? Where should she shop for baby clothes and furniture?

She had the overwhelming urge to share her news. To shout it from the rooftops.

Calm down, Kelsey.

After she climbed out of the shower and dried off, she realized she hadn't thought to grab any clean clothes. She wrapped the towel around her, and cracked open the bathroom door.

From the front room she heard Sadie say, "Come on, Trent. You can help Grandma and Grandpa get things together in our room."

The boy chattered something about visiting his Aunt Dara, and then Kelsey couldn't hear them anymore.

Otherwise the coast was clear, so she slipped across the hallway into her room.

Just as she was about to drop the towel to pull on a T-shirt, there was a light knock at the door, and Kade opened it. For a moment he stood in the doorway, drinking her in with his azure eyes. An almost pained expression crossed his face, his desire and need as clear as if he'd told her in words.

She straightened and dropped the T-shirt, her pulse hammering in her throat. "Kade."

Warmth flushed over her from head to toe, and she couldn't take her gaze from his.

Easing into the room, he shut the door, never taking his eyes from hers. The lock clicked, and in one long stride he stood inches from her.

He caressed her cheek with his finger, his touch sending shivers throughout her. "Darlin'. What you do to me."

Then his arms enveloped her. She forgot about the towel and it dropped to her feet as she wrapped her arms around his neck. She couldn't help herself. He held her tight, his blue shirt and jeans rough against her breasts and thighs, his buckle scraping the delicate skin of her belly. They kissed, his need matching hers with such intensity that she was wild with it.

Hard. Fierce. Demanding.

To hell with everything. She needed him.

"My God," he whispered against her mouth. His hands cupped her naked hips and he pressed her close to the thrust against his jeans. "You burn me up."

She brushed her lips over his cheek, softly kissing his stubbled face, leading to his ear. Like hers, his hair was wet and he smelled of soap. He lowered his head and captured her nipple in his mouth. Her knees weakened and she moaned as she melted against him.

"I need you so much." He moved his tongue to her other nipple and she could barely control the cries building up in her throat. "Tell me you need me like I need you."

"Yes, Kade. Now."

She helped him peel off his clothes, running her hands over his bare chest, his hard thighs. They were unrestrained in their haste, and sank to the rose rug. He grabbed a condom, and it was all she could do not to tell him it wasn't needed.

Not yet. Wait for the right moment.

He slid into her and she knew he filled her so completely, in every way. Her body, her heart, her soul.

And when she came, it was like it all fused together, and every part of her became one with Kade.

I love him I love him I love him.

When their lovemaking ended, they were both breathing hard, a sheen of perspiration coating their skin. Even then, he didn't stop kissing her. It was like he couldn't get enough. He kissed her lips, her cheeks, her ears, her eyebrows, her throat.

"We need to get dressed," he finally said with obvious reluctance. "Though I would give anything to stay right here with you."

"Mmmm." She nuzzled his neck, drinking in his scent. At that moment she knew that even if he didn't share her love, she would take whatever part of him that he gave her, for however long it would last. "Let's stay like this. No one would miss us, would they?"

"Temptress." He rolled away, eased to his feet, and started putting on his boxers. He looked so good to her that she could barely take her eyes off him.

She stood while she fastened her bra and then stepped into clean panties. "Who seduced whom, might I ask?"

With a laugh, Kade pulled on his jeans, watching her dress. "You were naked."

"I was not." She sniffed and slid into a pair of shorts. "I was wearing a respectable towel. And you barged in."

His voice was muffled as he yanked a T-shirt over his head. "You left the door unlocked." He pulled on his shirt over the T-shirt.

Shaking her head, Kelsey buttoned up her blouse. "I didn't expect a lecher like you to just waltz in here and seduce me."

"Lecher, huh?" With a grin he brought Kelsey close and kissed her so long and passionately that her limbs turned to gelatin.

"Wow," she whispered as she clung to him. It was a few seconds before her legs would hold her up.

Just as she was about to tell Kade that she wanted to go somewhere special to talk with him, to tell him about the baby, he interrupted her thoughts.

"I'm going to miss you." He stroked damp hair from her face, his features suddenly serious. "I can't stand to be away from you."

"Are you—" Hair at her nape prickled as a chill crept over her. "Are you talking about when I leave for San Francisco?"

"Yes and no." He brushed his lips over hers. "I came in here to tell you—and then lost my head."

Her soul turned to ice and she stepped out of his embrace.

Kade reached for her hand. "You need to fly to San Francisco with my family tonight. I've made reservations, and—"

"You what?" She shrugged away from him and planted her fists on her hips. "You think you're going to ship me off like a piece of luggage?"

"You don't under—"

"No man is ever going to tell me what to do again." Her voice rose. "We may have had sex, but that does not give you the right to order me around."

"Damn it, Kelsey." He clenched his jaw, his face hard. "I got a call today. A man threatened my family."

A frigid wave of fear crashed over her, chasing away her anger. "Oh, my God."

Kade ran a hand through his hair. "The son of a bitch said if I didn't turn in my resignation, he would come after my family. He named everyone." Kade grabbed Kelsey by her shoulders. "Including you."

"Me?" She shook her head. "That doesn't make sense."

"Somehow they know that you're my woman." He motioned to the door. "Now let's go. There's not much time. Chuck's driving you all to Tucson and flying you out to San Francisco to stay with my sister, Dara, where you'll be safe."

My woman. He called me his woman.

She closed her eyes and took a deep breath. When she opened them again, she said, "I'm staying."

Kade clenched and unclenched his hands as Kelsey stood there, her brown eyes flashing defiance. He all but wanted to shake some sense into her. "This is serious. These bastards threatened you, too. I need you somewhere safe while I hunt them down."

Kelsey shook her head. "I have two more interviews to do and I am not going to let anyone run me off."

"This is serious." Kade's voice was practically a growl. "It's not a joke."

"I'm not joking." Kelsey narrowed her gaze. "I'm more than capable of taking care of myself."

"Don't you understand?" Kade's tone turned almost pleading. "I couldn't bear it if anything happened to you."

Kade's words poured into Kelsey's heart. Half of her wanted to give in, to let herself be shuttled off safely away from the bad guys. But the other half of her knew she had a job to do.

The thought of being too far from Kade while he faced danger—no. Not happening.

Kelsey shook her head, more vehemently this time. "I'll be fine."

Kade crossed his arms over his chest. "You can't stay here."

She tilted her chin. "Are you telling me I'm not welcome in your home?"

He grabbed his socks and boots and started pulling them on. "You know that's not what I meant. They could come after you here."

Kelsey flipped her hair out of her face, trying to control the emotions inside her. "I'm not going back to San Francisco until next weekend."

Kade took a deep breath and counted to ten as he finished putting on his boots. "Then we need to take you to a hotel."

Kelsey seized a pair of sandals out of the closet. "Are you going?"

"No." He scowled. "I'm staying here."

She pursed her lips. "Fine. I'll check into a hotel on my own."

"Tonight."

"Tomorrow." She spun and marched out, carrying her sandals.

"Well, hell," he muttered as he followed her from the room.

Chuck, Sadie, and Trent were packed and waiting when Kelsey and Kade stalked into the living room.

"Ready, Kelsey?" Chuck asked.

"I'm not going," she said as she gave him a hug. "I'm checking into a hotel tomorrow."

Kade stood behind her with his arms folded, his brows furrowed, and jaw set.

Sadie glanced at Kade, then hugged Kelsey. "You sure you don't want to come with us? I bet you'd be an excellent tour guide."

Kelsey smiled. "One of these days I would love to show you around the Bay Area. But I have a couple more interviews and a deadline to meet."

Sadie patted Kelsey's shoulder. "You go ahead and use my vehicle while we're gone."

"Thanks." Kelsey squatted down in front of Trent. "Hey, Taz. Take care of your grandparents and I'll see you soon."

The boy threw his arms around Kelsey. "You promise you'll still be here when we get back? 'Cause I'm really, really, really going to miss you."

"I'll try." She pulled back. "I'm going to miss you, too." She ruffled Trent's hair. "Can you do something for me while you're on the plane?"

"What?"

"Draw a picture for me, okay?"

"Sure." Trent nodded, and brushed hair out of his eyes. "I've got my crayons and coloring pencils and paper packed in my backpack. Wanna see?" He started to unzip his pack, but Kade grabbed him by the waist and swung him high. Trent squealed with laughter.

"Slow down, pardner." Kade hugged him tight. "You need to get to the airport so you can catch that plane and go see your cousins and Aunt Dara."

Kade set Trent down, hugged his mom, then helped carry their luggage out to Chuck's truck. Sadie promised to keep the cell phone on, and to call Kade once they hit the freeway, and again in Tucson and in San Francisco. Dara and the kids would be meeting them at the airport.

He breathed a sigh of relief as the red taillights disappeared into the night.

But Kelsey. He turned to her and frowned. How could he keep her safe?

Chapter 30

The following morning was muggy and overcast, and Kade was sure it would rain later. After feeding the livestock for Chuck, Kade cleaned mud off his boots before he entered the house. His footsteps echoed as he walked to his bedroom.

Last night it had seemed that she had something to tell him, but instead they made love again and again until they were too exhausted to move.

He stopped at the doorway to his bedroom and found Kelsey still sound asleep. This time they'd slept in his bed. Where he wanted her always. She made him feel so good, just by being there. In a couple of strides he reached the bed, leaned down, and whispered, "Rise and shine."

"Mmmm." Her lashes were dark against her pale skin, and her chest rose and fell.

Bedsprings creaked as Kade sat and shook Kelsey's shoulder. "Get up, sleepyhead."

"Leave me alone," she mumbled, and turned her head away.

"Gotta get you out of here." Kade tried pulling the covers off, but she snatched them back.

"Go away."

"Nope. Out of bed."

"A little longer," she moaned.

He leaned over and kissed her ear. "I know how to wake you."

A sleepy smile teased the corners of her mouth as he nipped her earlobe. She grabbed a pillow and covered her head with it, swatting his face in the process.

Kade couldn't help smile as he pulled on his T-shirt, bulletproof vest, and overshirt. When he finished dressing, he lifted the pillow and nuzzled Kelsey's neck. She smelled so good, her skin warm against his nose. "Get up, honey. I've got to get going."

Another groan. "I will. Gimme a minute."

"Only one." He tossed the pillow aside and brushed his lips over hers before he grabbed her cell phone and placed it in her hand. "Call me at work and let me know when you make it to the hotel."

"All right." She wrapped her arms around his neck and kissed him back.

As she settled against the pillow, he wanted to tell her then. Wanted to tell her how much he loved her. Was she ready?

"You need to go to work." She captured his hand and brought it to her lips.

"And you need to get your pretty ass out of bed."

"Okay."

She looked beautiful and innocent, her hair splayed across the pillow, her lips soft and swollen. He didn't want to leave. Wasn't sure he should. Or could.

Last night they'd waited up until Sadie called to let them know that she, Chuck, and Trent had arrived in San Francisco and were safe and sound at Dara's. He was relieved they were out of danger. Why did Kelsey have to be so stubborn? Why couldn't she have gone to San Francisco, where she would be safe?

Fear settled in his chest, a hard lump that wouldn't go away. "I'll call in and tell Mikey I'll be late until we get you settled into the hotel."

Frowning, Kelsey shook her head. "Absolutely not. I'll call you when I get to Nicole's B and B."

He knew he would only make her angry if he pushed the issue. It was enough that she would at least be away from the house. She would be safe in Bisbee.

"I expect to hear from you by noon," he said. "If you don't catch me on my cell phone and I'm not in the office, leave a message with Daryl."

She smiled. "Gotcha, cowboy."

Kelsey had fully intended to get up when Kade left. But it felt wonderful lying there, thinking about him, her lips still tingling from his kiss.

He had smelled delicious when he came in from feeding the cattle. Of sweet oats and the promise of rain on a morning breeze. She thought about the feel of his hand in hers, the texture of his callused fingers against her lips, the soft hair on the back of his wrist.

She moved her hand to her belly. He'd given her the world, and she hoped he'd be as happy as she was when she told him. Last night she had wanted to share the news with him, but she wasn't sure what his reaction would be and she wanted to wait until she could sit him down and have some serious alone time. Not in-bed time.

While lying there, thinking about the reason he wanted her to go stay in Bisbee, she realized what Kade's Achilles' heel was, and her smile faded.

His love for his family. His concern for others. Whatever it was he felt for her.

The bastards knew exactly how to hurt Kade—by threatening his family. But Kade wasn't one to back down.

He would die fighting to protect those he loved. And to protect those who loved him.

The thought chilled her.

She held a fist to her aching heart. She couldn't bear anything happening to Kade. Couldn't bear losing another person whom she loved so intensely. How could she walk away and hide in a hotel while he risked his life? Shouldn't she remain at his side? But if she stayed, would that only put him in more danger?

The past few days weighed her down, and she closed her eyes against the relentless images. The threat to Kade's family. Acknowledging her love for Kade. The pregnancy.

So tired. Her thoughts moved to the only close friend she had who had gone through a pregnancy. She remembered how exhausted Theresa Cortez had been in her first trimester. The woman could hardly keep her head up or food down for three months, practically from the day she'd gotten pregnant.

Thunder rumbled outside as Kelsey snuggled into the pillow and drank in Kade's earthy scent, which clung to the sheets. She needed to keep her promise to him and get to the B and B so he wouldn't worry. She would just rest a minute longer. The heaviness in her limbs dragged her further down, deeper and deeper, until darkness enveloped her.

* * *

When Kade arrived at the station, he headed straight to Miguel Martinez's office.

"Everything okay?" Miguel asked, his green eyes narrowed. He sat at his desk, resting his chin on his steepled fingers.

"Got my family off to Frisco." With a frustrated sigh, Kade ran his hand over his head. "Kelsey refused to go because she wants to finish her damn feature. But she agreed to stay at a hotel in Bisbee."

Miguel frowned. "A man matching Gordo's description was seen in the vicinity of the phone booth the call was placed from yesterday. Again, José Hernandez. I put Sal and Don on him, but they've come up empty."

Fury simmered in Kade's gut. "What about Bull Stevens?"

"Everything's been quiet at his ranch." Rubbing his palm over his stubbled cheeks, Miguel added, "But we tapped an interesting phone call yesterday that might connect him to the threat."

Kade clenched the back of a chair, his knuckles white against the dark upholstery. Before he could respond, Daryl Jones paged him over the intercom.

"Phone call on line six for Agent Owen."

Miguel pointed to the telephone. "Take it here."

Kade grabbed the receiver. "Owen."

"This is Juarez," the informant said in Spanish. His voice trembled. "I have information concerning those who wish to do your family harm."

Clenching the phone in his hand, Kade said, "What do you know?"

"Mario's at noon. Come alone."

The line went dead.

* * *

"I think another agent should go in with you," Miguel said again when it was time for Kade to head to Mario's. "We can put someone in undercover."

"It's only an informant," Kade replied. "It's a public place."

"But it's the first time he's insisted you come alone, correct?" Miguel said.

"Juarez isn't a concern." Kade shook his head. "If anyone goes inside with me it'll scare him too much to talk."

Miguel picked up his frog paperweight and ran his thumb over the smooth glass. "I'll have a couple of vehicles keep an eye out as they drive by."

Kade nodded and headed out of the building, then strode through the rain to his truck. The drive took less than five minutes, and right at noon, he took his regular booth at Mario's Cantina. He shook rain from his hair and combed it back with his fingers. Mari didn't appear to be working, and another waitress took his order.

Fifteen minutes later, Kade checked his watch. Juarez was late, which wasn't like him. He studied the regulars, several of whom were already bombed off their asses, and it was barely after noon.

Speaking of noon, he should have heard from Kelsey by now.

Outside the open door, relentless monsoon rains pounded the sidewalk. A breeze swirled in, the scent of rain mingling with the cantina's odors of cigarettes and alcohol.

Another ten minutes passed and unease twisted in Kade's gut. Something wasn't right. He stood to leave and dropped a five on the table, then caught the smell of cheap perfume.

"Señor." Mari came up to him and laid her hand on his arm, her dark eyes wide and lips trembling. "A man. You were here with him before. He is in the kitchen and asked that you come at once."

Hair rose at Kade's nape. "His name?"

"Juarez." Her gaze darted to the back room and then to Kade again. "He said that he cannot risk being seen out here."

Keeping his right hand close to the Glock holstered at his side, Kade followed Mari through the doorway. The kitchen floor was littered with scraps and smelled of sour beer and stale grease. He glanced behind him as they turned a corner, then back to Mari.

She stopped in front of a dingy room. Kade caught a glimpse of papers piled on a desk and an empty chair.

Her eyes darted toward the office. "He's in here, señor."

As he eased up to the office, an enormous man rounded the doorway. Before Kade had a chance to react, he saw the flash of metal. Blinding pain splintered his head as the man slammed the butt of an automatic onto the side of his skull.

Chapter 31

The crack of thunder jarred Kelsey awake and she bolted upright. "Kade," she cried, holding her hand to her pounding heart.

Panic clawed its way up her throat.

She glanced at the digital clock on the bureau. Twelve thirty? How had she slept so late? She took a deep breath, then exhaled. Nothing was wrong. It was just the time making her nervous. She'd promised Kade she would go to Bisbee and she should have been gone already.

A flash of lighting and another rumble sent shock waves through her. Thunderclouds darkened the sky and rain poured in thick sheets.

She needed to call Kade. Let him know she was running late.

Still naked, Kelsey scrambled out of bed and grabbed Kade's robe. His scent enveloped her as she tied the belt and looked for her cell phone. He'd just given it back to her . . . There. She snatched it up and called his cell phone. No answer. More panic grabbed hold of her, and she hurried to the study, where she flipped through the card file. She dialed his work number and tapped her fingers as she waited for an answer.

"Border Patrol. Daryl Jones here."

"This is Kelsey Nichols. Is Kade Owen available?"

"Nope," the agent said. "He's out of the station right now. Do you want to leave a message?"

"Yes." She closed her eyes. "Please tell him I'm running late and probably won't be leaving the ranch until after one. I'll call him later."

After Daryl repeated the message, she hung up and took another deep breath. Kade was fine. She just needed to get to Bisbee so he wouldn't worry.

Kelsey hurried to take a shower and then packed enough clothes for four days. She French-braided her hair to keep it out of her face. After putting on her bra and panties, she pulled one of Kade's blue T-shirts over her head. It was baggy on her but made her smile when she smelled his wonderful scent. Then she tugged on loose jeans, socks, and tennis shoes.

When she was ready, she grabbed her laptop bag, purse, and suitcase, locked the front door, and headed through the rain to Sadie's SUV. The rottweiler trailed after her. Kelsey tossed everything onto the floorboard of the passenger side and slammed the door shut.

She rounded the vehicle and grabbed the handle to open the driver's side door when Roxie's bark caused her to jump. The dog bounded into the driveway and growled. The sound grew more ominous and threatening as Roxie stared down the road that led to the ranch.

Kelsey's heart thudded as the dog's deep-throated bark pierced the rain. Then she saw it. A car she didn't recognize tearing up the dirt road, about a quarter mile away.

Oh, my God. What if it was the men who had threatened Kade?

She thought about jumping into the SUV but knew the car could cut her off before she made it to the main road. With only stunted paloverde and mesquite bushes surrounding the property, there would be no place to hide a vehicle, and they would see her before she had a chance to get far.

Kelsey spun and ran onto the lawn, toward the front door. No. Not the house. If those were the men after Kade's family, the house would be the first place they would look. The ranch was so far from town that no one would have a chance to get there before anything happened.

She dodged around the house and eyed the barn. No, she was likely to sneeze so much they would hear her.

Trent's hideout.

Wet leaves and branches slapped her face as she raced through the orchard and into the windbreak. Her foot slid on the wet grass and she tumbled to the ground. Without pause, she scrambled to her feet and hurried on until she reached the playhouse. She scurried through the door and collapsed onto the floor. Trembling, she struggled to catch her breath.

"Calm down, Kelsey," she murmured as she wiped rain and mud from her face onto her sleeve. "It's probably neighbors coming to visit Chuck and Sadie. You're overreacting."

But even as she said the words, her gut told her differently. The same instinct that told her Kade was in trouble.

"I need to try to call Kade—"

Kelsey put her hand to her forehead. Her phone. She'd left it with everything else on the floorboard of the SUV.

In the distance she heard a car's engine and squeaking brakes. Roxie continued to bark, more ferociously than Kelsey had ever heard her before. A sound like a gunshot echoed across the yard and the dog yelped.

Silence.

Kelsey clapped her hand to her mouth. *No.*

Her entire body shook and she wanted to curl up in a ball and hide. But she needed to see who was out there. Needed to figure out what to do. As she scooted closer to the window, she remembered Trent's binoculars. Fortunately, she didn't have to dig far into the toy box to find them. Kneeling, she brought the binoculars to her eyes and pushed open the shutters, just far enough to allow her to see.

At first Kelsey saw nothing, but as she adjusted the lenses, the image of an enormous man swam into view. It was the man who'd almost run her off the road on John Stevens's ranch. The name Gordo popped into her mind—it had to be the man Stevens had been talking to on his cell phone.

Beside Gordo was a man whose face reminded her of a lizard. Lizard was waving a handgun and pointing to the house. Gordo shook his head and walked to Sadie's SUV. He yanked open the door, searched the vehicle, then slammed the door shut again. Lizard gestured to the muddy ground. Gordo nodded and they both started across the lawn toward the house.

The two men reached the front door and jiggled the handle. Kelsey heard the faint sound of glass shattering as Lizard used the butt of his gun to break a glass pane in the door. He reached through the broken glass, unlocked it, and walked into the house.

Anger churned in her stomach. How dare they violate Kade's home? She kept the binoculars trained on the house, occasionally catching glimpses of the men through the windows. Searching for her or one of Kade's family members.

Kelsey set down the binoculars and pressed her palms to her temples. What should she do?

Rain beat on the roof of the playhouse and lightning struck so close that for a moment Kelsey was deafened by its thunder. A rain-drenched breeze swirled around her and chills crawled up her spine.

How was she going to get out of this alive?

The searing odor of ammonia assaulted Kade's nostrils and his eyes snapped open. Blinding light caused him to shut his eyes again, but not before he caught the image of a hand waving smelling salts under his nose.

His temples throbbed as he struggled to remember where he was and what had happened, and he had a strange feeling in his head. Like he was underwater.

"Wake up, amigo." Sal's voice.

Kade brought his hand to his forehead and blinked until he was able to focus. He was sprawled on the floor of the Cantina's office, Sal crouched beside him. In the background he heard the hum of voices, and vaguely made out an agent questioning someone in Spanish. It sounded like Don Mitchell.

"How many fingers am I holding up?" Sal asked.

"Three, to go along with your three fucking eyes," Kade mumbled.

Sal grinned and pressed a cloth to Kade's forehead. "Your pupils are dilated. You've got one hell of a lump and a bruise, but you might get lucky and walk straight in a few hours."

Kade took the cloth from Sal and groaned as he eased himself up to sit with his back against the desk.

"Did you get a look at the guy who hit you?" Sal asked.

Pain slammed into Kade's head when he tried to nod. "Damn," he muttered. "I only got a glimpse, but the guy looked like those surveillance photos of Gordo. Big belly, handlebar mustache, enormous gold buckle." Even as the words pierced his head, Kade said, "José Hernandez."

"Miguel had Don and me drive by to keep an eye out for you. About twelve thirty I headed in to take a look. When I saw you weren't in the bar, I called Don for backup and we found you back here." He motioned to a pile of ropes beside Kade. "The SOBs started to bind you, but I must've spooked them. They managed to escape out the back door."

"It was my own damn fault—I walked right into it." Kade scrubbed his hand over his head and winced when his fingers brushed the bump growing at his temple. "What's the time?"

Sal checked his watch. "Twelve forty."

Kade's shoulders knotted as he thought of Kelsey. She'd probably arrived at the bed-and-breakfast, so he shouldn't be worried. He reached into his back pocket for his cell phone, but it wasn't there. Probably left it in the truck.

"They pulled this off you but left it on the desk." Sal handed Kade his Glock. "Must've been in a hurry to get out of here."

Kade holstered the handgun at his side as he got to his feet. He still felt his second Glock secured at the back of his waistband but didn't mention it.

He grabbed the phone on the desk and called the station. When he asked Daryl if there were any messages for him, Daryl said, "Yeah. Got one from a Kelsey Nichols. Said she was running late and probably wouldn't get away from the ranch until after one."

"What?" Kade shouted, the sound of his own voice splitting his head. "Never mind." His hand shook as he hung up and dialed her cell phone. Went straight to voice mail. Then he called the ranch and let the phone ring at least twenty times.

No answer.

"Don called the paramedics," Sal said when Kade slammed down the receiver. "They should be here any minute."

"No time." Kade headed toward the door. "I'm going to the ranch. I think Kelsey's still there and I've got to make sure these bastards aren't after her. Call the Sheriff's Department and call for backup."

He didn't wait for Sal's reply as he ran into the thunderstorm. Sirens approached as he jumped over water flowing in the gutter and stumbled into his truck. Gritting his teeth against the throbbing pain in his head, he started the vehicle and swung into traffic. His reflexes were off, causing him to drive erratically, and horns blared as he weaved on the road.

Cursing the distance to the ranch, he fought to maintain focus and control of the vehicle. He discovered his cell phone wasn't in the truck, and he had no way to call Kelsey to see if she was still at the house. Even the pouring rain mocked him, the washes already running with water from the downpour, forcing him to slow down as he crossed them so he wouldn't flood his engine.

When he finally arrived at the ranch, he took a back road and parked behind a clump of mesquite bushes, hoping the dark truck blended in well enough and couldn't be seen in the rain. He grabbed his field glasses out of the glove compartment, pulled out his Glock, and hurried out of the truck, careful not to slam the door.

Rain poured and thunder rumbled as he waded through floodwaters and crawled to the top of the muddy dam. He prayed that he was wrong. That Kelsey wasn't in danger.

But as soon as he looked through the binoculars, he saw the unfamiliar car in the driveway—and Sadie's SUV still parked there.

He swung the glasses to the house and glimpsed a man through a window.

Rage seared him and he had to force himself to think calmly. Two men stepped outside the house, and he recognized the first—José Hernandez, aka Gordo. The other was the man who'd knocked him cold. The bastard gestured to the yard.

Kelsey must be hiding somewhere. Where would she hide? Not the barn. Her sneezes would bring attention to her immediately. Possibly the garden, but not enough cover. Certainly not the plane. She was terrified of it. If it was Trent, he would know to go to the playhouse.

The playhouse. It dawned on Kade that Trent had told Kelsey about his dad's instructions. Would she remember?

Gordo started searching around the outside of the house and the other man headed to the barn. Kade scrambled over the dam, slipping in the mud and sliding to the bottom of the incline. He fought another wave of nausea from the concussion, then crouched low and ran to the windbreak. The playhouse came into view. He raced toward it, then paused at the door. If Kelsey was in there, she might scream, thinking him one of the men hunting for her.

Lightning struck, close enough that the clap of thunder was unbearably loud to his pounding head. He pushed open the playhouse door and saw Kelsey on her knees, her back to him, her face in her hands. He eased into the doorway, and as she raised her head he clapped his hand over her mouth and pulled her close to him.

Terror ripped through Kelsey and she struggled against the hands that held her.

"It's me," Kade said, and released her.

Her limbs went slack with relief. She turned and threw her arms around him, pressing herself against his wet and muddy body. "Thank God you're here."

He kissed her forehead, but when he pulled away, his face was grim. "You were supposed to be in Bisbee by now."

"I overslept." She gasped when she noticed the wound on his head. "What happened? You're hurt."

Kade eased by her, mud covering the floor of the playhouse behind him. He picked up the binoculars and looked out the window. "Damn. They've spotted my truck." He dropped the glasses and took her hand. "Keep low." He pulled her through the doorway of the playhouse and into the storm.

While she crawled out, Kelsey wiped rain from her eyes and started to ask Kade how they would escape.

Her heart stopped as a figure stepped in front of them. She sighed with relief when she saw that it was Sal.

"Sal." Kade put his arm out to block Kelsey from walking forward. "What the hell are you doing?"

It was then that she saw the gun.

Chapter 32

Kelsey's heart pounded as her gaze snapped from the weapon to Sal's face, his expression ruthless in the pouring rain.

"You couldn't mind your own fucking business, could you, compadre?" Water dripped from the brim of Sal's hat as he narrowed his gaze. "I convinced El Torero and Gordo to give you a warning. A chance to walk away." Sal spit on the ground but kept his eyes on Kade.

Kade pushed Kelsey partially behind him. "Just walk away from Kelsey." His voice was as hard and cold as steel. "You and I will deal with this."

"Too late. The man wants the both of you taken to him." Sal pulled Kade's cell phone out of his back pocket. "You're going to visit El Torero now."

Kelsey's gaze darted from Sal to Kade and back, her heart pounding. What could she do to help Kade? To help them both?

"Drop your weapon, then hands up, palms facing me." Sal stepped closer. Pressed his handgun against Kade's temple.

Kade's Glock dropped from his fingers and spattered the mud at their feet. Slowly Kade raised his hands as Sal kicked the weapon aside, hard enough that it landed at least ten feet away.

"Don't move while I make this call, or you're dead." His cold gaze cut to Kelsey. "You run off and I'll shoot him."

Raw terror filled Kelsey while Sal punched buttons on the weatherproof phone, the electronic sound surreal in the pouring rain. In the distance, somewhere behind them, men shouted in Spanish.

She struggled to calm the fear raging within. How were they going to get out of this? If only Kade had his handgun.

His second handgun.

Slowly Kelsey raised her left hand that was hidden behind Kade's back. He stiffened as her hand moved under his overshirt. She kept her eyes focused on Sal. The man spoke rapid-fire Spanish into the phone, but it was so low and unintelligible that she wondered if even Kade could make out the words.

Her fingers eased over the rough texture of his denim jeans and then met cold metal above the waistband. She withdrew the weapon, afraid that Sal would hear the sound of the gun moving across cloth. But with the rain pouring down she knew she really didn't have anything to worry about.

She kept her eyes focused on Sal's, using every bit of her journalism skills to school her expression.

Her hand shook as she pushed up her baggy T-shirt and slid the handgun into her left front pocket. She prayed her shirt was loose enough that Sal wouldn't notice the bulge, especially with the rain making her T-shirt cling to her skin.

The front of her shirt dropped down just as Sal punched off the phone. "Let's go. But first I've got to pat you down, compadre."

Kelsey froze.

"I don't have anything else." Kade's tone was so calm and natural, not betraying any kind of concern. "Lost my backup when I slid down the dam."

"Bullshit." Sal gestured for Kade to turn around. "Keep your hands up. I'll shoot your woman. You know I will, Owen."

"You can see I'm covered in mud from when I fell." Kade turned in a slow movement.

As Sal patted him down, Kade stared at Kelsey, asking her with his eyes what she'd done with his handgun. She glanced at her pocket and he gave her a grim smile.

"Not even a knife." Sal stared at Kade when he turned around and met Sal's gaze. "I'll follow you to your truck and you'll drive. I'm parked by you."

"Tell me why you're doing this." Kade turned and lowered his hands.

"Don't fuck with me, Owen. Keep your hands up." Sal aimed his handgun at Kelsey's forehead and she swallowed. "Money. What else? Shit, man, I'll never get rich working for the government. I've already made more cash in the past few months than I could in an entire year as an agent."

"You've been tipping off the bastards." Kade raised his hands again. "You gave them the names of my contacts. My family. Kelsey."

Sal's dark eyes flashed and he nodded toward the dam. "Let's go."

"You'd be one of the last people I'd ever think would turn." Kade worked his jaw as he stepped forward.

"That's your biggest weakness." Sal grinned. "You're too damn trusting."

Before Kelsey could even grasp what was happening, Kade swung his right leg around and kicked the handgun out of Sal's grasp. The man howled and cradled his hand. Kade caught his balance on his left foot and then shot his right foot toward Sal, plowing his boot squarely into the man's midsection.

Air whooshed from Sal's lungs. He doubled over and dropped to his knees. Kade swung his foot again, connecting with Sal's head. The man fell to his side and lay still.

Kelsey dove for Sal's handgun where it had landed on a patch of wet grass. Her hands shook as she scooped it up and handed it to Kade.

Men's voices were approaching.

Holding Sal's weapon in one hand, Kade grabbed Kelsey's hand and pulled her through the windbreak with him.

"Damn," Kade muttered. "There's only one way we can get out of here now."

"How?" But even as she asked, horror slammed into Kelsey and she started to shake. She tried to stop running, but Kade pulled her forward until they burst through the trees, straight toward his plane.

"There's no way. I can't." Every part of her quivered as Kade yanked open the cockpit door. Flashes of flames and her sister's dead face filled her head.

Shouts erupted from behind them. She didn't have a choice.

It took everything she had to force herself to climb into the plane, knowing that this time they would be flying, not making love.

Kade helped her up and then dropped Sal's handgun between the seats. "Everything'll be okay."

Somehow she managed to get into the copilot's seat and buckled in. She shook so hard her teeth chattered. Clenching her eyes shut, she tried to fight the horrific images in her mind.

The engine roared to life, and she felt the movement of the plane as Kade guided it down the muddy runway.

OhGodohGodohGodohGod. Naya's voice rang in Kelsey's mind and she gripped her seat cushion so tightly her hands ached. Flashes of the plane crash erupted in her mind, and she could barely keep from screaming in terror.

"Keep your head low." Kade's voice was tight. "They're at the end of the runway."

She forced herself to open her eyes and saw his clenched jaw, his hands taut on the steering column. His normally tan skin was pale, the wound to his forehead vivid red. Mud and water dripped from his clothing onto his seat and the floor.

Kelsey looked out the window and choked back a cry as the men came into view and the plane began to lift from the ground. Both men aimed guns at the cockpit.

Glass cracked as a bullet hit the windshield. She screamed as another zinged by her ear. She heard the ping of more bullets against metal as the plane rose higher. Then nothing but the sound of the engine and blood roaring in her ears.

"We're okay." Kade reached over and squeezed her hand. Then he glanced at the gauges and cursed, his features growing tighter, more concerned than even before.

"What's wrong?" Kelsey's voice was barely a croak.

He gave her a sharp look. "We'll be fine. It just means that we need to head to the closest airport."

More panic gripped Kelsey. "What happened?"

Kade blew out a harsh breath. "They put a bullet in the gas tank. Rather than chance going over the mountains to Bisbee, we'll land at the airport outside of Douglas, by the prison."

Rivulets of water streamed down Kelsey's face and her wet

clothes clung to her body. His handgun dug into her hip, but she couldn't pry her fingers from the seat cushion to take it out of her pocket. He radioed ahead and she berated herself for putting him in such danger by not getting away from the ranch as she'd promised.

When he approached the field by the prison, an air traffic controller informed him that for security reasons they wouldn't be allowed to land and would have to go to the airport in Douglas. Kade argued that it was an emergency, but the controller insisted he take the plane to the next airport and that it would be prepared for the landing.

"What the hell?" he muttered. He cut a look to Kelsey and managed a small smile. "It's a slow leak. We'll make it."

She tore her gaze from Kade's and closed her eyes.

And prayed.

Chapter 33

Lightning flashed and the plane bounced with the turbulence. Kelsey gasped and Kade looked at her again. Her eyes were squeezed shut, her face ashen. He thought about the day he'd met the woman at his side. And now he wanted to spend the rest of his life with her.

He could only hope that would be longer than it took to get the plane landed.

"It's all right," he said. "We'll be there in just a few minutes."

She didn't answer, and he wished he could take her in his arms and hold her tight.

Head pounding, he struggled to concentrate and control his clumsy hands. That bang on the head must have banged up his coordination, too. He forced himself to focus on the air traffic controller's voice and the approaching landing strip. The blue runway lights blurred in the rain.

"I'm taking us down now. It might be a bit bumpy." Kade tried to keep his voice calm and soothing. His hands were a little shaky from the concussion, but he wasn't going to worry Kelsey with that. "We'll be fine, honey."

"I trust you," she whispered, but when he glanced at her, he saw that her eyes were still closed.

Steady. Steady. Kade gritted his teeth and eased the plane down.

The nose dipped in the wind, and the plane pitched. Kelsey's gasp was audible over the engine's noise.

He swore under his breath, fighting the wheel more than he should have. Five hundred feet. Four hundred. Rain made visual impossible. He was flying on instruments, and on his gut instinct. Hopefully the concussion didn't affect his instincts as much as it had affected his hands.

Two hundred feet.

One hundred.

The plane dropped hard, skittering. Kelsey screamed and grabbed her knees. He dragged hard on the brakes, his breath catching with each shimmy and bump until they rolled to a stop in front of the hangar.

Kade leaned back in his seat, his muscles slack with relief. He looked at Kelsey's pale face.

"Did—did we land?" she asked, eyes squeezed closed, lips trembling.

He squeezed her hand again. "We're safe."

She opened her eyes. Her breasts rose and fell as she took a deep breath. "I'm so sorry I put you through this. I should have listened to you and gone straight to Bisbee."

"Hey, it's okay." Kade hooked his forefinger under her chin. "I'm just glad we made it. Now let's get out of here." He grabbed Sal's Glock from where it lay between the seats and tucked it into his waistband at his back.

Damn Sal. Kade's lips drew so tight he was baring his teeth. How could he have been so blind that he'd never seen it coming?

After he helped Kelsey climb out of the plane, she flung her arms around his neck and hugged him tight. Rain poured down as he squeezed her to him and kissed her wet hair.

"Señor," a man said behind them.

Kade released Kelsey and spun around. Instinct had him moving his hand close to the Glock.

"We have been expecting you." Dressed in coveralls with the airport insignia, the man nodded toward the closest hangar. "Please come in out of the rain."

Kade nodded, his head swimming with pain from his injury.

They followed the wiry man into the hangar, which was so dim he could barely see. Only a black truck was parked inside the building. Kade's skin crawled.

Even as he reached for Sal's handgun and tried to push Kelsey outside, something struck him in the small of his back. His breath knocked from him, he pitched forward and hit the floor.

"Kade!" Kelsey screamed.

A boot pressed into his back.

"Don't move or I'll have your reporter shot," a familiar voice said as the man in coveralls frisked Kade, then took his Glock. The door of the hangar slammed shut, the only light coming from a single bulb hanging from the ceiling.

Kade's vision swam. He turned his head to the side—his blood ran cold as he saw the man in coveralls holding Kelsey by one arm, the barrel of an automatic to her temple.

"Get up, Owen," Stevens ordered, a toothpick hanging from the corner of his mouth. "Hands where I can see them. I've got this here gun pointed at your head. Don't want to leave a mess."

Heart pounding, Kade eased to his feet and faced Stevens. Dominguez stood about a foot away.

Kade's eyes met Kelsey's and he tried to tell her everything he wanted to say with that one look. Her lips parted, but she looked calmer, stronger than he'd expected. He tried to keep his face calm, but inside he was dying. One wrong move and Stevens could have her killed.

Kade fixed his gaze on Stevens. "How'd you track us?"

The rancher's face was impassive. "Valenzuela let me know you'd gotten away. I called in a few favors and had you routed here, everything kept quiet. I pump a lot of money into this town."

"What—" Kade fought for focus, his injury making it difficult to think clearly or even to speak. "What do you want with us?"

"Sorry, Owen. You should've turned in your resignation." Stevens cocked his head toward where Dominguez held Kelsey. "She'll come with me. For now."

Rage filled Kade. Adrenaline pumped through his body, making his vision sharper. He had to keep Stevens talking. Find some way out of the mess they were in. "What kind of man smuggles people across the border and leaves them to die?"

Stevens's tone was calm. "Payback for all the damage done to my property. Payback for the thousands of dollars I've lost. Might as well see some of the cash if they're gonna be crossing my land."

Kade gritted his teeth, then spoke. "You killed Pedro Rios, didn't you?"

Stevens rolled his shoulders. "Rios revealed too much to the reporter. He might've spilled his guts to the wrong folks."

Kade fought back a wave of nausea. "Don't add another murder to your charges."

A smile tugged at the rancher's mouth. "I've been doing this for years, and with you gone nothing'll change."

Kade shook his head. "You've been under surveillance. José Hernandez, aka Gordo, a known *coyote,* has been seen going to and from your ranch. Your phone has been tapped, conversations recorded. It's over."

The smile faded from Stevens's face. Kade's heart thundered as Dominguez suddenly looked nervous and his hand started trembling, the weapon still pointed at Kelsey's forehead. His eyes darted back and forth from Kade to Stevens.

Stevens worked the toothpick between his teeth as if chewing on what Kade had just said.

Kade lowered his hands. He glanced at Dominguez—the man's attention was on Stevens.

"With a name like Bull, it wasn't too sharp, allowing yourself to be called El Torero. A matador," Kade said. "And you left one of your toothpicks at the crime scene with Rios. A DNA test of the saliva on the pick'll prove you were there."

Stevens spit out his toothpick and gripped the automatic even tighter. "You'd better be shittin' me."

It was what Kade had been waiting for—to get Dominguez's attention completely off Kelsey.

Kade charged Dominguez, jamming his arm upward, away from Kelsey's temple. He drove Dominguez back, back toward Stevens and the other handgun.

Stevens fired.

Pain exploded in Kade's arm.

Dominguez slammed to the ground, striking his head. Hard.

Kelsey screamed.

A hot knife split Kade's chest. He felt the bullet before he heard that second shot, and then—darkness.

* * *

"No!" Rage swept over Kelsey, fast and furious. She spun around. "You bastard." With all the strength she possessed, Kelsey rammed her knee into Stevens's groin.

Total shock crossed his features. The weapon toppled out of his hand and he dropped to his knees.

"Son of a bitch." Kelsey reared back, and as Stevens tried to straighten, she kicked him in the balls again as hard as she could.

The man gasped and collapsed onto his side, curling into a fetal position, vomiting and whining.

Kelsey kicked Stevens's handgun to the back of the hangar, well beyond his reach. Then she kicked Dominguez's gun to the back of the hangar, near Stevens's weapon.

She pulled Kade's handgun from her front pocket and trained it on the rancher as she checked on the other man and saw that he was completely still—knocked out. She didn't have the slightest idea how to use the weapon, but Stevens wouldn't know that. She hoped.

Sirens approached as she ran to Kade and tried to keep the handgun pointed at Stevens. "Oh, God," she sobbed when she saw blood pooling across Kade's shirt and mixing with the mud covering his clothing. "Don't leave me. Please don't die. I love you, Kade. I love you so much."

His eyelids fluttered and his hand clenched hers. "I know, honey." A weak smile, then his face went slack and he passed out.

She caressed his stubbled cheeks, her lips trembling, hot tears spilling down her face. His skin was clammy. "Damn it, Kade. Don't you dare die on me."

Dominguez moaned beside Kade. She turned and saw that the rancher still writhed in pain on the floor. She held Kade's gun with both hands, keeping it pointed toward Stevens. Her heart screamed for help as she looked from the vomiting Stevens back to the other man, now moving.

Sirens wailed and brakes screeched outside the hangar. She checked to see that both Stevens and Dominguez were still down, then threw Kade's handgun to the back of the hangar near the others. She ran to the door and yanked it open and saw police cars and an ambulance crowding the runway.

"Help, please!" she cried to the first officer that approached her. "John Stevens shot Kade Owen. And there's another man that held a gun on me. Kade knocked him out, but he's coming around."

Officers poured into the building and in moments had cuffed Stevens and Dominguez. When the building was secure, paramedics rushed in and started attending Kade.

Everything was a whirl of action, flashing lights, shouts, conversations, and her cascading emotions.

Kelsey turned to follow when Don Mitchell took her by the arm.

"How is he?" Don asked.

She blinked, for a second unable to process his question, then told him what had happened.

She started to shake. "There's so much blood. He can't die. He just can't."

Don patted Kelsey's arm, then pulled her to him in an awkward hug and she sobbed against his shirt.

"Kade's one tough hombre." Don rubbed her back like an affectionate father. "He'll come through."

Unconsciously Kelsey clenched the fabric of his shirt—and felt something hard beneath it.

"His vest." She looked up at Don, hope blossoming within her. "He was wearing a vest. I'm sure of it." She broke out of the man's embrace, turned, and ran into the hangar.

Kade was lying on the stretcher, his shirt and vest gaping open, the paramedics working on him. An enormous bruise covered the left side of his chest, below his heart.

"He did. He had on his vest." Her voice quavered and she was dizzy with relief.

Don walked up behind her as one of the police officers came to Kelsey's side. "Sure enough did." The officer nodded toward Kade. "Saved his life."

"But the blood." Her knees weakened and she grabbed Don's arm to keep from falling. "So much blood."

"From the flesh wound to his arm," the officer replied as Don pulled Kelsey against him and held her up. "He's got a bunch of bruises and he's lost blood, but other than that, the paramedics think he'll be fine."

Kelsey's stomach roiled. She tore away from Don, ran outside, and vomited. Even after there was nothing left, dry heaves continued to rack her body.

Kelsey sprawled in a chair in the hospital's waiting room, her hair drying but her clothing still damp from rain. She was cold and exhausted, but all she could think about was Kade.

She drew the blanket that a nurse had provided earlier around her shoulders, seeking warmth even though nothing would take away the chill of her fear for Kade.

"You need to let a doctor examine you," Don said as he watched her.

"I'm fine." Her stomach churned again as she inhaled the horrid antiseptic smells, but she was sure there was nothing left in her belly to throw up.

"You're in shock." Don stood and started pacing. "That's why you're vomiting and still shaking."

Kelsey pulled the blanket tighter around her. She wasn't about to tell Don the real reason she was throwing up. Maybe shock had something to do with it, but she was pretty sure it had a lot more to do with her pregnancy. Not to mention the hospital's pea-green walls. They were ugly enough to make anyone puke.

"How did you know where we were?" Kelsey asked, trying to draw Don's attention away from her and how she was feeling at the moment.

Don shrugged. "When Kade tore home after you, Sal followed. I've had a strange feeling about him lately, so I checked in with Miguel and found out that Sal never called for backup like he said he did. So Miguel called the Sheriff's Department and also sent out the closest Border Patrol units. They arrived as Kade's plane took off."

Kelsey shuddered at the mention of the plane but only nodded.

"Sal had just put down the cell phone when the agents and deputies surrounded him and the other two men. They were all arrested." Don stared at a framed print of yellow gladiolas. "There was some confusion as to where Kade was landing, or we would've arrived sooner. We were misdirected to the wrong airport while you were told to land in Douglas."

Don sat in a chair across from Kelsey as he asked, "When's Kade's family getting home?"

"Late tonight," Kelsey said. "They have seats on the last flight out of San Francisco to Tucson."

A silver-haired woman in a white lab coat came through the

double doors into the waiting room and Kelsey sat up in her chair. "I'm Dr. Taylor," the woman said. "Is either one of you a family member of Kade Owen?"

Before Kelsey could speak, Don said, "This is his fiancée, Kelsey Nichols. The rest of Kade's family is out of town."

Kelsey blushed as the doctor shook her hand with a firm grip but didn't contradict Don. "How's Kade?"

Dr. Taylor smiled. "He'll be fine. He lost a lot of blood so we're going to keep him here a couple of days and then he'll be able to go home."

Kelsey's head spun and her stomach cramped. She was so relieved that she barely heard the doctor's explanation of the extent of Kade's injuries.

"May I see him?" she asked when the doctor finished.

Dr. Taylor nodded and indicated to Kelsey to follow her. "Only for a few minutes. He needs his rest to help him recover more quickly."

A humming noise filled her head as the doctor led her into Kade's room. Her chest tightened when she saw how pale he was. Bandages were wrapped around his upper arm. Bruises covered one side of his face and his eyes were closed.

Her hand trembled as she caressed Kade's cheek, his stubble rough to her fingertips. He opened his eyes and gave her a weak smile.

"Kelsey," he said, his voice hoarse.

"Shhh." She touched his lips with her finger. "Get some rest, cowboy." She kissed him and watched him drift off to sleep.

Chapter 34

Kelsey pulled off her glasses and set them on the desk. She was so tired that the words had begun to blur across the screen.

After leaving Kade at the hospital last night, she hadn't been able to sleep, too wired after the traumatic experience. Instead, she'd plunged into writing the story of yesterday's fiasco and sent it off to her editor. She'd deal with the feature article later.

Theresa had sent Kelsey a quick e-mail, promising to call. She'd raved over the article, apparently ecstatic over Kelsey's involvement in bringing down a notorious smuggler who just happened to be backing a candidate for U.S. Congress. But she'd also expressed her relief that Kelsey and Kade were both fine.

Of course Montaño had called a press conference, claiming ignorance of Stevens's activities. But the damage had been done, and it was possible that the mayor's candidacy for Congress was in jeopardy.

Once she had returned from visiting Kade in the hospital that morning, Kelsey had thrown herself into her work and finished the last of the interviews by telephone. She had a bit more to do, but it could wait until tomorrow, when she could think clearly. As clearly as anyone who'd just been through what she and Kade had been through could.

It was now late afternoon and Kelsey was ready for a nap. She yawned and started to get up but stopped when her cell phone rang.

She looked at the caller display, then said, "Hey, Theresa," as she put the phone to her ear.

"Girlfriend." Theresa's voice held excitement, as if she couldn't wait to give Kelsey some kind of news. "I wanted to call you first thing this morning, but I was practically held hostage by the boss woman herself. Do you realize that you're national news? Major U.S. media has picked up your story."

Kelsey didn't have the energy for excitement. Theresa had enough for both of them. "I've been too busy to think about it."

"Are you okay?" Concern came into Theresa's tone. "I should've called this morning, but I figured you must be all right to have written that article only hours after it happened."

"I'm fine." Kelsey gave a tired smile to herself. "I'm just tired enough to sleep for a week. Maybe two."

After they hung up, Kelsey stared out the window without seeing. She had more important things to think about than being picked up by the AP.

Should she risk telling Kade again that she loved him, and if he loved her in return, should she risk a future with him?

"Done," Kelsey said as she e-mailed the final draft of the feature to Theresa. She leaned back against the den chair and relaxed.

It was hard to believe that at this time one day earlier Sal had betrayed them, Stevens had held them at gunpoint, and Kade could have died. Her skin chilled and she shivered. No use thinking about that now. It was over and he would be fine.

The house was eerily silent. Chuck had headed to Bisbee to buy a new pane of glass for the front door. Sadie had gone to Douglas to run errands and then to see Kade. Trent was staying home with Kelsey since he had a cold and they didn't want to risk Kade catching it.

And if she could work up the courage, Kelsey planned to tell Kade how she felt when he came home.

Was she making the right choice? Could she do it—could she tell him that she loved him again? And what if he rejected her?

In her heart she knew Kade was the only man she'd ever love. And if there was any chance he loved her, she had to know.

Sighing, she rubbed her belly, trying to imagine what it would look like in a few months. She wouldn't tell him about the baby—yet. She wouldn't be able to handle it if Kade insisted that they get married based on his outmoded cowboy sense of honor and duty. But if he didn't want to continue their relationship she'd still allow him to be a part of his baby's life.

Kelsey wandered around the house, which smelled of ham cooking in the Crock-Pot and bread baking in the bread machine. Afternoon sunshine spilled through the windows on the west side of the house, giving everything in the living room a soft glow. To avoid seeing the boarded-up pane in the front door, she headed out the back door to the pond.

Monarch butterflies danced over Sadie's irises, zinnias, and roses. The flowers were a bright splash of purples, oranges, and reds in the midst of all the greenery. The bees' hum as they gathered pollen was oddly soothing as a warm breeze caressed her skin. She smelled wet earth and moss from the pond.

Roxie barked and hobbled past her to the driveway. The bandage on the dog's haunch was dusty but bright against her black hair. Kelsey still couldn't believe that Roxie had only been shot in the leg. Like Kade, the dog was injured, but she'd be okay, too.

Trent came out of the house, smiling and chatting. They spent the afternoon together, Kelsey following wherever the boy led. Even though he'd been sick earlier, he sure had a lot of energy now. She played with him in his hideout, tossed the ducks grain, helped him feed his potbellied pigs, and pitched a game of horseshoes in the windbreak.

It was almost dark when they finally walked back to the house. Trent slipped his hand into hers. "I told Dad I wanted to keep you."

Kelsey's heart twisted as she stared down at him. "That was sweet of you."

He sighed and hung his head. "I wasn't supposed to tell you that."

"Oh," she whispered.

Kade had told his son not to tell her that he wanted her to stay.

Her face felt frozen, her heart numb as they entered the house. "Trent, I'm not feeling well," Kelsey said. "I'm going to lie down for a while."

"You gonna be okay?" His little face puckered in concern. "You don't look so good."

She forced a smile. "I'm tired and need to rest."

After she kissed his cheek she slipped into the guest room and threw herself onto the bed. She wasn't going to cry. She was finished with crying over anyone.

Kelsey turned on her back and stared at the ceiling. The back porch light was on, shining through the leaves of the mulberry bush outside her window. Shadows winked and moved in a collage of light and gray above her.

Her head ached from holding back the tears, but her heart ached more. She felt empty. Hollow. Alone.

She placed her hand on her belly and caressed it. No, she had her baby. The precious life growing inside her. The gift Kade had given her.

Kelsey found the strength to smile. Everything was going to be all right.

The following afternoon, the Turners went to pick up Kade from the hospital when he checked out.

Kelsey stood at her bedroom mirror and studied her reflection as she brushed her hair. Thoughts of all the things Kade had said to her over the past couple of weeks flooded her mind. Showing her his property and talking as though he was including her in his plans. Picking out the stoneware pattern that she'd fallen in love with.

Calling her his woman.

"Damn it, Kelsey." She thumped the brush down on the dressing table. "You can't blow this chance. Just maybe Kade loves you, too."

The sound of someone clearing his throat caused her heart to drop to her belly. She cut her gaze to the doorway and saw Kade standing there with his good arm hitched up against the doorway.

Heat flushed over her from head to toe. "You heard that."

He gave a slow nod and the corner of his mouth twitched.

Well, he already knew she loved him—she'd told him that when he was shot—so what did she have to lose?

"I love you, Kade Owen." She stood a little straighter and faced him. "I need to know how you feel about me."

Kade smiled and in a few steps had his good arm wrapped around her shoulders and her body pressed to his. He squeezed her tightly to him and kissed the top of her head. "Don't you already know, honey? I've loved you from the beginning. I just had to wait until you figured out you loved me, too."

Kelsey sagged against him, almost unable to believe it was true. He did love her.

He lightly tugged on her hair so that she was forced to look up at him. "How could you not know? I said it in a thousand different ways."

Emotions swirled within her like one of their summer monsoons. Happiness, yet worry over what he'd think about her being pregnant.

Before she had the chance to say another word, he said, "Come on. I want to take you somewhere special." He turned away, heading toward his room, and tossed over his shoulder, "Pack your overnight bag."

Insisting that he could drive just fine with one good arm, Kade drove from the ranch toward Bisbee, but Kelsey couldn't help worrying about him.

He loves me.

They talked about nothing and everything. About her time with Trent and how much Kade disliked hospital food. Yet he didn't mention the future.

When they reached Old Bisbee, she smiled as she thought of the day they'd spent there. As Kade drove up the winding Main Street, memories assailed her. She saw the shop where they'd bought the rose-colored skirt and blouse. The museum. The café where they'd eaten lunch. The shop where they'd picked out the dinnerware.

The bed-and-breakfast where they'd stayed.

And then Kade parked right in front of it.

Kelsey turned toward him. "What are we doing here?"

He trapped her in his azure gaze. "I have something to show you."

Kade took her hand after they got out of the truck, and he smiled. Warmth seeped into her and she wanted to melt against him. Instead, she let him lead her into the inn, where he approached the guy at the front desk. The ponytailed clerk tossed Kade a key without either of them saying a word.

"What's going on?" she asked as Kade led her up the stairs.

"You'll see."

At the top of the staircase, Kade inserted the key into the lock of the same room they'd stayed in before. He opened the door and gently pushed her inside.

Kelsey stared openmouthed while the door closed behind them. Flowers completely filled the room. Bouquets of red and yellow roses sprinkled with baby's breath covered the vanity. Vases brimming with white lilies and orchids topped the bureau. Baskets of purple irises, blue bachelor's buttons, and pink carnations lined the walls. The only space left open was the bed and a pathway to it.

She looked up at Kade and saw him watching her, a silly grin on his face. "Do you like it?" he asked, his voice almost shy.

"I've never seen anything so wonderful in my life." It smelled like a florist's shop, sweet with the perfume of roses and carnations. "You did this for me?"

"It's only the beginning." He brought her to him and kissed her so thoroughly that her knees gave out and he had to catch her with his good arm. He started nibbling at her ear.

"Your injuries." She gave him a worried look. "Are you sure you're okay?"

"When I'm with you everything's fine." Kade tossed his Stetson on the table.

Kelsey shivered as he started unbuttoning her blouse. He undid the front clasp of her bra and she gasped as his mouth captured her nipple.

She held his face in her palms and drew him up just high enough to lightly kiss the wound at his temple, then the cuts and bruises on his face. When she helped him unbutton his shirt, she winced at the sight of the bandage around his arm.

Faster than she had time to think, they were both naked and tumbled to the bed. She kissed the bruises on his chest, her heart twisting at the sight of the dark purple-and-blue flesh.

He pushed her back against the pillow. "Let me," he murmured. His lips took possession of her, loving every inch of her body. He slowly eased down her belly, to the soft hair, to the delicate skin of her thighs.

And when his tongue met that most intimate part of her, he drove her almost to climax, licking and sucking her clit, and then stopped, slid on a condom and moved over her. She was burning alive for him, wanting him deep within her. She wrapped her legs around him, but he just braced himself on his good arm and smiled.

She slid her arms around his neck. "Don't stop."

"Say it," he whispered.

"What?" She squirmed under him, begging him without words to take her.

"Tell me you love me," he said. "Say it. I want to hear it again."

He lowered his head and captured her nipple in his teeth and she moaned as she murmured, "I love you, Kade."

He kissed her hard as he slid into her, filling her, his strokes slow and purposeful. She clenched his hips and raked her nails over his skin, urging him on.

"Look at me," he said, his voice husky.

She gazed up into his blue eyes, their normal brilliance clouded with passion. Shock wave after shock wave rolled over her as she climaxed. He groaned and his body convulsed as he found his own release.

Kelsey closed her eyes, feeling completely boneless. Utterly relaxed, with his heart beating against hers. She lifted her lids to see him watching her. "You don't play fair."

"I know."

He withdrew from inside of her but remained on top as he leaned over and opened the nightstand's drawer. Her eyes widened as he pulled out a red velvet box and laid it between her breasts. "Open it, honey."

Her hands trembled as she opened the box and saw an exquisite diamond-and-sapphire ring. She looked at Kade and saw him smiling at her.

"Marry me, Kelsey."

Her thoughts spun. "Wow," was all she could think to say. "Really?"

"I bought this the day after our stay here." He stroked her hair behind her ear and his face was suddenly serious. "Like I said before, I fell in love with you the day I met you. I've wanted to tell you so many times, but it never seemed to be the right moment."

Kelsey bit her lower lip, then said, "There's one thing I have to ask you. Trent said you told him not to tell me that he wanted me to stay."

Kade smiled. "I asked him to hold off telling you because I wanted to."

Kelsey sighed with relief. Even though he'd told her he loved her, a part of her had still held back, afraid to give in. "I was worried you didn't want me around."

"How could you think that?" He kissed her nose, her cheeks, her forehead. "Just the thought of you leaving rips me up inside."

The happiness welling up inside her made tears prick at the corners of her eyes.

"Hey, are you okay?" His blue eyes filled with concern as he brushed hair from her face. "If you don't want to live here, we'll move to Tucson and I'll get transferred there. I'd even move to San Francisco if it would make you happy. I just want us to be together for the rest of our lives."

Her eyes widened. "You would do that for me?"

"Absolutely."

She couldn't think of anything to say but "Wow."

He kissed her. "Say yes, Kelsey."

She put a finger to his lips. "I have to tell you something first. And then if you're as happy as I am, I'll say yes."

Kane gave her his lazy smile and ran his finger over the tip of her nose. "Deal."

"Remember when the condom broke?" She took his hand and moved it between them to her belly. "You're going to be a father again, sometime next April."

His jaw dropped, shock crossing his face. "You're pregnant?"

She nodded.

Kade raised himself up to run his hand over her abdomen. "Beautiful Kelsey. You're going to be a mother. You're going to have my baby. Our baby."

Joy filled her heart. "Are you happy about it?"

"Hell yes, I'm happy. I want us to have at least half a dozen more kids together."

Laughing, she nipped at his chest. "Half a dozen? Why don't we just start with this one and Trent, and go from there."

He took the ring from the box. The diamond caught the light, sparkling and glittering with brilliant fire. The sapphires surrounding it were as deep as the blue in his eyes. "Will you marry me?"

She nodded, so unbelievably happy. "Yes. I love you so much it hurts."

He slipped the ring on her finger and kissed her long and hard. The gold felt warm and solid, a bond made of love. It felt right.

"I love you, Kelsey," he said, his gaze fixed on hers. He kissed her hair. "You've made me the happiest man in the world."

Kelsey breathed in Kade's earthy scent and sighed. "You can't possibly be any happier than I am."

"Darlin', you have the rest of our lives to prove it."

Epilogue

One year later

"Trent, pick up your toys," Kade said as his son reached the landing. "You wouldn't want someone to trip over them and fall down the stairs, now would you?"

"Okay, Dad." Trent scooped up the action figures, tossed them onto the floor of his room, and dashed back. "Mom's feeding the baby on the balcony. When she's done, can we go over to Grandma and Grandpa's? Roxie had her puppies and Grandpa said I could have one if it was okay with you."

Kade grabbed his son and tickled him until he squirmed on the floor in fits of laughter. "He did, huh?"

Trent squealed. "Yes. And I want to name one Rex. Can I, Dad? Can I?"

Kade tousled the boy's hair. "Okay, kiddo."

"All right." Trent scrambled to his feet and ran to the master bedroom. "Mom! Dad said I could have one of Roxie's puppies."

Kade followed his son through the bedroom to the balcony. The sun was settling over the Mule Mountains, the sunset blazing across the sky in pink and orange streaks. Kelsey was reclining in her favorite chair, a soft smile on her face as she held their daughter over her shoulder, patting the baby's back.

"Mom, what do you think of the name Rex for the new puppy?" Trent asked as he gently stroked his baby sister's arm.

"Sounds wonderful." Kelsey hugged him, then looked up at Kade and smiled. "How was your day? No shower?"

Kade leaned over and kissed her. "Showered in the locker room." His heart swelled as he looked at their daughter. "Let me hold Naya."

"She's all yours." Kelsey handed the baby to Kade and he cradled his daughter in the crook of his arm and kissed the top of her head. Her features were so tiny and perfect. She was as beautiful as her mother.

"How's Daddy's girl?" He let Naya grab his finger with her tiny hand. She kicked and smiled, and made strange gurgling noises that filled his heart with intense joy. Her eyes were dark, and he fancied they would be the same chocolate brown as Kelsey's.

Trent ran his hand over the baby's soft blond hair. "Naya's cute for a baby, but she's not much fun. When'll she be old enough to play with?"

"Oh, give her a few months." Kelsey pulled Trent into her lap and hugged him. "And then she'll probably be into all your toys."

"Some things I might let her play with, but not my important stuff." Trent wriggled out of Kelsey's lap. "Can I call Grandma and Grandpa and tell them we're going over there in a little while to pick out a puppy?"

"Sure," Kelsey said with a smile.

"Did you finish those book reviews?" Kade asked Kelsey after Trent dashed out of the room.

She yawned and stretched. "I managed to e-mail the last one to Theresa while Naya napped."

Kade walked through the French doors into their bedroom and laid Naya in her bassinet. Kelsey followed and slid her arm around his waist as they looked down at their daughter.

"Do you remember when we made wishes at the lake on Trent's birthday last year?" Kelsey asked as she leaned against Kade.

"Mmmm," he murmured, and kissed the top of her head. "My wish came true."

She looked up at him and smiled. "I wanted a baby. A child, like Trent. But before I made that wish, I wanted to wish for you. I just didn't think I could have you."

He grinned. "Darlin', you had me wrapped around your little finger from the day we met."

She turned and eased her arms around his neck. "What did you wish for?"

"You." Kade brushed his lips over Kelsey's. "What do you say we take a nice long bath in that huge tub of ours, and start practicing making another brother or sister for Naya and Trent?"

Kelsey sighed and melted against him. "I'm all yours, cowboy."

Read on for a sneak peek at

Vampires Not Invited

by Cheyenne McCray

Coming Winter 2010
From St. Martin's Paperbacks

A Master Vampire living in the penthouse of the elite Hudson Hotel off Central Park.

Could things get any stranger?

Of course they could. This was New York City.

Arriving in the Vampire's personal elevator wasn't an option. Olivia, Angel, and Joshua were with me in the stairwell, taking the long way to get to Volod's lair.

Earlier today Joshua and I had continued "talking" with other Sprites. Even using bits of the information from Negel, we hadn't been able to get any Sprite to talk.

A couple of the creepy beings had looked shocked, if not scared, when they heard the Vampire's name, but still no one said anything. We'd been lucky with Negel.

Joshua's flail rocked at his side as we jogged the twenty-four flights of stairs to the penthouse of the Hudson. Shadow Shifters are as silent as Elves and Fae when they move, even when they're in human form.

I pushed long strands of my blue hair over my shoulder as I

glanced behind me at Angel. She was incredibly quiet for a Doppler as she followed. Like me, she wore a form-fitting black leather fighting suit—only hers showed even more skin than mine did, which meant hers showed a *lot* of flesh.

The barbs on the whip at Angel's side had a dull look to them that didn't begin to betray their deadly knife-edged sharpness. Her beautiful features were set, a determined spark to her diamond-bright blue eyes, her blond corkscrew curls spilling over her shoulders like pale serpents.

Angel was a squirrel in Doppler form and as a human looked like a cover girl for a cheerleader magazine. A former Harvard graduate and NASA intern, Angel was one of the toughest Trackers I knew. She'd saved my butt more than once during the Werewolf op. Just goes to show you can't judge a Doppler by her human appearance or her animal form.

Olivia took up the rear. I winced every time I heard one of her shoes make a whisper of a sound. A former NYPD cop, she was pretty quiet for a human. But some beings have super-incredible hearing and I just hoped the Vampire's hearing wasn't *that* good that they'd hear the slight sounds of Olivia's running shoes.

"Fourteenth floor and ten to go." I looked at the number on the door as we made it from twelve to the next landing. "The fact that all hotels don't have a thirteenth floor has got to be one of the silliest superstitions humans have."

"Humans have lots of silly superstitions." Angel's voice was deceptively innocent and sweet, and I glanced at her again. "And Brownies looooove to play up to them."

I grinned as we hit another landing. "If they knew that Brownies are behind just about every superstition or haunting, humans would really flip."

Brownies are Fae and some of the most devious creatures known to paranorm kind. I dislike them as much as I dislike Sprites. But they can be amusing at times—when they aren't being malicious.

"Not all humans believe in that crap." Olivia might not be what anyone would consider slender, but she was in such great shape she wasn't breathing hard. "Don't even go there."

"Keep your traps shut," Joshua grumbled. Angel flipped him off. I grinned. "The bastards may have lookouts."

Joshua stopped on landing twenty and I came just short of running into him. I took his flail automatically as he handed it to me. The full weight of it caught me by surprise and I almost dropped it. Thank goodness I'm Drow and not simply human because the thing was so heavy that I wouldn't have had the strength to hold it otherwise.

"Going ahead to scout." Joshua shifted—sort of melted away—and then I watched as a large shadow drifted up the stairs. Sometimes he blended with the stairwell shadows, sometimes not. And then he was gone.

Angel reached my side and gave me her whip. "Ouch," I said as one of its barbs dug into my palm and blood formed where the small cut was.

"Sorry, Nyx," she said just before she transformed into a blond squirrel, jumped onto the railing, and darted along it to cover the last few flights.

"What am I?" I muttered as I hurried up the stairs. "A coatrack?" As I moved I hooked Angel's whip on my weapons belt next to my right-side dragon-clawed dagger and gripped Joshua's flail in my left hand. The blackness of the metal was dark against my pale amethyst skin.

Within seconds I was up the last four flights and had reached the penthouse, Olivia right behind me. A strange yet familiar odor that I couldn't identify cloyed the air. I frowned. Why couldn't I place the odor. So familiar . . .

Joshua and Angel were nowhere to be seen. As a Shadow Shifter, Joshua had probably slipped beneath the door and into the Vampire's lair. But squirrels . . . I looked up at the low ceiling. Dust had been slightly disturbed on an air vent. That explained Angel's disappearance.

"Like we talked about, wait here," I said to Olivia. "I know you don't think Vampires are dangerous because of the pukes at the Pit, but I think we have more to worry about than anyone realizes."

She scowled and I cut her off before she could say a word. "Don't come in, no matter what." I grasped the handle. "Your job is to shoot anything that comes through this door. And make sure it's through the heart."

"Just get your purple ass in there," she muttered as she positioned herself to the side of the stairwell door, her Sig held in a two-fisted grip and pointed upward.

I called to my air element and felt its reassuring embrace as it cloaked me and my weapons so that I was invisible. Most paranorms can still see me when I use a glamour, but Vampires are different.

Vampires aren't born paranorms. They were once human and in some ways they have human weaknesses. So to them I'm invisible when I draw a glamour. Thank goodness for that favor.

With my free hand I tested the doorknob to the penthouse's emergency exit. Locked. Joshua must not have been able to unlock it for me. I needed to be cautious because someone could be on the other side and see the door. I might be invisible to them, but they'd know something was up. A door being opened invisibly was bound to draw attention.

First I reached out with my senses, using my air element to search the area close to the door. To my satisfaction, it was clear.

I focused on the lock and used a small amount of my air element to unlock it, cushioning the mechanism so that the sound wouldn't be heard. I used the same element to buffer any squeak the hinges might make.

Olivia couldn't see me anymore, but I looked at her over my shoulder before I slipped inside. Her features were set and grim.

The smell of Vampire—like old dirt and musty leaves—was strong as I eased through the doorway. Modern classic design greeted me. But more than that, startled me.

Stark white walls with black accent walls towered to the vaulted ceiling. Muted city lights came through opaque drapes on the floor-to-ceiling windows.

Touches of red, like splashes of blood, were scattered on dead-white furniture. Crimson pillows were arranged on white sofa cushions, and I noticed hints of red in every one of the black-and-white paintings arranged on the walls. An enormous flat-screen TV was built into the wall. And I mean *enormous*. Go-to-the-movies enormous.

It shouldn't have surprised me, but apparently I'd fallen for the old vampire stereotypes like everyone else. Like where would he keep a dusty old coffin in a place like this?

Voices echoed in the large room, words bouncing from one wall to another like the hollowness of a Ping-Pong ball. I caught my breath as I settled the flail and barbed whip against the wall, keeping them cloaked in an air glamour. Joshua and Angel should be able to see them—wherever they were.

I eased behind a potted black tree. The white pot was as high as my waist, and the tree itself was about six feet high. The tree was naked of any leaves and would have been worthless cover if I hadn't shrouded myself in a glamour.

My gaze narrowed at Volod and another Vampire as they strolled into the room. Volod's black shoes sank into the rich white carpet as he walked with his casual yet arrogant movements.

Dressed in a black button-down shirt and tailored black slacks, Volod looked like any one of New York's elite aristocrats—just a lot paler. He was outfitted from head to toe in Gucci, Ferragamo, and Versace. Obviously I have a well-trained eye for the finer things.

The other Vampire's white turtleneck sweater against the deadly white of his skin did nothing for his complexion—except make him look more dead. Is that possible? The fact he wore Levi's and Nikes as opposed to Volod's designer clothing might have indicated he was some kind of underling if it wasn't for the arrogant way he carried himself.

I peered at them both through the branches of the naked tree. It seemed bright in the room compared to the night sky barely visible through a slim part in the sheer drapes.

Despite my glamour, a tingling sense of danger rippled up my spine as I studied the two Vampires.

Volod picked up a smooth black statue of a nude female and trailed his white hand down the statue's curves. I swept my gaze around the room. Joshua might be one of the many shadows, and as a squirrel, Angel could be just about anywhere.

I reached out with my senses, using my air power to guide me. I found, but still couldn't distinguish, Joshua on the other side of the room. In another second I felt Angel's presence beneath one of the sofas.

Vampires have extraordinary senses, but I didn't think they were able to sense Joshua and Angel like I could.

"Do you truly think that bunch of garbage can do it?" the second Vampire said as he tossed a crimson pillow on the floor and settled back in an oversized white chair. His skin was nearly as pale as his seat. "Can we put faith in the stupid creatures?"

Volod set the black statue on a glass table and the thumping sound it made caused me to flinch. The irritation on Volod's angular features sent that creepy sensation up my spine again. "Questioning me, Danut?"

Danut didn't seem bothered by Volod's glare. Danut shook out his long black hair, which gleamed in the light. "If they complete their mission is it wise to give them the *permanent* ability, brother?" It shouldn't have surprised me that he and Volod were brothers. The resemblance was clear to me now.

Volod didn't bother to answer Danut's question. "As long as the Night Trackers remain ignorant, nothing will stop the Sprites from getting the information."

I caught my breath as thoughts spun through my mind. What was so important that he would be afraid of the Trackers finding out? I had a feeling that it had to be dangerous, whatever it was.

The Master Vampire turned to one of the windows, pushed aside the flowing sheer curtain. He studied the glittering Manhattan skyline through crystal-clear windows. The view through the windows made the city's skyline seem almost close enough to grasp each light in my hand.

"I have given the creatures what they need to accomplish this task and this task only," Volod said.

Danut said, "It was brilliant that you gave the Sprites the ability to escape the elemental magic containment as only Vampires can."

So many questions ran through my mind that I had to set them aside to concentrate on what was being said.

Danut grinned, baring his fangs. "The Trackers have no idea what will happen tonight at the Paranorm Center or what we have planned for the future."

Tonight. Something is going down tonight. I gritted my teeth, torn between listening to the two Vampires and rushing to the Paranorm Center to stop whatever they had planned. If only there were a way to contact Rodán without the chance of being overheard on my cell phone.

"All will most certainly change with what you have planned for the Trackers later." Danut's grin vanished. "But for tonight the Sprites will gain the archives."

Disbelief at what the Vampires had said caused me to shift my body backward. The Sprites in the detention center! How could we have not thought of that? I'd have bet my last Drow-mined diamond that the Vampires had intended to have the Sprites caught so that the creeps could go after something in the archives.

I clenched my hand around the hilt of my sheathed dagger. Just as we'd thought, the Sprite mischief hadn't been random. But the realization that Vampires were behind it all made my skin feel tight.

"We have played the part far too long." Volod slammed his palms on the windowsill. He bent at his waist as he braced his hands.

My heart beat faster, my breathing grew heavier, my palms becoming sticky as I digested what I was hearing. What ability had the Vampires given to Sprites to break free of their cells and to get past the guards?

The Master Vampire straightened, then went still.

At once I knew he was searching for me with his mind, his senses. Bless it. Volod had felt the strong shift in my emotions.

"You think you can enter a Master Vampire's domain and not be found out?" He looked in my direction.

My heart thundered harder, but I maintained my glamour. In a rush I sought out my elements with my mind and senses. I could use water from the pipes behind the walls, fire from the stove in the kitchen, and, of course, I had air.

In the flash of a moment it took me to reach for my elements, his hand shot up.

Invisible power slammed into me. I bit my lip to keep from crying out as the force of his power sent me skidding on my side on the carpet. The blast burned through my chest. Was my suit melting? It felt like the leather was sinking through my skin.

I rolled with the momentum of the power as it shoved me toward one of the floor-to-ceiling windows. My concentration on my glamour failed, and I could be seen again.

With a shout and cry, I flipped my body into a crouch, drew one of my dragon-clawed daggers, and faced Volod. Shards of pain raked my lungs as I dragged in harsh breaths of air.

"Tracker." Volod tilted his head and studied me, his hand still outstretched. He looked at me as if not concerned at all. "The strange one. The Drow female."

"This creature is a Tracker?" Danut laughed, obviously not feeling threatened by me, either. "A purple woman?"

Give me a moment and I'll show you purple when I shove your—

"What are you going to do with her?" Danut asked, looking at his brother in a lazy, bored way. "Fun and games?"

Volod's black gaze held mine. "What do we do with all trash?"

Volod splayed the fingers of his outstretched hand. "We dispose of it."

I surrounded myself with my air element, a thick cushion that would have protected me if I hadn't been so stupid and unprepared.

If I tried I couldn't have held back the dangerous white flash in my eyes. "Vampire scum."

I grasped the double-edged buckler from the front of my weapons belt and flung it at Volod's neck. My air element shoved the buckler faster than a human eye could see.

Volod wasn't human. Not for a very long time.

He caught the buckler right before the razor edge would have sliced into his throat.

In a blur he threw the buckler at me. I dodged it. The buckler sailed through the floor-to-ceiling window behind me. Glass shattered with a loud crack. Icy wind whipped inside the penthouse.

Danut shouted something. From the corner of my eye I saw Angel's barbed whip wrap around Danut's neck. Multiple lacerations. Blood streamed down his body. Blood splattered the white sofas. Angel would rip the Vampire's head from his body.

I didn't have time to take pleasure in the sight.

My target was too powerful to allow myself to be distracted.

Faster than any Olympic sprinter, I bolted for Volod with my dagger. Blood rushed in my ears. My skin tingled. I'd carve his heart out.

Air cushioned me. Knowledge that I was protected gave me more strength.

My gaze was focused on the Vampire's grim expression. His bared fangs. A red glint in his black eyes. He raised his pale hand as he faced his palm out to me.

I gripped my dagger. I was protected. Volod wouldn't be able to hurt me this time.

Five feet. Three feet—

An even more powerful invisible blast slammed into me.

It was as if I had no protection at all buffering me.

Breath rushed from my chest. Did my lungs collapse?

Fire. My body was on fire. Burning more, even more than the last time.

My concentration on my air element shattered. All elements.

The power flung my body backward.

No control. I had no control.

My back and head hit one of the massive windows.

Glass shattered as I was slammed against it hard enough to break its thickness.

Shards sliced my skin and dug into my flesh as I sailed through the window.

I screamed as my body started to drop.

Twenty-four stories.

For Cheyenne's Readers

Be sure to go to http://cheyennemccray.com to sign up for her *private* book announcement list and get *free, exclusive* Cheyenne McCray goodies. Please feel free to e-mail her at chey@cheyennemccray .com. She would love to hear from you.